9-76

AN INNER SANCTUM MYSTERY
BY
LAURENCE MEYNELL

Virgin Luck

SIMON AND SCHUSTER
NEW YORK   1964

ONE

A BROAD-SHOULDERED, square-chinned man was breakfasting with one eye on the clock and the other on the *Daily Mail* list of runners in the three-thirty race at Doncaster that afternoon.

The sunshine of a brilliant September morning flooded the small dining room in which he was sitting and a large tabby cat (Trigger) was pressing himself up against the windowpane from the outside strongly suggesting that it was time he was let in.

The man rose and opened the window.

"Come on in, Trigger, you old sinner. What have you been up to all night?"

The cat, probably out of a sense of decency, ignored the question and looked anxiously at the milk jug.

As he was pouring out a saucer of milk the man had a sudden wave of affection for the small secure things of home.

His wife was upstairs in bed enjoying her breakfast. The routine was for her to come down in her dressing gown, get his breakfast for him and then retire to bed with her own, a cup of tea and a piece of toast. He himself was still young to have done so well in his profession; they were lucky to have found Woods Den with its half-acre of orchard running up to the big beech wood at the back; a small bright motor-car (not yet a year old) stood waiting in the drive. These were the things which in a sort of summarized appreciation of luck and happiness were comfortably in the back of his mind as he poured out the milk for the cat.

"You'll make me late, Trig," he complained, putting down the milk jug and going back to his paper.

The clock on the sideboard said 7:40 exactly; the list of runners for the three-thirty at Doncaster said, among other things, "Blue Arrow" and the betting forecast said 8 to 1.

"Blue Arrow it is then," the man decided. Since this was part of the daily ritual he had a piece of writing paper and an envelope handy.

"GK 4171," he wrote. "Blue Arrow Doncaster 3:30 ten shillings to win. Sept. 3rd."

He sealed and stamped the envelope and addressed it:

EDWARD WEST
WESTBET HOUSE
LONDON W.1

His smile as he did this was partly a recognition of his folly in the matter. He had a passion for racing and for betting on races. But he had always had the sense to keep it within bounds. He kept careful records and in the last three years of his transactions with the great bookmaker firm of Edward West he was twenty-eight pounds and a few shillings to the good. If he had found himself beginning to be seriously on the debit side he would have given it up. Since in his particular profession gambling in any form was looked on with much disfavor he had made it a rule never to do any of it from his office. It was all done and finished with every day before he left home.

It was quarter to eight and he went upstairs to the bedroom.

His wife, Molly, lay in bed, a dark-eyed, dark-haired beauty.

"You look much too pretty to be there all by yourself," he teased her.

"Ring up and say you've got a streaming cold and you've decided to have a day in bed."

"It's an idea." He bent down and kissed her. "Goodbye, darling."

"Goodbye."

"See you at six or thereabouts."

"I'll be waiting."

As he came down into the small hall the telephone began to ring. He immediately mistrusted it. A purely social call was hardly likely before eight o'clock in the morning and in his profession a call at his private house was likely to mean trouble.

"Cotterfield 464," he said.

"Sorry to trouble you at home, Inspector. Verney here."

"What's the trouble, Jock?"

"Murder, I'm afraid."

Detective Inspector Walter Gibson glanced automatically at the clock—7:48. He felt a stir of excitement. If this was a murder (and Sergeant John Verney was hardly likely to make a mistake in the matter) it would be the first which he had had to handle personally.

"What's the story?"

"I've only had it on the blower so far, and I thought I'd ring you at once so as to catch you before you left home. A Mrs. Sanders rang up. Pretty agitated, of course, but sensible enough. She goes in daily to tidy up and so on for a chap called Chess in Heath End Cottage—"

"Where's that?"

"You know the Rising Sun at the top of Leather Lane? It's about half a mile beyond that, on the top road. Stands back a bit. Out-of-the-way sort of place."

"And what happened?"

"This Mrs. Sanders went in as usual at about seven-thirty—"

"Early for a daily, isn't it?"

"She gets his breakfast, apparently. And the first thing she saw when she went into the living room to pull the curtains and so on was Chess lying stretched out on the floor, dead."

"How was he killed?"

"Hit on the head, she says. But she's a bit upset about all that."

"Who is he?"

"Chap called Arnold Chess, sir."

"Was he living all alone? No family or anything?"

"No. He lived by himself. I knew him a bit. Well, just to nod to."

"Is he retired or what?"

"No, he wasn't retired. He wouldn't be above fifty I'd say. Might be a year or two more. He went up to London every day. I believe he had some sort of job with Edward West the bookmaker."

"With Edward West?"

"That's right, sir."

Gibson hoped the sergeant hadn't noticed the slightly startled note in his query. Nothing in it really, of course, he assured himself, still it had given him a bit of a turn to be holding a letter addressed to Edward West in his hand and at the same time to be hearing that one of the firm's men had been murdered.

"This Mrs. Sanders—know anything about her?"

"Not a thing, sir."

"She has called in all the neighbors by now I take it and made a party of it?"

"I don't think so, sir. It wasn't five minutes after finding the body that she rang here, she said, and I told her on no account to touch anything or to interfere in any way. I don't think she wanted to by the sound of it. She'll be in the kitchen having a cup of tea if I know anything about it."

"You'd better get over there at once, Jock, and I'll go straight from here. What arrangements have you made at the office?"

"Wallis will be taking over in any case at eight o'clock, sir, and I can bring Chambers out with me."

"You're likely to go a bit short of sleep today."

"I'll manage."

"Let the doc know."

"I'll give him a ring straightaway, sir."

"What on earth was all that telephoning about?" Molly called from upstairs.

"Shop," her husband shouted. "Nothing to worry you. Go on wasting your morning like the wanton hussy you are."

"I like that! I'm getting up this moment to have my bath."

"I'm sorry I'll not be there to help you."

Leather Lane and the Rising Sun, Gibson thought as he went out to the car. He prided himself on his knowledge of the district but he had to admit that Sergeant Jock Verney could give him ten points in a hundred in the subject.

He turned left out of his drive leaving the mile run into Cotterfield itself behind him and heading for Farthing Green and beyond it to Leather Lane.

He stopped at Farthing Green post office to put his letter in the box.

"Next collection 10 A.M.," the enamel slip told him, so that was all right. His letter would be in the head office in Cotterfield before midday and would be time-stamped 12:45.

Whatever might have happened to one of its employees presumably Edward West would still function; the three-thirty at Doncaster would still be run; and with any luck, Blue Arrow would win it.

Leather Lane was a long winding road still rural in that it had no pavements and was innocent of any lighting. It was lined by well-trimmed hedges and behind the hedges were the herbaceous borders, the greenhouses, the tennis courts, the swimming pools and the half-timbered Tudor-style residences of the commuting fraternity. Not of course the lesser fry who caught the 8:30 or the 8:33 at the latest; but the more solid and successful ones who could afford to wait until the 10:30 (one stop only: "the directors' special") and who read *The Financial Times* in its uncrowded carriages.

But when at the top he reached the Rising Sun and turned

left along the top road the character of the neighborhood changed at once.

No expensive Tudor residences up here. Hardly any residences at all in fact. This had all been common land until fairly recently and it was now largely neglected with only an odd cottage here and there mostly standing some distance from the road.

The inspector drove along slowly keeping a sharp lookout and presently he saw a rustic sign proclaiming "Heath End Cottage."

He stopped his car outside on the road and walked up the short drive in case there might be tracks or footprints in it.

The cottage was small and homely looking; the garden neat and well cared for.

Weekend gardening type, Gibson thought, himself a keen gardener. Wonder how his roses are doing?

He went round to the back door, knocked and poked his head in.

Sergeant Jock Verney's surmise was shown to be correct. A short, capable-looking little woman was sitting in the kitchen drinking tea. She looked shaken and the inspector wasn't surprised. When you see death and particularly violent death for the first time it is apt to be a bit upsetting.

He smiled at her and she half got up.

"Mr. Gibson, isn't it?" she asked.

"That's right," the inspector said, reflecting not for the first time that more people know Tom Fool than Tom Fool knows. "And you'll be Mrs. Sanders?"

"Yes, sir."

"I understand there's bad news here," Gibson said, conscious that it was rather a feeble gambit, but not knowing how better to open the conversation.

"I nearly fainted when I saw him, sir. Nearly fainted right off."

"Well, that's not surprising, Mrs. Sanders. And you rang up the station straightaway, eh?"

"Oh, at once. I got on to the police at once. I always say any business like this and it's best to let the police deal with it. It's their job."

"Quite right. I'll go and have a look at things. No need for you to distress yourself any more if you'll just tell me where it is."

Mrs. Sanders came with him into the minute space which was called a hall.

"In there, sir," she said. "It's in there."

Gibson opened the door and went in gingerly.

It was the typical cottage room made more comfortable; a sofa, an armchair, a television set, a log basket by the fireplace (some of the logs lying on the floor) and close to the log basket the body.

Stepping carefully the inspector crossed to it and looked down inquisitively. A little blood and a crumpled heap that in death looked almost pathetically small.

One thing was certain, he had a murder on his hands.

His first. At thirty-six he was young to hold his rank; on his way up he had seen a number of unpleasant sights and not a few extraordinary ones; but he had never before had a murder all to himself and been in charge of it.

Controlled excitement, but still excitement, overcame the slight feeling of nausea with which he came out of the living room.

Mrs. Sanders was still in the hall and he took her back to the kitchen to ask some questions.

"Now, Mrs. Sanders. Take it easy. This sort of thing isn't nice for anybody. Especially for the first person to find it. Just take your time and tell me about it in your own words."

Mrs. Sanders had not much to say, so that the fact that she said it all twice at least wasn't as tedious as it might have been.

She lived "across the common" and had done so for fifteen years. Her husband, an ex-roadman, was retired and a semi-invalid. He never got up before midday. She helped out their pension money by "doing" for various people. For the past two years she had been coming five days a week to Mr. Chess. Not all day, of course. Mornings only. And a couple of hours a day, no more. Mr. Chess was all alone and it was a great help to him to have somebody to get his breakfast before he went off to get the London train.

Lots of dailies wouldn't come in as early as seven-thirty, but she didn't mind. She was always up early herself, being a farmer's daughter, and there was no breakfast to get for her husband who didn't eat it.

"And this morning?"

"I was over here as usual."

"At seven-thirty."

"Within a minute or two. Must have been. I didn't look at a clock special, of course, but I never vary much."

"How did you get in?"

"I've got a key. Mr. Chess gave it me soon after I started for him. It's easier for us both. I can lock up after I've finished and come over during the day to see to anything."

"And what happened? You didn't see anything unusual or out of the way?"

"No, nothing. I wasn't looking out for anything. I just did what I always do. Turned the grill of the electric cooker on and then while that was warming up went into the living room to draw the curtains and get the grate done. But then, of course, well, I saw him."

"And Mr. Chess, what was he like?"

"He was a very quiet gentleman, very nice."

"He didn't have any family?"

"Not that I ever heard mention of. Very much on his own he was."

"Did he entertain? Friends and so on?"

"I've never seen anyone in the house but himself."

The inspector was still asking questions when he heard a car in the drive. Sergeant Jock Verney knocked and came in by the back door.

"I've put Chambers outside the front door, sir, is that all right?" he led off.

Gibson nodded and asked, "Everything all right at the office?"

"Everything under control, sir."

"Good. You had better come and have a look in the living room—"

The two men were gone for the best part of ten minutes and when they came back Mrs. Sanders was standing with her hat and coat on.

"I hope as you'll be able to let me go home now, sir," she said. "I've got my husband to see to and I don't want to be mixed up in all this more than I've got to be."

"Quite right, Mrs. Sanders," Gibson agreed at once. "You'll have to give evidence of course at the inquest, but that will only mean saying what you've been telling me. Now if you leave your full name and address with Sergeant Verney we needn't trouble you any more for the present."

"What about the key, sir?"

"Oh, yes. We had better have that."

When Mrs. Sanders had gone the two men sat down in the kitchen.

"Pity this isn't a whodunit," Gibson said, "then we should have six characters all living close at hand and each with some perfectly good motive for bumping the little man off."

"At the moment we don't seem to have anybody," Jock Verney said.

"So far. Still, there's always the machinery—"

"Aye, the good old machinery."

"Let's set it in motion then. I take it you've contacted the print people and the photographer?"

"They'll be out here together about half past ten, sir."

"And the doctor?"

"He should be here any minute now."

"Good. Don't let anybody touch anything till I've seen the chief. I'll fix the inquest date with the coroner. And will you arrange a relief for Chambers for as long as we want anybody here?"

"Right-o, sir."

"I'll run over and see the chief now and I'll be back as soon as maybe, half an hour's time, maybe."

"I don't suppose Exhibit A will have got up and walked away, sir."

"No, poor sod," Gibson said with rough compassion. "We've all got to come to it but it's not much fun when it happens like this."

Privately Sergeant Jock Verney doubted if it was much fun at the best of times; but he didn't say so.

Walter Gibson made his way toward Underwood, the newly built and rather imposing house in which his superior officer the chief constable of the county lived.

Traffic was sparse and he pushed his car along fast, turning over in his mind as he sped along the exciting possibilities, and the vast amount of dull slogging work ahead of him.

He remembered having read somewhere that all science could be reduced to the taking of measurements; in the same way he thought all police work really came down to asking questions.

How? When? Where? Why? Get sensible answers to these four queries and inevitably the ultimate answer of all—to the fifth question, who?—must begin to appear.

Why? Walter Gibson wondered. On the surface Arnold Chess seemed a decent little chap, more harmless than most and not likely to be the object of robbery—why should death have come to him in Heath End Cottage last night?

Few questions in life can be disposed of by very simple answers.

To find out the answer to his question Detective Inspector

Walter Gibson would have had to go back three years in time and to have looked at life through the eyes of a twenty-one-year-old girl of striking appearance who was boarding a London omnibus in Shepherd's Bush.

TWO

ELBOWS," the fat woman in front of me said. "Some of them are like savages."

She was just about right too; but how was I to know there would be such a hell of a queue for the bus at Shepherd's Bush at ten minutes to nine in the morning? I ought to have got up earlier, of course. The number of things I ought to do in life and didn't (and naturally vice versa) was astonishing. As my father took great pleasure in pointing out.

Not that he was going to worry me any more. I had moved to Shepherd's Bush to get away from him once and for all and I had just spent my first night there. "Clean comfortable homely room for Young Professional Lady." I suppose I qualified as a Y.P.L.

Anyway there I was installed in Panter Street.

True, Mrs. Mason had looked a bit doubtfully at my legs which are long and in sheer nylon generally earn a second glance from most men.

"There won't be any gentlemen callers will there?" Mrs. Mason asked, and I could hear the massed ranks of nonconformity and its celebrated conscience at the back of her voice. And I ought to know about nonconformity. My father was a great chapel-goer. A strong believer in teetotalism, abstinence from tobacco, and generally making life hell for everybody. One of the elect, no doubt. Only I didn't elect him.

"Gentlemen callers?" I repeated to Mrs. Mason in as shocked a voice as I could manage. "Of course not." I was already wondering how long I could stick it there; but the point was that 52 Panter Street was *somewhere,* and I had been lucky to find it straight off. I realized that. So far it had lived up to its claims. My bedroom and the bathroom were both clean; my bed comfortable.

So I had nothing to grumble about. I was free and established, on my own, and I was on my way to the first morning of a new job. A temporary one. "Don't be late," the agency had warned me, which was why I had to do a bit of elbow work with the fat woman in front of me in the queue and get ahead of her in the general scrimmage.

"Thasserlod," the Jamaican conductor said. Was he Jamaican? He was coffee-colored anyway and he had long supple fingers and a sinuous sort of hip line when he walked. And it obviously gave him one hell of a kick to order the white trash about.

The fat woman lost by a short head and coffee-face grinned happily at her discomfiture. I was sorry I couldn't lip-read. Under her breath she was saying what I felt must be some very unchapel-like words.

I smiled at her through the window just to show there was no ill feeling. I could afford to have no ill feeling. I had made the bus; she hadn't. She was Jack; I was all right.

All right so far anyway.

What the Jimmy Mancroft Ltd. Theatrical Agent was going to be like and how the job there would turn out I had yet to discover.

Not that I was worried much. When you are twenty-one and your measurements are 36″ 22″ 34″ you can afford to tell life to take a running jump at itself occasionally.

Which is precisely what on the previous afternoon I had done in quite a big way.

"Where to, please?" the conductor asked the bulky man sharing the seat with me.

"Theyton Place."

"Where's that, man?"

"You're a conductor and you don't know Theyton Place?"

The Jamaican grinned hugely.

"Can't have heard of everything, man."

"Fivepenny," the large man said in disgust, "and there's a request stop not twenty yards from it."

He got his fivepenny, I got my ticket to Piccadilly Circus, and the conductor moved on still greatly amused.

"Bus conductors!" the man next to me growled. "Give 'im 'alf a coconut and 'e'd swarm up a tree and sit there scratching 'is arse for a week, perfectly 'appy."

I could see his point of view; but actually the spade looked pretty happy as he was, which made me think that maybe he, too, had got successfully away from something at home. Good luck to him if he had. That made two of us.

Home for me was, had been, 18 Hansbeck Road.

You can walk down Hansbeck Road and still count a large number of lace curtains and aspidistras. It's a place where the zombies come pretty thick. At the far end of the road is Ellerton Street, with Ellerton Street Chapel halfway down it. The chapel at which Councillor Jesse Barton (my father) is such a respected pillar. It's a great "thou shalt not" place. No smoking, no joking, no parking, no poking—nothing. They might just as well have written that up on their wayside pulpit as most of the fire-and-blood messages that get put up there.

And beyond Ellerton Street, dodging past a pub or two and a café and the usual spatter of standardized shops, you come into Welbeck Road where the well-known local firm (see occasional references in the *South London Gazette*) of J. L. Barton, Builder, Contractor, Repairs our Specialty; Estimates Free is to be found.

Estimates might have been free, but nothing much else was.

I don't suppose there has ever been a competition for the meanest man in South London, but if there had Councillor J. L. Barton would have won it easily.

"Don't you feel any affection for your father?" one of the family zombies asked me once. I had a good look at the question (I was fifteen then) and I just had to say no, I didn't. Which made me out a pretty ropy sort of heel according to their reckoning. But upstairs in my room by myself I asked aloud what I should have asked downstairs, only I hadn't had the nous to. "So, if a child doesn't feel any affection for its father whose fault is that?"

Because at fifteen you want affection. Unless she's pretty hard-boiled a woman wants affection all the time. Which gets you into a lot of trouble but is probably worth it on the whole.

Mother, of course, just didn't count. Jesse L. Barton had got her where he wanted her from the start. "Let me not to the marriage of true minds admit impediments"—I shall never forget reading that for the first time. The public library was about half a mile away from us in the High Street and at seventeen I suddenly found out about reading. I wouldn't have told them at home that I was reading poetry for anything. I didn't tell anybody. I just read it. At that point in my life I had never been drunk. In fact I had never had an alcoholic drink of any sort. It isn't easy in 18 Hansbeck Road where there was a half bottle of whisky kept locked up ("for medicinal purposes") in the sideboard in the dingy brown dining room.

But I knew what being drunk was like when I read poetry. I was still going to the high school then and I used to walk there and back every day shouting the stuff out inside myself. And occasionally aloud. "Let me not to the marriage of true minds admit impediments," I said, and stopped stock still all of a sudden in the middle of the pavement staring with unseeing eyes at some poster or other.

I was thinking of Father and Mother. Good God, I thought, is this the marriage of true minds? Is this what the words mean? Is this what it comes to?

You can be hard-boiled and modern and independent and all the things they like to label you (some of them true) and still have your dreams and ideas.

At seventeen, surely, you're entitled to a dream or two?

At the high school they ran a commercial class for the last year and I took it.

Father wanted me to and, come to that, I wanted to myself. Just occasionally what we wanted ran together. But even when we wanted the same thing it wasn't necessarily for the same reasons.

Still, I may as well be fair to myself; only half my reason for joining the commercial class was Mr. Lewis. The other half was a genuine desire to learn some commerce.

Mr. Lewis was generally supposed to be thirty-two and at least half the girls in the commercial class had, or thought they had, "a thing" about him. He used to take us on five afternoons a week. He always had very white cuffs and when he was talking he had a trick of taking his glasses off and swinging them in his hand. He wore a large ring with a black stone in it and looking back on it I can't imagine what we all saw in him. But he must have had something because he was the beginnings of romance for quite a few of us.

The trick was to make a nonsense of something you were doing and to stay behind to discuss it with him.

We all did it and he must have seen through it, of course; but as far as I knew he never took any sort of advantage of it. He would laugh and have a joke with you but that was as far as it went. Maybe he just wasn't interested. Maybe he was scared. Twenty-four adolescent females, some of them highly sexed for their age, are probably enough to put any man off his stroke. At the time we liked to think that he was playing hard to get so we tried all the harder to get him.

A girl called Nancy Ellward was my chief rival; sometimes she hardly bothered to have an excuse for staying behind.

She had very large eyes and used to black her eyelashes. "Mr. Lewis," she used to say and her voice would sort of die breathlessly away. Very effective.

I think Nancy's essential makeup must have been pretty well on the same lines as mine.

More fun than being dumb and unresponsive, I suppose; but it can land you into one hell of a lot of trouble.

Maybe she got further with Mr. Lewis than I did. I was certainly scared that she might be doing so at the time, and it made me jealous.

So one Wednesday just before the end of class when Mr. Lewis, who had been walking round looking at our individual work, left a book behind on my desk I covered it with a sheet of foolscap and didn't say a word to anybody.

Wednesday was our late day. Class didn't end until a quarter to six and at five forty-five this particular day Mr. Lewis shut up shop finally.

"Can't stay for any questions," he said. "Sorry, you inquisitive and provocative people; but this evening I've got to get home."

Nancy, who had her questions, her large eyes, her blackened eyelashes and her breathless voice all ready, was obviously disappointed. But it suited me all right. In my bag I had a small blue-covered copy of Vince's *Dictionary of Commercial Terms* with "M. F. Lewis" written on the flyleaf.

I hung about a bit talking to various girls and then at the bus queue deliberately let one bus go by before I caught the next.

I didn't get out at my usual stop but went on right to the top of Church Hill and along to the Memorial Park.

I got out here and started to look for Wellington Crescent.

We all knew Mr. Lewis' address of course, but none of us had ever been to his house.

So I reckoned I was making history.

Wellington Crescent wasn't difficult to find and I went along it rather excited.

There was a car outside No. 3 and I didn't know whether this meant guests or whether Mr. Lewis had a car of his own. As far as we knew in the commercial class he didn't; but then we didn't know much about him.

I was just a bit scared before I rang the bell. Well, maybe not scared exactly; but when he asked as he almost certainly would, "But why on earth didn't you keep the book and give it to me in class tomorrow?" what was I to answer? "I thought you might greet me with a welcoming smile, throw the door wide open and invite me in"?

And actually that was exactly what he did.

He opened the door himself and goggled for a second or two. Whether this was due to the fluttering business I was trying to do with my eyelids or just plain dismay at seeing one of the commercial horde up there at his private hideout I didn't know.

"Good lord, Liz, what are you doing up here?"

I showed him Vince's *Dictionary of Commercial Terms.* He stared at it.

"Why on earth didn't—" he started to say it; but then he stopped and smiled at me. He didn't go on. Funny how sometimes you can realize that you are behaving like a complete b.f. and somehow not mind. The other person is so decent it doesn't matter.

Mr. Lewis smiled at me. "Nice of you to have brought it up all this way, Liz," he said. "Come along in and have a glass of sherry with us. My brother's over from South Africa."

When we got inside No. 3 the South African brother and his wife were there and Mrs. Lewis.

She was a legendary figure to us down at the high school.

We all knew she existed but none of us had any idea what she was like. I had now. She was small, plump, not particularly good looking and frightfully nice.

"Here's one of the minxes from my commercial class," Mr. Lewis said. "I left a book behind which I particularly didn't want to lose and she's taken the trouble to bring it all the way up here to me."

Everybody said how kind it was of me.

Mr. Lewis grinned at me; he didn't exactly wink but I could tell he wanted to.

"They're good minxes on the whole," he said. "This one is called Liz. What about a glass of sherry, Liz?"

"I should love one."

I hoped it didn't sound as though it would be the first I had ever had.

"Sweet or dry? George has brought me three of each so I'm well off."

George was in the wine trade apparently so the stuff didn't cost him anything.

Sweet or dry? I hadn't a clue. But all the same I somehow sensed that in a way it was a test question. It was the sort of thing that I ought to know about. That I wanted to know about.

"Why not try the dry?" Mr. Lewis said.

I nodded. "Just what I was going to say," I told him.

I didn't get home till nearly eight.

Thank goodness Aunt Ella was there.

"Where have you been?" Father asked.

"School. Commercial class. Where else?"

"Don't ask me, young lady. I'm asking you."

"Well, of course I've been to school."

"And you came straight home, I suppose?"

It wasn't very clever of Councillor Barton to put his question that way. Even if Aunt Ella hadn't been doing all she could behind his back to warn me I could gather by now that something had gone wrong.

"Why shouldn't I have come straight back?"

"I tell you not to keep asking me things. I'm asking you. Why didn't you come straight back home?"

"Who says I didn't, anyway?"

Mother, of course, was standing like a dumb cluck terrified there was going to be a row and even more terrified of doing anything to prevent it.

"Oh, nobody, nobody. Only your friend Nancy Ellward rang you up and I gathered from her that you left the high school sometime before six!"

I thought it was pretty dim-witted of Nancy but on the other hand I could see that she might have answered the question before she had time to twig that there was danger about.

Except that there is always danger about when you've got a father like mine. She ought to have known that.

"Six is two hours ago," Father went on. "So where have you been?"

"If you want to know I've been up to Mr. Lewis' house with a very important book which he left behind by mistake and which he particularly wanted this evening. *A Dictionary of Commercial Terms.*"

I knew that would impress Father. The words commerce and business had a sort of hypnotic effect on him.

"And if you don't believe me," I went on, "you can ring up Mr. Lewis and ask him."

"Now don't be rude. I never said a word about not believing anybody."

"You obviously thought I'd been somewhere where I shouldn't have been—though I don't know where that would be around here."

Unfortunately I was standing rather close to him and I suppose if you don't smoke or drink yourself your nose gets extra sensitive.

He suddenly pushed his face right into mine and sniffed.

"Have you been *drinking?*" he asked.

I told him I had had a glass of sherry (as a matter of fact I had had two).

"Am I to understand that one of your teachers, a master at the high school, has been giving you alcoholic liquor?"

Well, there you are. You can see the setup. Up in Wellington Crescent with Mr. and Mrs. Lewis and the two people with them it had been fun and I felt I was getting somewhere. I was a person; one of them. Down in Hansbeck Road it was all this "am I to understand?" business and a glass of dry sherry had been "alcoholic liquor."

So we had a row, Mother fluttering about ineffectually on the edges of it and Aunt Ella doing her best for me.

By and large spinster aunts may not amount to much but I'll always be grateful to Aunt Ella.

She was Mother's sister and there was one good thing about her—she hated her brother-in-law.

Whether this was because she had been looking forward to sharing a sisterly existence with Mother and Father had butted in and made it impossible I don't know.

Perhaps she just couldn't bear the thought of his sharing a bed with Mother. Anyway she hated him.

She stood up for me in that particular row, just as she had done in lots of others. And it riled Father pretty badly. Any sort of opposition always did. It was obvious that Aunt Ella wouldn't get anything left to her in his will.

Not that this particular row worried me much. For one thing Father was in a difficulty. True, I had been *drinking,* which was terrible (two very small glasses of dry sherry, enough to damn anyone for all eternity by his standards); on the other hand it was all tied up with Mr. Lewis who taught us our commercial course and commerce was a sacred subject. Very difficult.

I got tired of the whole thing. I was seventeen and the days of Father enjoying himself with a hairbrush were over. I walked out while he was still in full spate and went up to my room and read Dylan Thomas . . . "when I was a windy boy and a bit." I wasn't sure what it meant but most of it was good to say over and over again, aloud. Even if you didn't understand all Dylan Thomas was saying you knew he was on your side against the zombies.

When I left the high school I went into the office in Father's business.

Of course it was a stupid thing to do, but it isn't always easy to avoid doing stupid things.

Father and Mother both pressed me to and in some ways the job suited me. There it was ready-made and waiting; and it was handy.

And to my surprise Father didn't try to beat me down about money. He gave me the same wages that he would have given to any other girl coming in from outside. So I didn't really have much to grumble about.

J. L. Barton, Builder and Contractor, was prospering and although I never officially saw any of the accounts it wasn't difficult to get the general impression that Father was making quite a lot of money.

There were three typists. Miss Castle, who must have been fifty, did Father's letters and any stuff he didn't want the rest of us to know about. She was a great buddy of his in chapel circles. One of the blood-and-fire and isn't-modern-youth-awful brigade. Then there was a girl called Sheila and myself. I typed estimates and specifications mostly . . . "finish in three coats best gloss paint to client-selected color," that sort of thing.

I dare say it was all right as that kind of job goes. If you like that kind of job. Which I didn't much. But after all I had to make a start somewhere.

Father was becoming quite a big bug locally and he was beginning to be talked about as the next mayor. The chapelists would probably be behind him to a man. I didn't go to chapel any more. I stopped going the same week that I started my job with J. L. Barton's.

Of course there was a row. But it was only halfhearted. I didn't flare up or anything, I just said I wasn't going.

Father told me all the things that would happen to me if I didn't go; but by this time I had had a good look at the chapel-goers and it didn't seem to me that they were any better than anybody else. So I didn't see the point in going. I stayed at home and read Dylan Thomas . . . *when I was a windy boy and a bit . . .*

Poor Father! I suppose he traces everything that has happened to me since back to that dreadful decision not to keep on going with him to the dismal little building in Ellerton Street to listen to somebody talking about hell-fire.

Nancy Ellward had got a job with Jean's Beauty Salon in the High Street. She didn't get as much money as I did even, but she was mad about the work, and she reckoned that when she had been there three or four years she would set up on her own.

In spite of the fact that we had been rivals over Mr. Lewis we had become good friends. I don't suppose Father approved of her; he certainly wouldn't have if he had had the slightest idea what her conversation was like, but her father was a solicitor and to know the Ellwards was considered to be a bit of a feather in one's social cap locally.

That first autumn Nancy and I started to play badminton on Wednesday evenings. There was a hall in Goldhurst Road, only a threepenny bus ride away, which the club we had joined used to hire on Wednesdays.

"But I'm no good at badminton," I told her when she suggested it. "I'm not sure that I know how to play, exactly."

"I'm not sure I do. But we can soon learn. And there'll be some men there anyway."

I saw the point of the argument and we joined. It wasn't bad fun, either. As Nancy said, "It gets you away from home, anyway."

There was suddenly a lot more work than normal in the office as Father had managed to get the contract for putting up a row of shops with flats over them on a site that had come into existence when the old fire station was demolished.

This was what brought Louis Armstrong into the firm.

His name really was Louis Armstrong and heaven knows he must have got sick enough of being asked where his trumpet was.

He was about thirty (thirty-four to be precise, as I discovered later) and he was always whistling. Not out loud errand-boy whistling, but quietly, under his breath, especially when he was looking at a plan or studying the figures on an estimate.

Father had brought him in to help with this shops-plus-flats development scheme and an office was made for him by clearing out a lot of old correspondence files and junky furniture from a sort of alcove off the room where Sheila and I worked. Miss Castle had a desk in Father's room, "the inner office."

Funny how a thing can hurt you like hell at the time and when you look back on it from only a year later perhaps it's as dead as ashes. You just can't see how it mattered.

I fell for Louis the very first day that I saw him.

"This is Mr. Armstrong," Father said. "He'll be working in the little room that's been cleared out and if he wants any letters or specifications typed one of you two will have to do them."

And that one will be me, I determined straightaway.

There's no sense in being the boss's daughter and getting no benefit out of it and I had already got Sheila pretty well where I wanted her as far as work went.

Louis saw me looking at him and smiled.

Later in the afternoon of that same day he came out to dictate a letter. Sheila had taken a specification into the inner office and was probably getting hell from Miss Castle who would be going through it with a fine-tooth comb.

Long may she continue to get hell, I thought, as Louis perched himself on the edge of my table.

"Have you time to take a letter, Miss Barton?"

"Yes. Sure. Plenty of time."

"I can easily wait till the other girl's back if you're busy."

"I'm not busy. I'd like to do it for you."

"What's her name, by the way?"

"The other girl? Sheila. Mine's Liz."

"Miss Barton to me. You're the boss's daughter." But he was grinning when he said it.

I don't suppose that Father often made mistakes in picking people to work under him and he certainly hadn't made one with Louis Armstrong. He earned every penny that he was paid and a good deal more. He was out of the office a good deal, on the new site I suppose, and when he came in there was always a flurry of work.

I did it for him.

"For heaven's sake let me give some of this to Sheila," he'd say.

"Not on your life," I told him when I handed a typewritten letter to him. I would take good care that my fingers touched his beneath it.

The first time that happened he drew his hand away quickly and I got quite a thrill from knowing that he was afraid. He was scared because I was a woman. If he was scared, then I *was* a woman. It sort of confirmed my womanhood.

After that first time he would occasionally let his fingers stay there touching mine while he looked at the letter, reading it.

Luckily the alcove that had been cleared out for him was frightfully cramped so when I moved round his chair it was delightfully easy to press myself against him. He didn't press back but he didn't draw away so I reckoned I was making progress.

31

I was just a hot little bit throwing myself at the head of the nearest presentable male.

Only it wasn't quite like that. That wasn't quite all. I wouldn't have been throwing myself at his head if I hadn't felt something about him. Even if it was only a teen-age infatuation.

Nancy and I had started badminton in September and even now looking back I can remember what a wonderful autumn it was that year. All through September and October and well on into November. The days were full of bright sunshine, with the afternoons definitely warm; and then when we were waiting for the Goldhurst Road bus, bonfire smoke would drift over from the allotments behind the chapel and you felt sad and happy all mixed up inside you. At least, I did, because everything I did or saw was connected in my mind with Louis Armstrong to whom as yet I hadn't spoken one single word outside the premises of J. L. Barton.

I very nearly spoke about him one day to Aunt Ella. She used to come to the house regularly in spite of her dislike of her brother-in-law and at some stage of every visit she was sure to find herself in the kitchen doing the washing-up.

She and I were both smoking. Father knew we smoked in the kitchen. He didn't like it but he couldn't very well do anything about it. In the drawing room he would have kicked up such a fuss that it wasn't worth trying.

"Men," Aunt Ella said, "you've got to humor them."

I said I supposed so.

"What about you?" she went on brightly. "I don't see any boy friends coming round to the house."

"Is it likely with Father here? If he saw me talking to a boy on the street corner he'd think we were just going to jump into bed or had just come from it."

"Liz, really—"

"But wouldn't he, Aunt Ella?"

"Yes, probably he would. It's just the way his mind works."

"Well, good luck to him."

As a matter of fact I had a sudden suspicion that perhaps I wasn't being quite fair to Father. My own mind did quite a lot of work on the jumping-into-bed theme.

"Did you have lots of boy friends, Aunt Ella?"

"Not lots exactly. No."

"One?"

"Yes, oh yes, I had a person I was very fond of, once."

"Just one particular one?"

"Somebody I was very fond of."

"What happened?"

"He married somebody else. Nothing very tragic about it; he wasn't killed flying, or he didn't get cancer. None of those things. He just fell in love with somebody else and married her and I should think they are very happy."

"Poor Aunt Ella!"

"Oh, well—some of us are born that way, aren't we? Follow the man who was born to be king, not the woman who was born to be a failure. Nobody can help the way they are made, can they? Just wipe these two plates again, young lady, or you and I will both be getting into trouble."

One Wednesday evening right at the end of October I was waiting at the usual bus stop for Nancy; one Goldhurst Road bus had already gone by and we looked like being late and it was raining.

When Nancy arrived I was going to have something pretty forceful to say on the subject of people who couldn't come on time.

She wouldn't have heard me if I had. She was too excited. There was a street lamp just by the bus stop and her dark eyes shone in it.

This colored boy she was mad about was frightfully clever. He was studying law in Lincoln's Inn and her people couldn't stick him. It was no good, they just could not stick the idea of her going out with a colored boy. And he was the most wonderful dancer. "Honestly, Liz, it's like dancing in a dream." And what with late lectures and things Wednesday was just about the one night in the week he could be certain of getting off which suited marvelously because Wednesday was rock and roll night at The Goldfish and that's where she was off now to meet him.

"The point is, Liz," she went on, "that at home they are used to my being out on Wednesdays. As far as they are concerned I shall be up at badminton with you. So if anybody should ever ask you anything, not that they ever would, but you would always say we were at Goldhurst Road together as usual, wouldn't you? And you'll be all right because you get on marvelously with anybody and if ever you get the chance of going out with a colored boy you take it, Liz, they've definitely got something . . ."

Which is how conspiracies are hatched. In one way I was all for it. One girl can always be relied upon to help another when it comes to covering up for a bit of fun. All the same I felt a little flat at the moment. I wasn't keen on going up to Goldhurst Road all by myself, it was beginning to rain like stink and there was Nancy simply streaking off along the street toward The Goldfish where she was due to meet the boy with the snaky hips who danced like a dream.

So it looked like a blank night for me and I wasn't particularly interested in the old black car which pulled up just beyond the bus stop.

Until Louis Armstrong stuck his head out of the window and called out:

"Are you waiting for a bus? Would you like a lift?"

Twenty minutes later we were sitting in the saloon of the Three Kings at Weddy Corner.

"What will you have to drink, Liz?"

"Sherry. I always have sherry."

"Dry?"

"Yes, I like mine dry."

When I had got into his car and shaken some of the rain off myself he asked where I wanted to go to.

"Home?"

"No, anywhere but home," I told him. "Where are you going to?"

"I—I was going up to a pub I know, at Weddy Corner."

"The Three Kings?"

"That's it."

I knew the Kings although I had never been in it.

"Sometimes I go up there for a meal," he went on, "especially if things are a bit difficult at home."

Home? I didn't know he had a home. For some reason or other I had always imagined him living in digs.

"I always thought you lived in digs. Nobody ever tells me anything."

He laughed. "I'm a married man, Liz."

Well, that was O.K. by me. All the more exciting if he was married. Only not for him apparently. We ate ham sandwiches and he drank whisky and I had two sherries. And he told me all about himself.

I didn't know then that men are apt to tell you all about themselves in pubs. Not that Louis got maudlin or even half tight. He was just unhappy. His wife was six years older than he was and for some reason which nobody could understand (and that included her) every now and again she would start on a terrific jag.

"It's something medical, I suppose," he said. "Too many glands of one sort or not enough of another."

On that particular Wednesday she had been blind drunk at three o'clock and she was now sleeping it off. When he got home no fire lit; no meal prepared; nothing except a smell of drink and his wife snoring on the bed.

So he had come out to forget it for a bit.

And at the Kings he *did* forget it for a bit. The place was pretty full and people were laughing and we felt (I felt anyway) that it might have been a thousand miles from Hans-beck Road.

I made all the running. Looking back on it now I can see what a decent type Louis was and how well he behaved.

I told him all about badminton on Wednesday nights and how Nancy had got herself something else to do.

"So now I've got to go up to Goldhurst Road by myself every Wednesday and pretend she's there too."

He cut one of his sandwiches in half.

"And I just don't want to go there by myself. In fact I'm not going. So I'm going to have every Wednesday night free."

"But, Liz—"

He didn't run me right home, of course; he dropped me at the bus stop where he had picked me up and by that time I knew it was all settled even if he didn't.

On Wednesdays he was to tell his wife that he was work-ing overtime at Father's office; I would be going out to bad-minton as usual; and we would meet at the bus stop at six-thirty.

We never went anywhere too local, of course. Always ten minutes or so away in the car. Sometimes we went to the pictures; sometimes we sat in a pub (usually the Kings) and talked; once he took me greyhound racing and I made fifty-five shillings.

And except that he occasionally kissed me good night nothing happened between us.

"Louis, Louis kiss me, kiss me."

"Liz, how old are you?"

"Seventeen. Nearly eighteen. I'm not a kid any more."

"Of course you're not. You're a lovely young woman. But I'm thirty-four, Liz. Twice your age."

"I don't care if you're a hundred. I love you."

"Liz, Liz—"

"I do, I do. I love you."

"Take it easy, Liz. It's wonderful for me to have this one

day a week out and to be able to talk to someone—you don't
mind me telling you things, do you?"
"Tell me anything, Louis, anything, anything."
"Ah, not like that, Liz."

That was how the winter went by. November and December. I gave Louis a silver cigarette lighter for Christmas. He didn't want to take it.

"It's too expensive, Liz. You're a frightfully extravagant person."

"Yes, I am. I'm extravagant and passionate, Louis, and I love being like that."

It wasn't much good being extravagant and passionate in Hansbeck Road; but just at the moment I was all right.

Louis was my dream.

"How's badminton?" Nancy would ask on the telephone. We used to ring one another up once a week to make sure there hadn't been a slipup.

"Fine. There's a new member. A Captain Porter. Frightfully military and dashing." I've always been able to invent stuff like that.

"What about you?" I'd ask, doing my best to sound casual and disinterested.

"My dear, Chicky is too wonderful."

"Dancing?"

"And everything."

In the office Louis was extremely correct. I loved it. It was a sort of game. I thought of us as being in a TV play all the time and people watching us and saying, "Isn't she wonderful the way she doesn't show any emotion at all?"

Halfway through February I got a letter from the badminton club saying what a good season they had had and reminding everybody that Wednesday, 17th March, would be the last evening until next autumn.

I had completely forgotten that it packed up during the summer, and I couldn't think what to do.

However, I needn't have worried. I've found out since then that very often when you are dithering about, wondering what to do, life does it for you.

It certainly did that Thursday evening.

Aunt Ella was coming over and I wanted to wash my hair before she came.

"Where are you going?" Father asked as I was leaving the drawing room.

"I'm going to wash my hair."

"Didn't you do it last night?"

"Last night? Yesterday was Wednesday. Badminton."

"Oh, yes. How's badminton going?"

"Fine. I love it."

"Is that girl—"

"Nancy—"

"—Nancy. Is she any good at it?"

"She's better than I am, anyway."

"Do you and she play together as a rule?"

"Sometimes. Sometimes we split up."

"Liar!"

I suppose I ought to have been suspicious of all the talk about badminton, in which normally Father took no interest whatsoever; but it had sounded harmless enough and I hadn't suspected the land mine until it exploded.

"What a liar you are."

I looked at him steadily. He had a very thick neck and a heavy face. It was quite white with rage now and his eyes seemed to be sticking out.

I had a feeling then that this was going to be the final flare-up.

But I thought I might as well fence for time a bit and try to find out how much he knew.

"I haven't the vaguest idea what you are talking about. Not a clue."

"No? Perhaps you are aware that your friend, Nancy Ellward, has a father. Not that you think anything of fathers, of course. We know that. Fathers are just there to pay the bills."

"What about Nancy's father?"

"Last night he happened to see his daughter out with a colored man when she should have been up at the badminton club. With you. That's what about him."

"Last night?"

"Yesterday was Wednesday. Remember? And you came in and told us what a good evening it had been at the badminton club."

"I didn't say Nancy was there."

"Do you know a Mr. Hayward?"

"Mr. Hayward—?"

"He's the secretary of your club. In case you've forgotten."

I *had* forgotten; but why say so?

"Of course I know him."

"Mr. Ellward has been in touch with him and it seems that Nancy Ellward hasn't been to the club for at least three months."

"Good gracious."

"Neither have you."

I stared at him without saying anything for a moment or so. However good your imagination is there are situations when it is extremely difficult to know what to say. Which was why Father was waiting with such a pleased look on his face.

"Is that what Mr. Hayward told you?" I asked him.

"That is precisely what Mr. Hayward told me when I spoke to him on the telephone this afternoon. That you had not been to Goldhurst Road any single Wednesday for the last three months."

"Well, he ought to know," I said, "being secretary."

"Where have you been?"

"I've been going out with somebody."

"A man?"

"Of course. I'm normal, aren't I?"

"How dare you answer me like that."

Well, there we were, on the "how dare you" basis now. I don't say Father wasn't justified. From his point of view he was justified. Only I wasn't looking at it from his point of view. I was looking at it from mine and I didn't see much future in Hansbeck Road.

Of course there was the prize flare-up of all time. Outraged virtue went to Father's head in a big way. Also curiosity. Whom had I been going with all this time? That was what he wanted to know.

"Another colored man, I suppose," he said. I told him I hadn't been lucky enough for that.

"Lucky?" He almost screamed.

"Well, Nancy tells me they've definitely got something for a girl."

Naturally I didn't tell him it was Louis and in the end I went up to bed almost before he had finished laying down the new list of regulations I was going to have to keep in future: in the house every night by ten at the latest and even then not go out unless I said where I was going and whom with and so on.

Before this Aunt Ella had turned up, and she and Mother had had an hour's lecture about the iniquity of young people today and how it was all the fault of women for not keeping up the moral atmosphere of the home.

So while I was undressing I made up my mind to go. I suppose you would call it running away from home. Only that sounded much more melodramatic than it actually was.

After all I wasn't exactly a kid any longer; I could get a job anywhere as a shorthand typist, and it just happened that there wasn't any love between me and the people who had brought me into the world. I didn't see why there should be. It doesn't work that way with kittens and young birds. As soon as they can fend for themselves they get shoved out into the world and the best of British luck to them.

I could fend for myself and I wasn't waiting to be shoved out, I was going.

And I knew where I was going. This wasn't the first time that I had thought about launching out on my own and I had always been keen on starting in Shepherd's Bush. There wasn't anywhere particular that I knew of there, but somehow it appealed to me. And I didn't think it would be too expensive.

And I knew just how I was going to set about getting a job. Sheila, who typed alongside me in the office, had been away with jaundice and Father had had to get a replacement for her. This was a pretty tough sort of character, about twenty-five percent more efficient than Sheila, who told me she never took anything but temporary jobs. She reckoned it was more fun.

"You see lots of different people and lots of different work and on the whole you get better money. People are in a hole because somebody has folded up with illness or something of the sort, like your girl here; they've got to have somebody pro tem and so the agency can twist their arm a bit. The agency takes a percentage off what you get, but even so you generally come out pretty well."

All that remained was working out the actual business of getting away from the house. I got that settled during the night as I lay awake looking up at the dark ceiling and thinking how glad I was that I had finished once and for all with Hansbeck Road.

The rule at breakfast time was everybody down and seated at the table at eight o'clock or else . . . or else there would be moral indignation and a scream about laziness from Father who from what one could gather used to get up at six and do half the housework when he was a boy. I didn't notice him doing half, or come to that any, of the housework now, but he was certainly all set to start eating his breakfast at eight every morning.

Next morning I just didn't get up. Presently Mother came padding up as I knew she would. "Father wants to know . . ."

"Tell him I've got the curse badly and I'm staying in bed for a while. I'll get down to the office as soon as I can."

This was a relief to her, I could see. I did get the curse badly at times, and this was an excuse which couldn't very well be questioned.

All the same she had to come padding back.

"Father says there's a lot to do at the office and to get down there as soon as you can."

I nodded. I didn't say it. I didn't say what I was thinking about the man she had been silly enough to marry. It might have shocked her.

I heard front-door noises at eight forty-five. Councillor J. L. Barton going off on schedule to do some more highly profitable contracting and estimating.

Mother came up immediately afterwards with a cup of tea and to say that she would be going out soon to do the shopping and probably I would be getting up before long?

I told her probably I would.

At nine o'clock the front door closed again, this time behind Mother off to the shops early to see if she could save a penny or two on the bills because the household accounts came in for severe examination every week.

It can't have been more than twenty minutes later that I was in the High Street carrying my one and only suitcase crammed with all I could get into it.

My running away from home was as undramatic as that. I simply put the things I thought I would want most into an old suitcase and walked out.

In a way that suitcase was a symbol for me of Hansbeck Road. It was old and disreputable and because the lock was uncertain you had to have a strap round it. One of the things I wanted most in life and which I had already promised myself I would have one day was good luggage. Brand new, white, smart stuff that would let the porters at the air terminal and the staffs at the hotels know that you were somebody.

But at the moment it was the old suitcase which luckily was a huge one. There wasn't much I didn't manage to cram into it. Nothing essential anyway, and I carried two coats.

I had to go down the High Street for a short stretch because there was no other way of getting to the Underground station and I must get to the Underground in order to get to Shepherd's Bush.

Mother was almost certain to be somewhere in the High Street and naturally I didn't want to run into her. Not that I would have been persuaded not to go, but simply that it would have meant a scene and I didn't want any scenes. I just wanted to clear out. No fuss, no drama and once the moral indignation brouhaha had died down great relief for all concerned.

The danger of running into her wasn't particularly great as the odds were that she would be in one of the shops, Sainsbury's or the Co-op, while I hurried by outside.

"Liz."

I stopped abruptly. I had been so keen on looking out for Mother that I had forgotten other people might be about as well.

It was Aunt Ella. Staring at my dirty old suitcase bulging under its holding strap and at the two coats over my arm and with comprehension already showing in her eyes.

"Liz . . . what . . . you're . . . ?"

I nodded. "Quite right, Aunt Ella, I'm going. I'm off. I've had enough of it. Especially after last night."

She took a deep breath.

"It just doesn't make sense hanging on there," I went on.

"They don't get any pleasure out of me and I don't get any out of them. I'm off on my own."

"Good for you, Liz; oh, good for you."

Well, that was a relief, anyway.

"Do they know?"

"No, I'm supposed to be in bed feeling moldy. I just walked out."

"Where are you going, Liz? What are you going to do?"

"Not to worry about that, Aunt Ella. I can get a job tomorrow without any trouble. I shall be all right."

"What about money?"

"I'm O.K. I'll get by."

She thought of something suddenly and looked up. We were standing directly outside Barclay's Bank.

"That's my bank," she said. "Come on in."

Inside she bought a check form for twopence and wrote it out, "Cash. Fifteen pounds, Ella Dangerfield."

She gave the fifteen pound-notes to me, and for the first time since I had made up my mind to go I felt a bit shaky. When somebody's unexpectedly kind to you it often gets you that way.

"Look, Aunt Ella, I—"

"No, no," she insisted. "Take it, take it. I wish I could make it more. I ought to have done what you're doing a long time ago. Go and live on your own and good luck to you."

Outside her last words were, "Never tell them I gave you anything, will you?"

"I shall never see them again," I told her. "Don't worry. Look after yourself."

She gave me a bit of a smile and I could see she wasn't far from crying and that's how I left her.

All that I had had in my bag up till then was eight pounds that I had got saved in my stocking drawer. Which had never looked very reassuring as total working capital to start on. Eight plus fifteen was twenty-three which was a lot more promising.

If I had seen a taxi at that moment I think I would have hailed it and damn the expense.

But taxis weren't common along the High Street, and the Underground station was only five minutes' walk away, so I said "Shepherd's Bush" to the man behind the grille and as he passed the ticket out he can't have had any idea what he was doing.

As I say there wasn't anything dramatic about it. I expect that hundreds, probably thousands, of people do the same every year in London. Pack up and push off. Start out for themselves. But all the same it was exciting. *I* was excited, anyway. Hansbeck Road, the chapel and the local cinema were one world. But there were others. And I meant to get into them. Luxury? All right, call it money if you want. Money came into it of course. Money was the main difference between the world I was leaving and the one I meant to get into. Money and what it did to people. I wanted to be with people who didn't care. People who kicked life around instead of being kicked. People who sent a thirty-word telegram to wish somebody else a happy birthday. People who had swimming pools; who went to first nights; who traveled with four brand-new rawhide cases and had their names printed on their labels; who had lovely tiled bathrooms and huge baths and let the scalding hot water run right up to the top and over the top if they happened to be doing something else at the moment and forgot about it. . . .

Not that Panter Street looked much like that when I got to it.

Two minutes outside Shepherd's Bush station there was a small stationery and tobacco shop with paperbacks in the window and a couple of glass-fronted cases hanging outside.

The top case had half a dozen of the unobviously obvious sort of card in it. "Young blonde model gives private French lessons, ring Bay 36312." "Strict ex-governess free for part-time employment. Ring—"

I wasn't interested in these. It was the lower case that interested me and there the very first thing I saw was "Clean comfortable homely room for Young Professional Lady. Apply Mrs. Mason, 52 Panter Street. 5 mins."

A man selling papers told me where Panter Street was and at No. 52 Mrs. Mason, having looked a bit dubiously at my nylon-clad legs, agreed to let me have the room.

So I was in; and it was barely an hour since I had walked out of Hansbeck Road.

I paid Mrs. Mason a week's money in advance, told her that I had a typist's job at the War Office and went out to get a cup of coffee before tackling the agency Sheila's temporary replacement had told me about.

THREE

Love? You tell me what it is and I'll tell you whether I was ever really in love with Jimmy Mancroft. Let's say I learned a lot from him and leave it at that.

Jimmy had a lot of talents. He was good at making love, cooking, spending money and losing his temper. And if things didn't go just the way he wanted them to he could sulk better than most spoiled kids of ten.

There was no difficulty at the Agency for Temporary Clerical Posts as it rather grandiloquently called itself. I happened to walk in—though I didn't know it at the time—just as Jimmy had done a raving mad and a for-God's-sake-send-me-somebody-or-I'm-sunk act on the telephone.

I expect Mr. Clore of the agency was tired of Jimmy and as I walked in at that moment I got the job.

There were normal inquiries about my speeds which I answered truthfully and my experience which I took more liberties with.

"Ever done any theatrical work?"

"Not actually theatrical work."

I wasn't sure whether Mr. Clore would understand what that meant. I didn't. But Mr. Clore wasn't feeling at his best. He looked as though he might have had a whale of a party the night before. There were bags under his eyes and he gave the impression that the whole thing was a bit much for him.

"At any rate you would find theatrical work interesting, wouldn't you?"

"Definitely."

"And after all it is only temporary—I'll get a form ready Miss—"

"Barton."

I read through the form before I signed it. Not that it made much difference because if I had to sign the form to get the job I intended to sign it anyway. It seemed to me that Mr. Clore was going to make a pretty good thing out of the labors of Miss E. Barton. No wonder he could afford expensive hangovers. Well, good luck to him. I had to get a start so I signed.

"Jimmy Mancroft's up to Nottingham this afternoon," he said. "I suppose one of his people is playing there. But he'll want you first thing tomorrow. Deeley House, Shaftesbury Avenue. Ten o'clock. Don't be late, will you?"

I shook my head. I wasn't going to be late. He needn't worry.

Mr. Clore had a good look at me.

"You'll get on all right with Jimmy Mancroft," he said. "I should think."

I wasn't late. Thanks to elbowing the fat woman out of her rightful place in the bus queue at Shepherd's Bush I was in plenty of time.

Deeley House isn't much to look at. Go through a narrow entrance between a shop where they sell musical instruments and a window full of clothes I wouldn't want to be seen dead in and you're in a dark hall looking at a board with a lot of unlikely-sounding names.

"Third Floor, Jimmy Mancroft Ltd. Theatrical Agent. No. 7. British Council for Improvement of International Understanding. No. 8," was what it said.

There's a crazy lift which you work yourself and which I was scared to take that first morning (I thought it might get stuck halfway up) and you find yourself on the third floor with the British whatever it was for not throwing atom bombs about on one side and Jimmy Mancroft Limited on the other. A two days' pile of letters on the floor outside the B.C. for the I. of I.U. and two milk bottles outside Jimmy Mancroft's.

Not that milk was his staple drink by any means, but he certainly liked his cup of tea occasionally.

When I went in Jimmy was in an attitude completely characteristic of him. He might have been posing for a portrait. His left hand was outstretched stubbing out a half-smoked cigarette in a huge glass ashtray on his desk, his right hand had a telephone to his ear.

That man spent his life on the telephone and most of the time that he was telephoning he was smoking.

"That bitch Tandy," he said, putting the telephone down. "That false red-ripe, false-hearted bitch. We had an up and downer more than a month ago and she won't speak to me. I can sign her up for a wonderful part in Messel's new film and she just won't say yes or no. She won't say a bloody thing. Hell's tits to her. Maybe she isn't all that wonderful after all. Do you think she is?"

There was only one Tandy I knew about and that was Tandy Sellman. I had seen her in *Wise Men Never Try* and I thought she was marvelous.

I said so.

Jimmy nodded gloomily. "Yeah, yeah. Of course she's marvelous. You're quite right. And this part would suit her like a glove. Just up her street. Most likely she'll take it. She *will* take it. By the devil's flaming eyeballs she *must*. But will she say so? She knows that it would be the best thing that has ever happened to me so she won't say a darned thing. How mean can you get? I suppose you're from the agency?"

Yes, I told him, I was from the agency.

He took time off from being worried to have a good look at me. I was beginning to wonder when he would notice I had taken some trouble about turning myself out that morning.

Jimmy smiled.

"Well, they show signs of sense occasionally I must say. Can you type as well?"

That was just the sort of thing Jimmy said. Even at that early stage I realized that.

I told him I could type.

He reached for a cigarette and pointed with it to his desk which was a shambles.

"Come on then," he said. "Let's tackle it. I was up in Nottingham yesterday and Oxford the day before that and I never answer letters till I have to anyway. Give me a light."

What he said about not answering letters was obviously right because there was stuff there that ought to have been dealt with weeks before.

Jimmy may have thrown it all on a pile out of his way but now that he was coping with it he did so highly efficiently.

He knew what he wanted to say and he said it, which is how I like dictation to be.

About every ten minutes the telephone went and dictating would be interrupted while I was half trying to make out what the heck the word in the middle of the last sentence was and half trying to listen in and to pick up clues as to who was on the other end of the phone and what Jimmy was talking about.

It was interesting but not very rewarding.

". . . let him stew in it then. He must be the worst actor God ever inflicted on the West End of London and he deserves to be in a mess . . ."

"Cheltenham? My dear boy, lovely; but how the star-spangled blazes do you imagine I can afford the time and money to whirl up to Cheltenham with you and pour out my fortune into the bookmakers' satchels?"

He dictated till eleven.

"Tea," he suddenly said. "I suppose you can make tea?"

I told him yes, I could make tea.

"Versatile, aren't you?" he grinned at me. "I shouldn't

wonder. Vile stuff tea but at times necessary. Do you suppose that moron Tandy will ring me?"

"Can she get the part except through you?"

He shook his head. "Not a hope. As far as that goes I've got her here," he pressed a well-manicured thumb down on his desk.

"Then she'll ring."

"We hope."

While we were having tea I asked him what had happened to his regular secretary.

"She wasn't regular. At least not as regular as all that. She fell down the stairs and broke her virtue. She went off in a huff. She was afraid I wasn't going to seduce her or something."

The telephone rang and he motioned me to answer it.

"If it's Tandy Sellman I'm engaged on the other line but you're sure I'll speak to her."

It wasn't Tandy S.; it was an accountant from Blackfence & Co. who wanted to know when the returns for income tax were going to be sent in.

"Tell him to sod off."

"Mr. Mancroft has got the matter in hand," I said, "and we'll be sending the returns along shortly."

"They are more than three months overdue," he pointed out.

"Mr. Mancroft has been exceptionally busy lately, but he hopes to get round to it soon."

"You're going to earn your money, I can see that," Jimmy said, grinning at me as I put the telephone down.

I was sent out for lunch at half past one and Jimmy ate some sandwiches in the office.

At three he suddenly announced that he had to go out.

"Only up to Regent House to see Hopper Hunt of L.D.A. I don't believe Tandy Sellman is going to ring now. If she does tell her that I've been called away on important business to Pinewood but that I'll be in tomorrow morning."

He hadn't been gone five minutes when Tandy rang.

I recognized her voice immediately; one of those highly exciting voices that start men thinking along the right lines straightaway.

"Is that half-witted agent Mancroft about?" she asked.

I went through the important business at Pinewood routine and I am not sure how you gather from the way a person listens that they aren't believing you, but somehow I did.

"Is that all true or is he skulking about the office somewhere?" she asked.

"He definitely isn't in the office, Miss Sellman."

"How did you know who it was speaking?"

"I recognized your voice."

"I don't recognize yours. You're new there, aren't you?"

"I only came in this morning."

"Jimmy hasn't had time to ask you to sleep with him yet, I suppose?"

"Not yet."

"Don't worry. He will. Well, you can tell him I'll take the part in Messel's new picture."

"Oh, Miss Sellman, that's fine."

"What's fine about it?"

"Well, I mean, you were so marvelous in *Wise Men Never Try*—"

"You liked it, did you?"

"I loved it."

"Tell Jimmy Mancroft that in spite of his being the most damned awkward agent in the business I'll take the part and he can go ahead with the contract."

Ten minutes later a brainwave struck me. There was a short list of frequently used numbers by the telephone and when I thumbed it open at H the first name I saw was H. Hunt, L.D.A., REG 51421.

I dialed it and a man's voice answered at once.

"Hopper Hunt here."

"Is Mr. Mancroft there, please?"

"More or less."

Hopper Hunt's voice sounded as though the cupboard behind the safe was open and the bottle of Scotch was on the desk.

"Who wants to speak to him?" Hunt demanded.

"Miss Barton."

". . . *your past rapidly catching up with you, old man,*" I distinctly heard Hunt say as he handed over the phone.

"Hallo," Jimmy's voice was tentative and defensive. "Who is that please?"

"Liz Barton."

"I'm afraid—*who* did you say?"

"It's your secretary, Mr. Mancroft."

After a moment's pause Jimmy's voice roared out in what was by now becoming a familiar fashion.

"Why in the name of all the archangels couldn't you say so before? What did you say your name was—Barton? What a fantastic name. What are you chasing me over here for? Is it the union's time for you to go home or something?"

"Tandy Sellman rang up."

"When?"

"About ten minutes ago."

"Did you tell her I should be in the office tomorrow morning?"

"No, I don't think I did, actually."

"For God's sake. You're fired. I knew that damn agency wasn't any good. You can pack up and go. What *did* you tell her?"

"I told her I thought she was marvelous in *Wise Men Never Try.*"

"And I suppose she said her darling fans were too, too wonderful. God, what mush!"

"Actually she said she was going to take the part in the new Messel film."

"She said *what?*"

"She said she was going to take the part in the new film and you could start drawing up the contract right away."

It seemed that I had hardly put the phone down before he was back in the office. I had to recount every word that Tandy Sellman had said and when he had absorbed that we got to work on the contract.

"These things take time to draw up," Jimmy warned me. "You have to bind these ruddy stars hand and foot. You have to tie 'em up in every detail. We shall be hours doing this."

As I still had a wodge of letters to type this wasn't very good news, but doing the contract was quite interesting and we weren't interrupted too badly by the telephone.

One of the calls reminded Jimmy of something he had obviously forgotten.

". . . The Fortune, seven forty-five? Of course I hadn't forgotten," he lied valiantly, ". . . no, as a matter of fact she can't . . . naturally I've got somebody else." He covered the mouthpiece with his left hand and shot across at me:

"You doing anything tonight?"

I shook my head.

"Naturally I've got somebody else," Jimmy went on down the phone. "A very attractive girl called Liz Barton . . . Leicestershire? God knows, very likely she is. You'll fall for her in a big way . . . No, nothing will persuade me to put on a dinner jacket . . . oh, we'll eat afterwards somewhere, I'll fix that . . . meet at The Fortune seven-thirty, O.K. . . ."

He put the telephone down and smiled at me.

"Tubby wanted to know if you were one of the Leicestershire Bartons. Are you?"

"I wouldn't know."

"None of his business anyway. He's God's own most pathetic snob. But he's got money and he thinks the theater's wonderful. So he's to be cultivated."

"I gather I'm being asked out to a party?"

"Quite correct. *Where Is She Now?* at The Fortune which isn't even half a good play but I've got to go and see it for various reasons. And supper afterwards. Probably at the Casse Croûte. Aren't you a lucky girl?"

"Supposing I don't want to go?"

"Don't be a b.f. And don't get any silly ideas about Tubby Waller; he'll fall for you all right, so let him fall."

"But I'm not to be interested in him?"

"You couldn't be, Liz. He's not your type." Jimmy leaned across and pinched me hard. "I'm your type."

At six o'clock I went on strike and said I wanted to go back to my room to change.

Jimmy was genuinely surprised.

"We can go on working here till after seven and then slip along to The Fortune."

"Not me. I'm not going like this."

"What's wrong with you? You look charming."

"Thanks for the testimonial. But I'm not going to the theater like this."

"Women! I'm going just as I am."

"You're a man, you're different."

"Don't start giving me lessons in elementary biology."

"I wouldn't have thought you needed them, Mr. Mancroft."

He laughed. "How right you are. You'd be surprised how right you are. Or maybe you wouldn't. Difficult to tell with you Leicestershire Bartons. And by the way it's 'Jimmy' if we are going out in a party together. Which we are."

It shook him when I demanded a pound from the petty cash, but as I pointed out Shepherd's Bush was a long way off and girls who were going to the theater didn't travel by bus. At least this one didn't.

Although only ten hours had passed since I left the place, No. 52 Panter Street seemed like a strange and foreign world. Or maybe it was Jimmy Mancroft and Shaftesbury Avenue that was the strange and foreign world. Anyway there were clearly two worlds; of that I was more than ever aware now, and I knew which one I intended to belong to.

I didn't have time to spend wondering what I was going to wear. I only had one dress that was suitable. It was an olive-green semi-evening affair which I had bought at C. & A. in Oxford Street three months before and which suited me perfectly. It was one of those lucky buys which every woman makes occasionally.

Not expensive but just right.

I had a bath, changed, did my hair and was down in the minute hall with its depressing brown wallpaper by a few minutes after seven.

Mrs. Mason appeared up the basement steps.

"Going out?"

"To the theater."

She sniffed. I could see that she had strong zombie tendencies too. Maybe all landladies have.

"I didn't know you'd be one of these people who come in late," she said.

"I won't wake anybody."

"And if you put on the light please be sure to turn it off again. Otherwise I'm afraid I shall have to charge extra."

I nodded.

"Are you going in the Underground like that, without a coat or anything?"

"I'm not going by Underground, I'm going by taxi."

"*Well!*"

Jimmy was waiting in the foyer of The Fortune when I arrived. I don't know how it was that he wasn't in the bar. It is just possible that he thought I would be glad not to be left on my own and was looking out for me. But only just; he wasn't noticeably unselfish.

There were a lot of people milling about. *Where Is She Now?* was obviously doing well.

There's one feeling that you can't mistake. It's like nothing else in the world. The feeling of excitement and urgency that pervades a whole theater when the play's a success.

Jimmy pushed his way across and had a long, frank stare at me. And Jimmy knew about women and how they ought to look in their clothes.

He smiled and nodded and that moment of warm approval must have gone a long way toward deciding the ultimate course of the evening as far as I was concerned.

"You'll do, Liz," he said, "you look fine. You'll look a damn sight better than most of the others."

"Is it a big party?"

"Ten of us. Let's go down to the bar and put in a little serious drinking before the mob arrives."

"Sherry?" he said when I told him what I thought I wanted. "You don't want sherry. Too damned livery. Besides you can't sit out a play like this on a dry sherry. What you want is a brandy and ginger ale."

He was perfectly right, too, which I realized as soon as I started to drink it.

"Here's lots of fun, Liz."

"Lots of fun, Jimmy."

By the time we were all in our seats and the curtain went up I had had two brandies and ginger ale and a far worse play than *Where Is She Now?* would have seemed good to me.

As a matter of fact anything would have seemed good to me that evening. I hadn't been with people of that sort before. I never heard anything but Christian names and I never did sort everybody out properly. I took a quick look at the four other girls in the party and to my immense relief I could see that I needn't worry.

My inexpensive olive-green number from C. & A. was going to hold its own all right. There was one girl, Sonia, in black, who would have knocked spots off nearly anyone, anywhere; but I was as good as the others.

To start with I was sitting between Jimmy and the man who seemed to be convinced that he knew my family in Leicestershire, Tubby Waller, a tall, fair-haired, middle-aged man of about twenty-six who talked like a politician addressing a not very intelligent meeting and dragged as many titles into his conversation as he could:

". . . *She* married a chappie who became an admiral," he would say.

Good luck to her (whoever she was), I thought. I could see that marrying an admiral was probably a very sensible thing to do. No doubt you would get as many brandies and ginger ale as you wanted.

". . . wasn't he the Barton who stood for Parliament?" Tubby would say tentatively.

"Was it that one?" I asked and very nearly burst out laughing at myself. I hadn't a clue what he was talking about but that, obviously, was the way to keep the ball rolling with Tubby.

"Perhaps it wasn't," he said, "I think you're right there. Was it Harry who—"

"*Ssh*," went some angry female behind us who wanted value for her seventeen and six and Tubby's sandy eyebrows went up in pained surprise.

We all went out for a drink during the second interval and as I seemed to remember somebody advising me never to mix my drinks I naturally had a brandy and ginger ale.

When we shuffled back into our seats there was some slight confusion and although I was still next to Tubby on one side Sonia was on the other.

A good-looking bitch this Sonia, but rather harder than most nails. She turned and took a little long feminine look at me. Top to toe. Hairdo to stockings and shoes. She didn't miss much. I bet she could have written out an inventory there and then of everything I was wearing, where I got it from and what it cost. She didn't like me. So she smiled sweetly.

"How's life with Jimmy?" she asked.

"I wouldn't know."

"You soon will. Don't worry. And incidentally, and just for your own private ear, he's a bastard."

"Incidentally just for your private ear," I told her, "he's my boss."

"You must be a Girl Guide working up for your loyalty badge. How frightfully quaint. But I don't think it will get you very far. On the whole Jimmy isn't keen on Girl Guides, I wouldn't say."

I enjoyed *Where Is She Now?* I hadn't often before seen a play from the stalls of a West End theater and it was no good anybody trying to tell me I ought to be blasé and bored. This was life and I was living it.

Afterwards two of the men had cars and the rest of us packed into a taxi and so we all arrived in Chelsea at the Casse Croûte.

"They've a very reasonable Nuits St. George here," Jimmy said. Good for them, I thought; I was all for being reasonable. Up to a point.

Tubby gave us a lecture on the lesser vineyards of some particular valley or other and Sonia told us about the private sex life of the leading actor in the play we had just seen which apparently centered in the barman at a West End theatrical club.

Somebody wanted to know whether I did a job and if so what and while I was taking a sip of Nuits St. George to give myself time to think out the proper answer Jimmy, who seemed to be fully engaged in noisy conversation with the other end of the table, cohered and chipped in. I learned very early that there were no flies on Jimmy when it came to handling situations.

"I've created a new part for her," he said in the mock-heroic tones which enable you to get away with most things among the educated English. "I've made her my P.A. My personal assistant."

"I've never heard it called that before," Sonia said, which of course got a laugh from everybody. Including Jimmy. But I saw his eyes. No laughter in them. Jimmy was quite cross. "He'll give that smart little bitch a beating up some day," I thought, "and I hope I'm there to help."

When we came out the air was deliciously cold after the fug inside and the stars were bright in a dark sky.

Everyone began to sort themselves out and to say good night . . . marvelous . . . lovely, wonderful, God bless, be seeing you . . . whirl away . . . we all suddenly had a new surge of affection for one another. You can afford to when you aren't going to see one another again for some time.

". . . if you ever *are* in Leicestershire again . . ." Tubby was saying.

Yes, yes, I told him; certainly if I ever am in Leicestershire again (never having been there in my life) certainly I will. I hadn't a clue what it was that I was supposed to do, but the Nuits St. George had made me very reasonable and I was anxious to see Tubby's fat, white old-young face look pleased.

". . . don't forget Hurlingham on the twentieth," one of the girls—Nell—screamed out as she got settled in the front seat of a car.

The engine revved, a taxi loaded up and drove off. Sonia, in black velvet and a six-tie sable wrap I'd have scratched her eyes out for, plus her partner stood on the pavement. So did Jimmy and I.

"Wallis is getting a taxi," Sonia announced.

In point of fact Wallis had already got one. Probably if you were Sonia's knight-in-attendance you had to be pretty efficient or you got hell.

"Shall we all pile in and drop you two at your different addresses?" Sonia suggested.

"Not to bother," Jimmy told her easily. "It will take you miles out of your way. You two drive off in state and Liz and I will catch a cab on our own."

"It's such a lovely night I wouldn't mind walking a bit," I said.

"You only do that when they run out of petrol," Sonia told me. "You'll learn."

Sonia's taxi drove off and in response to Jimmy's uplifted hand another pulled up.

"Walking's not a bad idea," he said, "as an idea. Jump in."

"Where to, sir?" the man asked.

"Three Merton Mews."

Most men get amorous in taxis. But not Jimmy. Not on that particular evening anyway. He lit another of his interminable cigarettes and flicked the match across the inside of the cab.

"Sonia's got a one-track mind," he said. "She thinks I'm taking you home to spend the night with me.

"Which of course I am," he added as the cab turned out of Chiltern Gardens into the narrow entrance of Merton Mews.

Merton Mews, or Jimmy's part of it, consisted of two rooms one above the other. The best part of it was the size of the rooms. They were both really big. Downstairs was the living room plus a minute kitchen; above, which you reached up a staircase like a thing on board ship, was the bedroom with the bathroom and loo combined next to it.

What Jimmy liked was light. It was the first impression I got of the place when he opened the narrow front door and knocked down the switch. The tiny hall and the big room it opened into were both flooded in brilliant light. In the middle of one wall there was a picture with its own light above it. It drew my eyes at once. I couldn't make out what the hell it was. An abstract I supposed. Yet the more you looked at it the more you couldn't help feeling that if only you looked a little bit longer you would see what it was really meant to be. Something would emerge. Right up to the end I still felt that. Though I never made up my mind what was most likely to emerge. Sometimes I thought it was a nightmare sunset (moonrise?) in a spooky wood and sometimes I was almost certain I could see a dwarf (two dwarfs?) crossing a black and white paved courtyard.

"Childe Roland to the Dark Tower came," Jimmy said once when he saw me looking at it.

"Is that what it's called?"

"It isn't called anything. But that's the sort of thing it makes you think of."

He was right too . . . *Childe Roland to the Dark Tower came. When I was a windy boy and a bit . . .*

Not that we sorted all that out on that first night. I just looked round the room in the way you do when you come into somebody else's little world for the first time. Table, chairs, sofa, pictures, books, curtains, lamps—the same toys that we all have but what has this particular child made of them?

One thing the child Jimmy had was a long green shelf with all sorts of glasses on it. Including two large balloon glasses which he now brought down with care.

"I'm going to have a small brandy," he said, "and so are you."

"Good show."

The question of whether I stayed the night or not (i.e. the question of my virtue) didn't seem to have been discussed at any particular point.

There I was in Merton Mews, and there obviously I was going to stay.

I put in a pretty strong plea for going back to Panter Street and collecting some night things plus something to get up in tomorrow but Jimmy would have none of it.

"Not at half past one in the morning," he said. "The only sensible thing to do now is to get into bed. And one good point about this flat, if you can call it a flat, is that the bed is really marvelously comfortable."

It was too.

It didn't take long to get into it either. Especially as Jimmy gave me enthusiastic assistance in getting undressed.

"How's life with Jimmy?" the Sonia bitch had asked.

"I wouldn't know."

"You soon will." Which turned out to be among the world's most valid prophecies. She ought to take to crystal-gazing, that girl. Because here I was, five hours after she had said it, finding out.

I thought it was marvelous, and Jimmy didn't seem dissatisfied either.

Finally he went to sleep before I did and just before I dropped off I thought back over the last forty-eight hours and could hardly believe all that had happened.

Forty-eight hours ago I had been in Hansbeck Road, surrounded by zombies. Where the hell was Hansbeck Road anyway? I didn't believe it existed. And the zombies were scattered forever. . . .

"I'll come down with you to collect your stuff in case the old harridan turns nasty," Jimmy said in the office next day. "We'll go at half past twelve or thereabouts."

But of course we didn't. The telephone rang all morning and a man called Benny Lane came in about a quarter past twelve and as they went out together Jimmy called out:

"Sorry, Liz, no can do. I'm lunching with Benny. I probably won't be back till around three."

So I took another pound note out of the petty cash and went off in a cab to Panter Street by myself.

I got in and upstairs without anybody seeing and I was halfway through changing into a blouse and skirt (junior executive stuff) when Mrs. Mason shambled into the room.

"Well," she said.

I laughed. I could afford to laugh.

"You've been out all night."

"Naturally." (I was bustling about all the time getting changed.) "A man took me back to his mews and so I spent the night with him there."

She didn't know whether to burst out into moral indignation or to ask me what it was like.

So I made up her mind for her.

"It was lovely," I told her.

"I hope you're going to leave this house at once," she said.

"I am. Don't worry. You've got a week's money, so you've nothing to grumble about and I've found somebody to live with."

"It's all this television," she said.

"Balls."

FOUR

THE EARLY MORNING in Merton Mews generally tended to be a bit chaotic. Jimmy was as unreliable as hell over a whole lot of things, but there were a few points he was adamant about. One was getting to the office by nine forty-five every day. It didn't matter how late we had been up the night before, or how little sleep for one reason or another we had managed to get, we had to be in Deeley House by a quarter to ten.

"Not that any of the lazy so-and-so's I represent are even awake at that hour," Jimmy used to say. "Most of them regard nine forty-five as the middle of the night; but I like to get the post out of the way and be settled in before the phone starts ringing."

As a matter of fact he wasn't being quite fair because I used to shudder sometimes at what was expected of girls, even quite big stars, whom he signed up for filming work. "On set ready made-up by seven-fifteen." "On set" probably meant Pinewood. And the girl would be starting out from Chelsea or Earl's Court or maybe even Islington. Deeley House by nine forty-five was luxury compared to that sort of thing.

One of Jimmy's peculiarities was that he couldn't, or at any rate wouldn't, drive a car. Which must have cost him a lot of money because whenever we went out anywhere, which was pretty often (we were scarcely a pair of home birds), we went by taxi.

I never found out what was at the bottom of this anti-car phobia of Jimmy's.

Men are unwise and curiously planned
They have their dreams and do not think of us.

I came across these two lines in a play called *Hassan* shortly after settling in Merton Mews. There were books everywhere, mostly plays, poetry and theatrical autobiographies. One of them was this *Hassan* thing published way back in 1923. I read it right through twice without stopping one evening when Jimmy was up in Nottingham. When I asked about it he said it was terrific poetry but a poor play.

I wouldn't know about that because I never saw it acted but when I read, "Men are unwise and curiously planned/ They have their dreams and do not think of us," I thought, You can say that again, for me.

Not having a hot little Bugatti or something of the sort tucked away in the mews complicated the getting-up program. Even Jimmy's extravagance didn't run to taking a taxi every morning to the office, although we occasionally did, so it meant catching a Number Nine bus at about nine twenty-five.

Working backwards this meant starting breakfast not later than five past nine (nine-ten we discovered cut it too fine) which in turn meant getting up, for me at any rate, at half past eight.

Like a lot of men Jimmy was very easy to get into bed and very difficult to get out of it.

We often made love to one another in the mornings, maybe at half past seven or eight, which was nice as far as it went (and with an expert like Jimmy that was pretty far) but which made the business of getting up half an hour later worse than ever.

Jimmy had a wooden clock that he bought in Bavaria; you could set it to any hour you liked and a little man with a red cap, a sort of gnome, popped out and rang a bell.

Jimmy had a hate-love complex about it.

"That bloody little man," he would exclaim most mornings, "what a fantastic noise for any human being to devise!" But he wound it up faithfully every night and he wouldn't have been without it for the world.

As soon as the bell started ringing Jimmy used to go into action; verbal action only of course.

"God, another day! How you can expect me to get up after what you've just done to me I don't know (never a word about me getting up first after what he had just done to me!). Go on, you slut; you wanton, you man destroyer. Get up and get some clothes on and start things going."

If there is one thing a woman doesn't want to do just after someone has made entirely satisfactory love to her it is to jump up and start bustling around.

But I had to get into the bathroom and out of Jimmy's way and perform a combined dressing and getting the breakfast act and have everything ready on the table by nine-five when his lordship would be ravenous to get at it.

The bath was the only really unsatisfactory feature of the place. It was much too small, so that you couldn't stretch out in it and wallow. Why Jimmy, who liked his comfort above all things, didn't have it changed I don't know. He was always talking about doing it.

"Some day I'm going to get the most luxurious bath you've ever seen," he'd say. "Big enough for two of us to be in together."

But all the time I was in the mews with him he never did.

By nine-thirty we slammed out of the flat leaving chaos behind us, the bed not made, all the breakfast things on the table, pots and pans all over the kitchen. And like that it would stay until Mrs. Mount came in, usually at twelve but some days not till three, and did an hour's clearing up and cleaning.

Mrs. Mount was a cockney character who lived round the corner in, believe it or not, Goodmount Street.

"Must 'ave known I was living there when they christened it," was her crack. She was slapdash, untidy, heavy handed, dishonest as the day is long, uncharitable as hell (which made her entertaining to talk to) and what we would have done without her I can't think.

What she helped herself to in the way of drink and cigarettes was nobody's business, but as Jimmy used to say, "Learn from the Chinese" (Jimmy was a great admirer of the Chinese). "The Chinese know that everything in life has a squeeze attached to it. This is old Ma Mount's squeeze. We can't do without her and she knows it. Hence she squeezes and enjoys it; we are squeezed and try to look as if we did."

What Jimmy said when I first showed up in his office about never answering a letter until he had to didn't turn out to be strictly true. In many ways he was an annoying person to live with (which of us isn't?) but I soon found out that he was a highly efficient theatrical agent.

"While these bastards lie in bed and natter and play golf and waste their money at Hurst Park I'm driving myself silly getting work for them," he used to say; and there was a certain amount of truth in it, because Jimmy never let up. The job was always with him. Three evenings a week on an average he would have to be at the theater. Sometimes at a first night, sometimes at a revival; sometimes just to see what sort of performance a particular actor or actress gave. And if he wasn't at the theater he would be glued to a play on television.

He couldn't always take me with him, but when he could, he did. After his fashion, and allowing for the fact that he was a man, James was reasonably dependable. For a man.

"Frailty, thy name is woman!"

When I first heard that (Jimmy and I had gone to the Old Vic where Tandy Sellman was playing Ophelia. The Messel film which was going to make a fortune for everybody, including Jimmy, had been indefinitely postponed. "Why?" I asked. "God knows," Jimmy told me, "nobody knows. A million reasons. No reason at all. Show business, there you are, that's it, show business.")—when I first heard the tag about frailty and woman I couldn't believe it.

Back in the mews next evening I looked it up.

I had never read *Hamlet* before, and there it was. Ham.: 1. 2. 146: "Frailty, thy name is woman!" written by a man of course—Honest Master Shakespeare with his Dark Ladies and Dear Boys and all the rest of it in the Sonnets. I laughed like a drain.

The only thing I really disliked about Deeley House was that crazy lift that must have been put in when good Queen Victoria was on the throne and not quite the newest model, I wouldn't think, then.

I was terrified that it might stick halfway and I shouldn't be able to get out.

I'm as normal as they come about most things but I've got this claustrophobia thing. Sometimes quite badly. People get the wrong idea about it. It isn't just being in a small space that worries you. It's when you can't see a possibility of getting out that you feel you can't stick it. For instance an ordinary railway carriage is a lot smaller than a coach on the Underground. But if you are in an ordinary railway carriage you know that you can get out. All you've got to do is to get to the door and open it. Just because you can do it you're O.K. In the Underground you're shut in. *Wham,* the doors slide to and you're in the steel box. You could beat your hands raw against it and you could never get out. If you suffer from claustrophobia that's the feeling that gives you hell. You start to think about it, you see yourself up against the curved steel doors hammering on them and you begin to get hot and your heart starts to thump and your mouth goes dry.

I never told Jimmy this, and I used to go up and down in that lift with him, but I hated it.

He had to go away fairly often usually to Oxford or Nottingham. This was always on theatrical business, to see some show before it came in to the West End, and sometimes he would take me with him. If he didn't and I was left behind for the night alone in Merton Mews he used to issue the most terrifying warnings about how I was to behave and next day he would go all through the place like a ferret looking for any suspicious signs.

He never found any, of course. Jimmy had got me all wrong, as I tried more than once to explain to him. Because I had gone to bed with him the first time he asked—though strictly speaking he didn't even ask, it just happened—he thought I was the sort of girl who would do it again, just as easily, with anybody else. I wasn't.

Jimmy was the end of zombiedom for me. It's difficult for a woman to analyze her feelings about the man whom she loses her virginity to, and I seldom bothered to try to analyze what it was I felt for Jimmy. I was too busy enjoying the new world which unwittingly, because it was the world he was used to, he had thrown open to me, or more correctly thrown me into. We formed an enthusiastic working partnership both in office and bed.

So, like I said a long way back, you must tell me what you mean by love if I'm going to be able to say whether I was ever in love with Jimmy or not. Which obviously means that I wasn't.

You're never in doubt, you never have to fiddle about with definitions, when the real thing hits you.

As I was to find out later. You lie awake most of the night sweating over something that he said or didn't say; the party was sheer hell because he was there and didn't speak to you; the knives turn in your heart when you see him smile at another woman; when he hits you, physically or mentally, you don't mind, the point is he's doing it to you and not to anybody else so you enjoy it.

No woman in love ever needs any explanation about drug addicts. Something has got you by the throat, but, by God, you want it to have you by the throat—the thing is killing you and you like it that way.

So I wasn't in love with Jimmy.

But I was teamed up with him and when, on the point of leaving for Oxford or Nottingham, he would say, "No funny stuff, Liz. If anybody rings up you tell them that I'm here in the flat beside you and we are shortly going to bed together." I used to tell him he could save his breath, I wasn't that sort of girl.

"All I can say is you look that sort of girl, you look splendidly lascivious."

"Thanks very much."

"It's a compliment really."

"It sounds like it. You know what you look like?"

"Tell me."

"You look like a man who drinks much too much, smokes much too much, who never takes any exercise if he can possibly avoid it—"

"Fancy you saying that!"

"—any outdoor exercise then. You look ten years older than you are."

That always got him on the raw. Very few men can stand being chipped about their age.

"Leave ages out of it, for God's sake," he would say. "We shall all be dead before we know where we are."

So on the evenings when Jimmy was away I didn't even try to see anybody else. I was only too glad of a few hours by myself in the flat; it gave me a chance to catch up on feminine chores which I didn't have time for when Jimmy was around.

If there wasn't any washing or ironing to be done I'd read. I found that by the time I had read half a dozen autobiographies of stage people I had read the lot. Essentially they were all the same: how bloody marvelous I was in twenty different parts; what a dedicated professional I am; and look at all the famous people, with titles, I've met in the world and as a final paragraph God bless everybody in or out of this wonderful profession. Plus photographs of the House Full signs when playing at the Ambassador's and one of the old Gaiety just before it was pulled down.

I soon had my fill of these, but Jimmy's shelves were stacked with plays and I never tired of reading them.

Or maybe I'd switch on an L.P. record and while I was listening to it stare at that crazy picture and try to make up my mind whether it really was two dwarfs or not.

"The point of the picture," Jimmy said once when I asked him about it, "is that it can be virtually anything you want it to be."

"I thought a picture was meant to represent something."

"So it is. This one represents a point of view."

"What point of view?"

"Whatever point of view it happens to set up in your mind. It suggests. It starts you thinking. What else do you want from a work of art?"

I could see that he had something there; he talked sense occasionally.

As a matter of fact what I said about never taking any exercise wasn't strictly accurate. It's true that Jimmy hated all ball games. He was almost fanatical about them. If somebody he wanted to get hold of was playing golf he used to surpass himself in picturesque language, and when the television seemed to have nothing on it but cricket he nearly went mad, but when the new artificial ice-skating rink was opened in Hallam Way (conveniently close to the mews) he got tremendously keen. We used to go there twice a week and sometimes he even cut a theater date for it. Luckily I had done a little skating with Nancy before we joined the badminton club so I wasn't a complete beginner. I expect the experts would have said that Jimmy was more enthusiastic than good but that didn't worry us and we had lots of fun.

It was at the Icedrome that we met Percy Mander.

"Well, well, well, look who's risking life and limb."

"This is Liz Barton," Jimmy said. "My secretary."

Percy smiled and rolled an eye at me. Naturally being a normal sort of girl I would have been disappointed if he hadn't but I just smiled sedately back.

Percy—Percy M. he was generally called—was on the fat side, especially considering his age; he can't have been over thirty-five and the hair was beginning to thin over his temples. He was very light in coloring, almost sandy, which I usually dislike in a man. But he looked good fun.

He didn't seem to have a partner and he sat with us for maybe ten minutes which I thought would annoy Jimmy who generally didn't like to miss any skating time. But he was unexpectedly amiable to Percy. Unfortunately Percy wasn't wearing skates so he couldn't ask me to go on the ice with him which I would have enjoyed; Jimmy was good at skating but he was a bit monotonous.

"Anything you can do for Sheila Dane?" Jimmy asked when Percy was beginning to go.

"Don't see why not. Have you got an angle? Give me an angle and I'll work in a para. or two."

Jimmy said there would probably be something in a few days and he would give him a ring.

"I'll look in and have a natter one of these mornings," Percy said. "Anything to get out of the bedlam at that office."

Sheila Dane was the rising starlet who was just about to make her first West End appearance in *Boy with a Trumpet*. She had a pretty useful start, of course, seeing that her father was Sir Donald Dane who was always being referred to as one of our leading actors and the doyen of the profession and so on but who, as far as I was concerned, was a pompous middle-aged bore.

Personally I didn't think much of Sheila Dane. She gave me the impression all the time of knowing that her father was the great Sir Donald so the rest of you can go and get stuffed. But Jimmy thought she was good. Or said he did. Most likely he only hoped she was going to be good because she was one of his clients. If Sheila Dane did well Jimmy did well so naturally he was all for cracking her up.

"What can Percy Mander do for Sheila Dane?" I asked.

"Percy's on the *Standard*. He helps to write that new entertainment gossip feature they've introduced."

"He didn't look like a newspaperman to me."

"What do you expect a newspaperman to look like? Printer's ink pouring out of his ears?"

"He didn't look hard-boiled enough to me."

"Everybody in Fleet Street is hard-boiled. Protective coating. They have to be to survive."

So Percy with his sandy receding hair was hard-boiled. The great Jimmy Mancroft had said that he was and that was that. But I didn't believe it.

A week later Percy M. came into the office.

"Is your lord and master in?" he demanded.

"Jimmy's out." (Jimmy might be giving me a whale of a time every night in the flat but I didn't regard him as L. and M. Definitely not.)

"The ends of the earth or up the street or where?"

"He's with Hopper Hunt of L.D.A."

"You'll be lucky if he comes back sober, then. Hopper knocks it back in a big way. Some of these boys must have zinc linings to their stomachs. We'll be carrying a story to-morrow about Sheila Dane."

"Good show."

"Thank God for that pet poodle of hers. The great child-torturing British public will lap up anything about animals. Say Alfred Munnings to a lot of people and they immediately think not of an artist but of the husband of the woman who owned a black Pekinese dog. Ever do any betting?"

He was sitting now and had pulled a midday *Standard* out of his pocket.

"Wolverhampton," he said, "what a place to go racing in. You ever been to that course they've got there?"

"I've never been racing anywhere."

"Oh, well. It takes all sorts. You're as bad as Jimmy."

I had heard Jimmy on the subject of racing. He was fanatical about it. Of course, way back in the land of the zombies in Hansbeck Road, bookmakers, whores, Roman Catholics, Communists and publicans all ran a perpetual photo finish for damnation. Put a bob each way on a horse and you were heading straight for hell. Good Christian stuff. So naturally I hadn't been brought up in a betting atmosphere; and the funny thing was that Jimmy, as un-zombie-like as they came in most respects, was almost as dead set against it. He wasn't the slightest bit interested in racing. If he had lived in a house slap bang on Epsom Downs he wouldn't have bothered to get up out of bed on Derby Day to watch the finish from his bedroom window.

"I accept the fact that one animal with four legs suitably encouraged by a severe beating from a jockey terrified of losing his percentage of the winning stakes can run faster than some other animal which isn't being beaten by quite such a strong jockey or with quite such a cutting whip."

"Come off it, Jimmy, the horses enjoy it."

"Of course they do. Just as any fox is well known to sign a document immediately prior to being torn to pieces by the hounds that it infinitely prefers such an end to the dull business of dying a natural death."

"All right, all right, you're a fanatic—"

"You must either be fanatical about something in life or a moron."

"Well, I'm fanatical about racing. For it. One horse can run faster than another. O.K. The point is *which*."

"I couldn't be less interested."

"A race-meeting's fun anyway."

"More rogues, thieves and active vagabonds follow in the wake of that noble animal the horse than you'll come across even in the theatrical profession. And that's saying something, by God."

That was Jimmy on racing; so what with one thing and another I had never had a bet in my life.

"You back Bobbity Bob in the three-fifteen at Wolverhampton today," Percy told me, "and you'll make yourself a bit of money."

Could be, I supposed. And a bit of money sounded as nice to me as to the next person. But somehow I wasn't interested. Not then. I could hardly foresee the time when I should be concerned with it all day.

And Percy was bored with it. He threw the midday *Standard* across the desk and lit a cigarette.

"You like it here? Are you, as they facetiously say, happy in your work?"

"Yes, actually I am. Very. Ought I to say 'sorry'?"

He grinned. "Damn nearly. In this rat race. Or perhaps it isn't so bad here as in Fleet Street. Been skating again?"

"We went last night."

"You and Jimmy?"

"We try to go twice a week."

"I never knew Jimmy was so keen on anything even remotely resembling sport. I used to skate like anything when I was a kid."

"In London?"

"God, no. Lincolnshire. Mewton we lived at. Just on the edge of the Fens. If it was cold anywhere in England by God we caught it there. It would cut the horns off a cow. And when I was a kid—six, seven, and eight, that sort of thing—we had one or two winters that were real freezers. Funny how most men look back to their childhood and see it in terms of long warm summer days with the sun shining all the time and I see frost and icicles on the guttering of the shed and a bloody great red sun trying to get through the mist over Mewton Long Fen.

"Skate? You could skate for three miles in a straight line there."

"Why don't you skate now, Percy?"

He made a puffing noise something between pah and pooh. Derisive anyway and rather sad. A man blowing away the remnants of things that have gone down the wind.

"Skate now? That's all over. They used to hold the championships on the Long Fen. My old man always had a go. Didn't do badly either. You'd hardly expect a parson to be good at skating, would you? Although, I don't know. Plenty of God-botherers have been useful at cricket so I don't see why one shouldn't skate."

"Your father was the parson at this place?"

"Still is. A good and holy man. And I mean that. Damn it, even after twelve years of Fleet Street you can still believe that goodness and holiness exist, especially when you see them walking about on two legs, can't you?"

"I expect, Percy."

"And much good it's done the old boy. A fat lot he'll get out of being good and holy. Unless there's another world. Is there going to be another world, Liz?"

Is there going to be another world? I hadn't the vaguest idea. I'd never thought about it. I couldn't care less.

"Search me. This one will do for me at the moment."

"And me; it's bloody well got to. It's the only one we've got anyway. And it won't last long the way things are going. You put a bit each way on Bobbity Bob and help yourself to a good time."

I didn't put anything on Bobbity Bob, partly because I didn't know how to, partly because I forgot and partly because Jimmy came back half tight and in a foul bad temper.

"Bloody numskulls," he said.

"Who?"

"You. Me. Everybody. The great British Public. 'Well, British Public (ye who like me not) God love you.' You've never read any Browning, I suppose? Of course not. Meat and strong wine. Not sweet enough for feminine taste. Stick to Rupert Brooke like all the rest of the women.

I often wonder when the Styx is crossed
And age-bent Charon, rowing back for more
Leaves me bewildered on that farther shore,
I often wonder in that lightless land
What ghostly head will nod, outstretched be what thin hand.

Don't tell me that isn't good, round, genuine vintage Brooke; and I ought to know, I wrote it myself before I left school. When I was seventeen. But Browning's another matter. Though why the hell I should use up valuable time giving you extramural lectures in poetry appreciation I wouldn't know."

Nor me, either. Except that I found it rather interesting. I made a mental note to have a look into this Browning character.

"Why has everybody turned out to be a numskull since you went up to see Hopper Hunt?" I asked.

"*Boy with a Trumpet* looks as though it will have to close."

"I thought it got rave notices."

"It did. For once that embittered band of myopic kitchen-sinkers, the dramatic critics, actually showed a bit of sense."

"Won't the notices pull them in?"

Jimmy lit a new cigarette from the stump of an old one and stubbed the old one out in his huge glass ashtray, already the graveyard of fifteen or so, and I had emptied it once.

I had been living with him for eight months now and it was the first time I had seen him look middle-aged. I felt a bit guilty. Maybe I was letting him overdo it.

He laughed. "You've got to laugh," he said. "A man's got to laugh. That whoreson troupe of lighthearted butchers, the critics, will do a real carving-up job on a play and the public will still come flocking in. Good, faithful wooden-witted clots thumping their pound notes down at the box office like good 'uns. Another time—*Boy with a Trumpet* for instance—the same critics will bend over backwards saying what a marvelous show it is and how to miss seeing it is the one thing nobody must do and the morons stay away in droves. In bloody droves. What can you make of that?"

"Show business."

"How singularly right you are. Show business it is. Break your bloody heart. And who cares? 'Theatrical agent dies of broken heart contemplating the folly of the goddam public and the lamentable state of the world of the theater'—you think that would rate more than a four-line para. at the bottom of the sporting page in the last edition? Not on your nelly!"

"What will happen to it now?"

"I still believe it's too good to fail. But if it's going to hang on it will have to be nursed. If a backer turns up willing to risk say four thousand in keeping it alive for a bit I believe he might well see his money back handsomely. It might easily catch fire and run away into a big success. Or maybe I'm just kidding myself because I've already got some money in it."

"Why don't you put up the four thousand yourself, Jimmy?"

"Because I haven't got it." He smiled at me suddenly. "Keeping you is too expensive."

Which was nonsense of course. I mean the part about me being expensive. And I didn't much like the expression "keeping you" somehow.

Boy with a Trumpet kept staggering on with public support growing slightly, just enough to persuade the management to keep it on and not enough to justify them in doing so. Everybody was on a knife edge about it.

"If I lose what I've put into that," Jimmy groaned, "I shall be broke."

I don't know about other theatrical agents' offices but Jimmy's was chaos one day and as quiet as anything the next. You either hadn't got time to go out and eat a sandwich even, or you were twiddling your thumbs with nothing to do.

Occasionally in the thumb-twiddling periods I used to look at the racing page of the *Mail*. Percy M.'s Bobbity Bob had won, I noticed, at seven to one, so if I had put a pound on it I would have won seven, if I had put ten pounds on it I would have won seventy and if I had put a hundred—the normal sort of daydreams about money. I hadn't actually put anything on it and as a matter of fact I still didn't know how to make a bet.

It was one afternoon while I was doing just that thing, reading through the racing news because I had nothing better to do, that the person-to-person call from Málaga (Spain) came.

"Would Mr. James Mancroft take a person-to-person call from the Golf Hotel, Málaga, Spain?"

I said I was sure he would. It sounded like business. The Golf Hotel, Málaga, Spain, sounded just the sort of place one of his clients might have whirled off to.

"Who is it who wants to speak to him?" I inquired.

"Mrs. Mancroft," and then just to emphasize, I suppose, that it wasn't a mother or aunt or any nonsense like that, "Mrs. James Mancroft."

There were no feathers handy for me to knock myself down with. But I must admit I was a bit shaken. This was the first I had heard of the existence of a Mrs. James Mancroft. Not a whisper from Jimmy. The old so-and-so, I thought.

I was sitting in the small outer office so I rang through and said, "Will you take a person-to-person call from the Golf Hotel at Málaga?" I paused to give more effect to the bomb and then exploded it, "Mrs. James Mancroft."

Jimmy didn't seem to notice the bomb. "Certainly, I will," he said, cheerful as a cricket. "Put her through at once. And by the way, Liz—"

"I'm still here."

"As soon as I'm through, get off the line, will you?"

"I'm not in the habit of listening to other people's conversations," I told him haughtily, and when the connection was made I clicked down the receiver very noisily so that he would be sure to hear it and then let it up again very carefully and quietly hoping that he wouldn't.

She was in the middle of telling him that he was lucky she hadn't made it a reversed charge.

"I wouldn't have taken the call if you had."

"Are you hard up, my poor lamb?"

"Moderately."

"No vast fortunes in the theater?"

"You know what show business is."

"Perfectly bloody. I always thought so. It's heavenly out here, Jay. Pure heaven."

"Is the naval commander type pure heaven?"

"Actually he isn't. Poor pet. He has turned out rather a flop."

"I'm crying my eyes out for you."

"In many ways he's frightfully limited."

"Don't go into details. I believe the Spanish are very particular about what is said over their phones. You might well find yourself in jug."

"Would you come and bail me out, Jay?"

"Most certainly and emphatically not. I don't care how many Spanish jugs you get into."

"Don't be vindictive, pet lamb."

"Why the hell shouldn't I be vindictive?"

"What's the weather like with you?"

"The weather? It's been raining incessantly for what seems like a week. I should think somebody has dropped an atom bomb somewhere."

"You haven't become an A-bomb bore, have you, Jay? You don't talk about them all the time, do you?"

"Practically incessantly. What do you talk about to your naval character?"

"Well, naturally things crop up."

"I'll bet they do."

"The sunshine is too marvelous."

"What is this, a meteorological report or something?"

"Don't be peevish just because you are having a lot of rain and we aren't—how are you, Jay, that's what I really rang up about."

"Curiosity or affection?"

"We don't have to be mad with one another."

"Don't we? I'm all right, Betty. Older, wiser, sadder. What else do you want me to be?"

"Have you got anybody in the flat to look after you?"

"Mrs. Mount comes in as usual."

"Hasn't she landed up in jail for thieving yet? I meant somebody for you, yourself. Somebody to keep you warm at night."

"Of course not."

I very nearly chipped in at that. Betty! I could just picture her, long brown limbs, the smallest of bikinis, in the sun at the Golf Hotel, Málaga, Spain. Stretched out on the beach with the unsatisfactory naval type by her side. A voluptuous bitch if ever there was one, I was willing to bet. I wondered what she would have made of it if after that traitorous "of course not" of Jimmy's I had chipped in with "liar." Probably she would have laughed like a drain.

"Take care of yourself, Jimmy."

"When are you coming back?"

"Back? Oh, Jimmy, Jimmy, probably never."

"Damn you to all eternity, then."

"That's what I feel like at times. That's exactly what I feel like at times. Damned to all eternity!"

Click, about seven pound ten's worth of scintillating conversation was over.

Jimmy came in and skulked about. He thought that I

had been listening in but he wasn't sure and he didn't know how to make sure.

I wasn't going to help him. Betty! in a bikini lying in the Spanish sun with her long brown legs stretched out alongside the man she had gone off with . . .

That night I made Jimmy make love to me as soon as we got into bed.

"You liar," I told him, biting his ear afterwards while he was still in my arms.

"So you were listening in?"

"Of course. You couldn't have told me, I suppose, that you were married?"

"Did I ever tell you that I wasn't? Have I ever asked you if you are married?"

"Don't be silly."

"What are you grumbling about anyway? Isn't everything pretty nice as it is? Are you dissatisfied, Liz?"

I couldn't honestly say that I was dissatisfied. Not at that moment, anyway.

"Men are unwise and curiously planned." You're telling me, I thought.

I thought over the situation a great deal during the next few days and I came to the conclusion that the only thing I really felt about it was my pride was hurt slightly. There wasn't anything about it that touched me deeply. For about half a day I tried to work up a tragic act about being the central figure in a tense situation but all that ended in laughing at myself.

The fact was that I wasn't in love with Jimmy and this made me realize it fully. And to be fair to him I couldn't even work up much in the way of a rage about it. "You liar," I had said with a certain amount of feeling when I had got him at my mercy that evening; but was even that true? We had come together fortuitously and I had gone into the business of living with him with my eyes open and I couldn't really grumble at the deal I was getting. In a way what had happened had cleared the air and I even felt more self-reliant as a result of it. Bikini Betty, who didn't seem to be getting on too well with the naval commander anyway, hadn't been able, presumably, to hit it off with her Jimmy and I was.

So to hell with her long brown legs anyway. All the same I suffered the eternal curiosity of the on-the-fringe female—*what was she like?* I would have given a lot to talk about Betty to Jimmy himself but he never opened up the subject and I didn't like to.

One day when Percy M. came in I got a chance.

Jimmy was at the far end of Piccadilly talking to some character in M.P.A. with whom he did business occasionally and Percy settled down in his chair.

"How's racing?" I asked.

"Are *you* making any money at it?" he countered.

"Me? I've never had a bet in my life. I don't even know how to."

"*O sancta simplicitas.* I wish I didn't. I wish I was completely ignorant of the fact that Cistercian Abbey is running in the three o'clock at Worcester today. Cistercian Abbey will win, it's bound to win, quite seriously and soberly there isn't another horse in the race that can beat it, ergo it must win."

"Isn't that a good thing to know?"

"But if I back it, which I shall do, it will lose."

"Don't back it then."

"I must," Percy said gloomily. "It's my only possible chance of getting even with the book."

I didn't get it. I didn't see how backing a horse you knew was going to lose (if you backed it) gave you a chance of getting level with the book.

"How long have you known Jimmy?" I asked him.

"Years. As long as I've been in the Street. A decade of mortal time."

"What was Betty like?"

Percy's eyes opened a little. "Jimmy's Betty?"

"I'm not interested in any other."

"Five foot two. Dark. And gave poor Jimmy hell."

"A bitch?"

"To be honest I've known bitchier; but she isn't anybody's sweet ray of domestic light."

"What happened?"

Percy spread his hands. "What does happen? The human situation begins. They were both so damned awkward to live with that in a way you would say they were ideally suited to one another. 'Let me not to the marriage of true minds—' "

"Good heavens."

"What's the matter?"

"Fancy you knowing that! When I was quite a kid, well, fifteen or so, I used to think about it."

"You were a bit precocious, Liz, that's your trouble."

"Could be. What about Jimmy and Betty?"

"They got on like fun one minute and fought like hell the next."

"Was Jimmy very fond of her?"

"Desperately, I should say, if I didn't want to hurt you."

"You won't hurt me, Percy. Not that way."

"Then I say it—desperately. If she ever shows up again you'll be out on your ear."

"Thanks very much."

"No good getting cross, Liz, it's the way it goes. It's the human situation. If I back a horse it loses; but if I don't back one I can't win anyway, can I? So how do I win? You can't be happy clammed up inside yourself and never loving anybody else; and yet when you start giving out and loving somebody you find that it can be the quickest way to get hurt there is."

"I shan't get hurt, Percy, if Jimmy's lawfully wedded wife turns up and demands her share of his bed. I shall walk out as happy as you like, fancy free."

"That's my girl."

"I've never actually owned a bikini but I can always buy one."

"What the hell has that got to do with it?"

"Nothing."

Three days after that Jimmy and I had our first real flare-up. In a way it was over business, which was silly. Because what the hell did it matter to me how James Mancroft Theatrical Agent Limited was doing? Except that when you attach yourself to anything you can't help rooting for it. Part of what Percy would call the human situation, I suppose?

Anyway it was a Friday morning and we had been to a first night on the previous evening (*The Worm in the Wheat* at the Criterion) and Jimmy had spent the whole time almost equally between cursing the critics and drinking in the bar. Well, that was O.K. What are critics for if not to be cursed by producers, promoters, agents, authors and actors? And what are bars for if not to drink in?

Next morning he had a hangover as big as a battleship, we were late for once at the office, and there was a mountain of correspondence to be tackled. Which I suppose explained why at eleven he chucked in his hand and said, "I'm going over to have a word with Hopper."

"Which means you won't be back till three or half past."

"What has it got to do with you when I get back?"

Jimmy had gone quite white and he was suddenly flamingly angry.

"All right. I'm only the secretary around here."

"And for God's sake don't start that nonsense either. You're my mistress. You hop into my bed every night and you enjoy it. And what sort of right does that give you to tell me when I can go out of the office and when I've got to get back?"

"O.K., Jimmy, O.K."

"Or watch every drink I take like you did last night?"

"That's childish. I wasn't watching your drinks and I just wanted to get back into our seats and see the play."

"If you wanted to get back and see that miserable apology for a play you must be a moron."

"So the critics can tear it to pieces, can they?"

"Go and get stuffed by the critics."

"No wonder she went off with a naval commander."

Jimmy leaned across my desk.

"Listen, eavesdropper, you say another word about Betty and I'll turn you over and spank you hard. Very hard."

He was very cross when he went out and I wasn't feeling all that settled either. There wasn't much I could do because Jimmy hadn't got round to dictating any letters, but there was always a certain amount of filing and tidying up to be done so I got busy on that and was still doing it when a short stocky man of about sixty came in.

He asked in a very quiet voice if Jimmy was in and I said no, was there anything I could do?

As it happened my *Daily Mail* was lying on the desk with the racing page uppermost. I hadn't in fact been reading the racing news but I was going to, because talking to Percy M. on the subject was beginning to make me take an interest in it and I wondered, if ever I wanted to make a bet, how to go about it.

The man who had come in looked a pretty tough type. But he was expensively dressed. He had a short thick neck and powerful hands. When you looked up into his eyes they shook you a bit. They seemed to go right inside you.

"Betting?" he asked with a bit of a smile.

"Thinking about it."

"I wouldn't if I were you."

A zombie? I wondered for a moment; but this man wasn't a zombie.

"I suppose some people do all right at it?" I said.

"They do—the bookmakers. Will Mr. Mancroft be long?"

I was feeling so cross with Jimmy that I nearly told him

if he waited till about a quarter to four he would probably be able to greet the eminent theatrical agent on his return from lunch (on Hopper Hunt's expense account).

But of course I didn't.

"I could give him a ring," I said. "I think I had better. Who shall I say it is who wants him, please?"—which seemed a hell of a roundabout way of saying "what's your name?" but that's how you get to talk in offices.

"Edward West."

The name didn't mean a thing to me. He might just as well have said "Alfred East," "Arthur North" or "Thomas South." His name was Edward West, so what?

I got on to Hopper Hunt's office and asked to speak to Jimmy.

"Are you ringing up to tell me you are burning the place down?" he inquired with a sort of ferocious geniality.

"I had thought about it; but somebody has come in to see you."

"Not Tandy Sellman?"

Ever since the failure of the Messel plan to get started Tandy Sellman had been a problem. Her Ophelia up at Stratford had been a flop and in any case was now over, and she was making poor Jimmy's life a misery explaining to him just what a wonderful, unappreciated actress she was and what a bloody useless numskull of an agent she had saddled herself with in him.

"Not Miss Sellman," I reassured him, " a gentleman called Mr. West."

There was a slight pause of somebody assimilating something they can't quite believe.

"You don't mean *Edward* West, do you?"

"That's what he said."

Another pause, then, "Has he said anything about *Boy with a Trumpet?*"

"No, he just wants to see you."

"By God, tell him I'll be there in ten minutes, less if it's possible."

"Mr. Mancroft coming back?" Edward West asked as I put the telephone down. He was smiling, slightly. Maybe he had heard what Jimmy said and how he said it.

"Just as fast as he can."

Mr. West drew a cigar out of his breast pocket where there was a small battery of them.

"Mind if I smoke, Miss—"

"Barton. Liz Barton."

"—mind if I smoke, Miss Barton?"

"No, of course not."

"Do you smoke in the office?"

"Sometimes."

He shook his head. "I don't let my girls smoke."

Zombie or not-zombie? Difficult to tell. As it happened a couple of telephone calls came in on top of one another so I was kept busy until Jimmy hurried in.

"Sorry to have kept you waiting," he said.

"Not a bit. I've been admiring the way your excellent secretary deals with her telephone calls."

Jimmy smiled so amiably at me that I took it our little dust-up had been forgotten in the general excitement of getting this West character, whoever he might be, into the place.

They went into Jimmy's office and I was free to get on with the filing and tidying up.

It was about half an hour before West came out with Jimmy fussing after him like a headwaiter after an important client.

I had got tired of filing and tidying and had been reading the racing news again but there was just time to slip the *Mail* under a pile of letters.

Or was there? It wasn't easy to be sure how much that man's remarkable eyes saw.

He stopped by my desk and said, "Good morning, Miss Barton. If Mr. Mancroft ever treats you badly don't forget you can get a job with me. I always notice the way a girl works on the telephone."

Smiles and laughs all round; but the moment the door was safely shut Jimmy turned on me quite sharply.

"How the hell did he know your name?"

"I told him. You were out of the office at Hopper Hunt's. Remember? So while he was waiting for you Mr. West asked my name and I told him."

"You know who that was, I suppose?"

"Mr. Edward West."

"But you know who Edward West is?"

"Not the foggiest."

"Ring up the Café Royal and book a table for two for luncheon. I'm taking you out. Mr. West seemed to like the way you handle a phone and he ought to know, he's got about two hundred of 'em in his office."

"Two hundred telephones?"

"Edward West, my dear innocent eavesdropping puritanically minded mistress, is one of the biggest bookmakers in England."

I must say I had to laugh at that, first of all Jimmy calling me puritanically minded after some of our sessions in bed and then Mr. West the great bookmaker solemnly advising me against betting. Now that Jimmy had told me I remembered having seen the name in newspaper advertisements, but I hadn't connected them.

"What did he come here for," I asked, "to give you a tip for the Derby?"

Jimmy laughed. "Rather better than that. He is going to put five thousand pounds into *Boy with a Trumpet*. He saw the play on Tuesday of this week and thought it wonderful. Somebody told him it was in danger of folding up so he came to see me about it.

"I told him quite honestly that if he puts five thousand into the play now he might, indeed, lose it all; but on the other hand he might double it in a year's time. Actually it doesn't matter much to Edward West which he does. When you are worth at least two million, five thousand is small change."

I had never before actually spoken to a millionaire. Of course you try to kid yourself that there's nothing in it; "he's just an ordinary person like you and me" and so on; but you don't quite succeed. A man worth two million isn't just an ordinary person in the world we live in, he's a man worth two million.

So *Boy with a Trumpet* was saved and Jimmy, who was very often right in theatrical matters, was right again. The play began to pick up and in the mysterious way which does sometimes happen, what looked like a certain failure, began to turn into an obvious success.

"Edward West's five thousand is going to be safe," Jimmy said. "Which doesn't surprise me; the boys with big money always make money. That's the way it goes."

"The human situation, eh?"

This particular human situation suited Jimmy too, because he had an interest in *Boy with a Trumpet* and when that had turned the corner and other business began to go right he started to look a lot less strained. I never really knew much about his finances. I guess that like many people in the world of the theater he handled a lot of money without much of it necessarily sticking. But although I lived with him for eighteen months I never knew what his income was. I didn't ask and he didn't say. Not that it worried me. Why should he tell me, after all? He paid me my salary at the office every week—and that wasn't large— and I didn't have any housekeeping expenses. I can't say that Jimmy was mean, but he wasn't extravagantly generous either. Perhaps he couldn't afford to be.

I certainly looked after his money for him. I mean from the housekeeping angle. I used to do the shopping on Saturdays. In North Street, just round the corner from the mews, and which was almost like a village street.

It had a pub on the corner, of course, The Compasses; a tobacconist and newspaper shop; a butcher; a greengrocer and a general household goods shop as well. For fish I had to go farther afield, usually into the King's Road.

As I say Jimmy wasn't mean but I took a pride in shopping as economically as I could and on the whole we did pretty well. If we had a meal in the flat (and very often we didn't) Jimmy did the cooking, at any rate to start with. He was a good cook and knew a lot about it. I wasn't, but in the end he taught me quite a bit.

If we went out anywhere to a meal, which was usually at night because lunch was often only sandwiches in the office, it was always to the Casse Croûte or L'Aiglon or the Rotonde, Jimmy's theory being that if you were going out anywhere you might as well go somewhere good and blow the expense; as he used to put it, "Any bloody fool can be uncomfortable."

One Saturday afternoon I got back early after my usual round of shopping in North Street. It had been one of the less frustrating days. The things that I wanted were in the shops and there weren't long queues waiting to buy them. Also it was fine and dry and the October sun was making a golden haze of London's afternoon. Jimmy and I hadn't been getting on particularly well during the past week. Nothing much. Just the pinpricks and irritations of two people getting on one another's nerves a bit. The human situation, I suppose. But coming back to the mews with all the shopping safely done and in such good time too, I felt as amiable as could be.

I knew Jimmy wouldn't be in because he had gone up to Regent's Park to see Sir Donald Dane who wanted to talk over some theatrical affair with him and had issued his imperial decree that he would be pleased to see Mr. Mancroft at three o'clock on Saturday.

Which incidentally was the cause of one of the minor irritations between us that week.

"Who does he think he is ordering you about like that?" I asked.

"It isn't a question of who he thinks he is but of who he *is*. Sir Donald Dane is the current lead of the acting profession."

"So what?"

"So, you stupid half-wit, he's in a position to tell people when and where he wants to see them and they go along. The same as I am going to do."

"Cap in hand."

It wasn't a fair thing to say and it riled Jimmy so there weren't any fond farewells and "good lucks" when he set out for Albany Terrace, Regent's Park.

But, as I say, by the time I had done my shopping in the warm afternoon sunshine I was amiable again, even if I was beginning to have a suspicion at the back of my mind that all good things have to come to an end sometime and my affair with Jimmy was no exception.

When I opened the door of the flat I heard the phonograph playing. "Burglars," I thought, "and they've had the cheek to put on an L.P."

Then the tune registered, "Lady in the Evening," and I tried to think, Jimmy's back earlier than he expected. But I didn't believe it.

I knew what had happened.

And when I went into the living room, sure enough, there she was. Five foot two and dark. As per schedule. Whether her legs were brown or not I couldn't see. And, of course, she wasn't wearing a bikini.

She had a good look at me. It was the most insulting thing she could think of, I expect. A real damned good, up and down, miss nothing, God-Almighty-what-the-hell-can-he-see-in-that-lot look. The sort of look that other bitch Sonia had treated me to in the theater way back now when it was all beginning.

"Well, well, well, how very interesting," she said. "You've been doing the shopping, I take it?"

I wished to God that I hadn't missed my hair appointment that Thursday and I felt certain that there was a ladder in one of my stockings.

"Yes," I told her, I had been doing the shopping.

"I do it every Saturday," I added, just so that she could understand the situation.

"Presumably you are Betty?" I said.

"I suppose he has discussed me with you?"

"Not one single word."

I think she was disappointed.

"And is it too much to inquire who you are?" she said. Wycombe Abbey or Cheltenham College, I should think, by her voice. And how she came to be mixed up with Jimmy in the first place I wouldn't know. Let alone run off with her naval commander type. But maybe quite a lot goes on outside the strict curriculum in these high-class places.

"Liz Barton," I told her.

She wrinkled her nose. "I don't think I know any Bartons—"

"Not the Leicestershire Bartons?"

That shook her. You could see it working. There might well be Bartons in Leicestershire chasing foxes like mad all over the place. And I might be one of them. She took another look at me.

"How's the naval commander?" I asked. "Still limited in some ways?"

That made her very angry.

"I thought you said Jimmy hadn't discussed me with you."

"He hasn't. I listened in when you rang him up from the Golf Hotel, wherever it was."

"Oh, you listen in to other people's conversations do you?"

"Naturally. Don't you?"

"I take it you're Jimmy's secretary?"

"That's what everybody has agreed to call it."

"Quite so. Well, I'm his wife."

She switched on the phonograph again and settled down to enjoy the rest of "Lady in the Evening."

I sat listening; well, not really listening much, for a couple of minutes. Then I got up and moved toward the door. She switched off the phonograph and said:

"Where are you off to?"

"I'm going upstairs to pack."

She nodded. "I should think that's an extremely sensible thing to do."

I thought so too. As Percy M. used to say, sometimes there's a time for starting and a time for ending everything.

In twenty minutes' time I was staggering up the mews dragging a bursting suitcase along. I found that I had acquired a number of new clothes while living with Jimmy so I had to leave a certain number of things behind. Well, if he ever wanted to get sentimental over some laddered stockings, a torn bra, and a ghastly brown cardigan he was welcome to. These foolish things!

I couldn't help feeling a bit not exactly sad but thoughtful about it all. On the whole Jimmy and I had got on well together; and even if I knew, and had known all along, that I wasn't deeply committed, my affair with him had been a tremendous thing for me. It had been the end of zombiedom.

But on balance I wasn't sorry. Time to pack and go. O.K. I was packing and going. It had taken twenty minutes, no longer, for a girl to get all she possessed in the world together and clear out from one aspect of the human situation.

I felt sorry for Jimmy, leaving him to the mercies of the tiger in the bikini, but that was his business. He had married her, and as far as I knew nobody had made him.

At eight o'clock that evening I rang up Merton Mews.

"This is Mrs. Jimmy Mancroft speaking. Who is that, please?"

"I want to speak to Jimmy."

That created a pause. I could almost hear her working out the possibilities and dangers.

"If you tell me he isn't there," I said, "I shall ring up every ten minutes till he is there. And by the way, don't get alarmed. I'm not fighting over him, you're quite welcome. I just want to say goodbye, that's all."

After a considerable interval Jimmy came on.

"Liz, where the hell are you anyway?"

"In a hotel in the Cromwell Road—if you want to know."

He didn't really, of course; but I suppose he had to start the conversation somehow.

"Look, I'm sorry about all this—"

"Not to worry, Jimmy."

"I suppose it had to happen some time."

"Too right it did, as the Aussies say."

"Still—"

"Forget it, Jimmy. The sands were running out anyway. Thanks a lot, it was fun while it lasted."

"Liz, what about Monday?"

"Monday?"

"What time will you be at the office?"

"I shan't be at the office."

"Good grief, now, have a heart—"

A bit humiliating for a girl to realize that a man can be philosophical over the loss of a mistress but as upset as hell when his secretary walks out.

"You can't just walk out on me like that."

"You'd be surprised."

"But what am I going to do?"

"Ring up the agency. You got one good secretary from there, didn't you?"

FIVE

IF YOU'VE NEVER spent a wet Sunday in a cheap private hotel in the Cromwell Road don't get into a state about it. You haven't missed anything. By Monday morning I'd have joined the Salvation Army if it had been the only means of escape.

"Miss Barton, there's a letter for you."

I hadn't even glanced at the green baize board with its crisscrossing of tapes and I wouldn't have unless the head jackie of the place had prompted me.

A letter for me? I didn't see how there could be. Nobody knew I was there. Except Jimmy and I didn't think that he was likely to write.

But he had. "No hard feelings, Liz. It had to end up like this sometime. I can see that you don't want to come back to the office, so here's a month's money. I doubt if the next girl from the agency will be so entirely satisfactory as you were, bless you."

Inside there were eight one-pound notes and a check for forty quid. Four weeks' wages.

I thought it was decent of Jimmy and it certainly cheered up that Monday morning.

"Quite a little windfall!" the landlady said, watching me with the pound notes and the check in one hand and Jimmy's letter in the other.

"The wages of sin," I told her.

She shuddered slightly. Whether at the whole idea or because she didn't think I was getting enough I wouldn't know.

Of course I could have gone straight to the agency where I got the job with J. Mancroft Limited, but somehow I didn't want to. Not yet, anyway. I didn't feel in a hurry to do anything. Except to get away from the Cromwell Road. And I was going about that in a leisurely sort of way.

It had rained hard most of the night and I had heard a lot of it because I hadn't slept well.

But the sun was shining now and leaves were being blown about the pavement and a lot of the front doors were painted bright new colors.

"Walking is quite a good idea—as an idea," Jimmy had once said. I had always thought so, and now there was nobody to stop me putting it into practice, so I walked.

By the Victoria and Albert Museum there was a street artist with half a dozen pictures. Not painted by him on the pavement, but movable canvases. The sort that they hire out (so I've been told) from a central agency for so much a day, together with a notice saying "all my own work."

Well, good luck to them if they do. I put a sixpence in his upturned hat and he said, "Thank you, miss. It'll be your lucky day today, you see."

Which of course was nonsense, but nobody ever minds hearing it said, do they?

When I reached the Brompton Oratory there was a small crowd of people standing about and a policeman waving traffic around what they were all looking at.

Being curious I poked my way in to have a look and rather wished I hadn't.

A woman had been knocked down and was lying at the side of the road. A young policeman was kneeling over her holding her wrist—feeling her pulse, I suppose, and by her head there was a large pool of very bright blood slowly running into the gutter.

She was gray-haired and her eyes were closed. I dare say she was dying. She looked like it. I don't see how anyone could have that amount of arterial blood let out of them and not be dying. Just beyond her was another gray-haired woman on her knees with a rosary in her hands. Prayers for the dying, I suppose. And the traffic was whizzing by all the time just missing everybody. It was all a bit gruesome to come across suddenly on a bright and windy Monday morning, and I must say I went on more thoughtfully. In the midst of life, etc. The only conclusion I could draw from it was that while you were alive you might as well enjoy yourself.

I felt I wanted to talk to somebody just to confirm that it wasn't me who was dying so when I reached Harrods I caught a bus and half an hour later I was in Shoe Lane.

It was eleven o'clock by now and Percy M. had that very moment come in.

He didn't look in quite such bad shape as the woman lying on the ground in Cromwell Road but Monday morning obviously sat pretty heavily upon him.

At first he thought I had come to ask him to work in some nice little bits about Sheila Dane or some other pet client of Jimmy's and he just didn't feel like working in nice little bits about anybody.

"Percy, are you busy?"

"Everybody's always busy in this madhouse."

"I know that. What about taking me out for a cup of coffee somewhere?"

He reached for his hat which only a few moments before he had thrown onto the stand in the corner.

"Jolly good idea." He opened a hatchway and bawled something through it to my Fleet Street counterpart in the next office.

"They can write the bloody gossip column themselves this morning," Percy said. "Let's go out."

"You were quite right," I told him as we sat down opposite one another. "Betty's back and I'm out on my ear."

He smiled at me, the friendly companionable smile of one trouper to another.

"What do I say?" he asked. "Bad luck?"

I told him I didn't honestly think I could say that I had had much bad luck so far.

"Do you want a shoulder to cry on, Liz?"

"I'm not crying, Percy."

"That's my girl."

"I want a job."

"Ah, a job—"

"I've got into this habit of eating."

"Inconvenient, isn't it? How soon do you want a job? Now, at once? And how badly? Desperately?"

I told him about Jimmy's letter that morning so that it wasn't exactly desperate.

"What sort of job?"

"Well, naturally, in an office. Secretarial of some sort. Only somewhere where something happens. I was wondering about in Fleet Street?"

Percy didn't seem to think much of Fleet Street; nor of a girl's chances of getting anything decent to do there.

"What's Jimmy doing in his office?" he inquired.

I told him I wasn't interested in what Jimmy was doing. "Probably feeling exhausted after a hectic weekend," I said.

Percy grinned. "A rum bird in many ways, our James," he said. "But then so are most men by and large."

"Men are unwise and curiously planned."

"You've got something there," he said. "But seriously, Liz, the Street isn't the best place to come looking for a job at the moment."

"I thought a shorthand typist only had to show her nose anywhere these days to be snapped up for good money with paid holidays, official tea break, luncheon vouchers and sleep with the boss if required thrown in."

"Up to a point. But not so much in the newspaper world. Newspapers are dying, Liz. Remember the *News Chronicle*? Remember *The Star*? Of course, you don't. Not really. Just names to you. On sale one day, Amalga-bloody-mated the next. In other words killed—murdered. What do you think happened to all the people who used to have jobs on them? They've been up and down Fleet Street like ants ever since, trying to get something. Anything. And not more than half of them have succeeded. There'll be Sunday papers dying the death next. Owning newspapers is a drug. Power. It's all happened before. It's happening now. Men who must go on buying up, buying up. More and more papers. A bigger empire. The Hitlers of commerce. And you don't build empires without something getting broken, somebody being lost in the process.

"If I had my time again I wouldn't come into the Street. I wouldn't come near the lousy racket—by God, no."

"What would you do, Percy?"

"Run a chicken farm on top of the Chilterns somewhere. Take a pub at Rye. Start up a garage on a bypass—"

"Sez you."

"Quite right. Sez me. Most likely I'd do just the same, of course. Why do you do anything in life? Any one of us. Because that's the way we're made. There isn't such a thing as pure luck in life. I'm convinced of that. It's all slanted luck. If you play cards you attract a certain kind of hand to yourself. If you back horses there's something inside you which makes you bet on a certain kind of horse, which generally loses. As far as I'm concerned, anyway."

"No winners lately, Percy?"

"Horses don't win races. Any of 'em. Some lose by smaller margins than others, that's all. By the way where are you living now that Betty is back in Merton Mews?"

"I've spent the last two nights at a private hotel in the Cromwell Road."

Percy's face fell. "That's bad," he said.

"I couldn't agree more."

"You know the old crack about the C. R.—a place that has length, but no point?"

I didn't know it, but I could heartily endorse it.

"The first thing is to get you out of the Cromwell Road," Percy said, "into a decent base. Then with a month's money in your purse you can take your time looking round for the sort of job you want."

That seemed sense, too.

"And there," Percy said, "I can help you, I think. If it isn't too late. These all-girls-together arrangements get snapped up in no time, but Carolyn was talking about it only last night. Where's a telephone?"

There was a telephone not ten feet away and even if Percy didn't have four pennies I did, so in no time at all I was listening to half a conversation and trying to guess at the other part of it.

"Is that the Topsail Travel Agency?"

Apparently it was.

"I'd like a word with Miss Hinde, please."

Somebody went off to fetch Miss Hinde.

"Carolyn? Percy here. You remember last night saying you were looking for a girl to join you and that chum of yours in your flat . . . no, I am not touting for advertisements . . . have you fixed anybody yet? . . . tentatively? . . . Forget her; scrub her out. She won't suit you. I can feel it in my bones. I've got the very girl for you. . . . O.K., O.K., O.K., get all the usual cracks out of your system and over with . . . just a friend, like I said. . . . Of course she's all right, she's a damned good sort . . . well, tonight, I imagine . . . six, half past? O.K. I'll tell her . . . don't worry, this will be O.K. And she's got pretty strong influence in the theatrical world. . . ."

He grinned at me as he put down the receiver.

"I haven't got any influence in the theatrical world, Percy."

"Of course you haven't. Nobody's got any influence any-where much. But it's just as well to let people think you have. That's how we all live. You be at No. 3 Tammerton

Square at half past six tonight and you'll find you'll be all right."

And I suppose you might say that that's how it all began.

Suppose Percy hadn't happened to be in that morning; suppose he hadn't been talking to Carolyn the very night before; suppose she hadn't happened to be in when he rang from the coffee place—I often play the "suppose" game.

Futile, of course, because in point of fact all these things had happened, and at as near half past six as made no matter I was walking along one side of Tammerton Square.

I fell for T. S. the very first moment that I saw it. London's full of little squares and I've been in lots of them, but Tammerton Square is the nicest.

It isn't a square, really; at any rate the gardens in the middle aren't square, they are oval. An oval piece of grass with a miniature pond and a little lead figure, a cupid, holding up a lily out of which a thin stream of water plays.

The door of number three had a speaking-tube arrangement. You rang the bell and a voice—Carolyn's voice—said, "Hallo, who is it?" You said who it was, there was a click and the door opened.

"Did you shut the door after you?" Carolyn asked as soon as I got up to the top floor. "Because Mrs. Nagelson gets frightfully peeved if we don't."

But Mrs. Nagelson didn't have to get peeved, because I had shut it. And I liked the sound of that "we."

There was never any question of my not "fitting in" at Tammerton Square.

Vicky, who was on holiday climbing somewhere, didn't appear for the first week so Carolyn and I had the flat to ourselves. When Paul wasn't hanging about, that is. Paul was Carolyn's own particular pet property and had great hopes of getting her to say yes, she would marry him.

I must say I thought he was on to something good; and from Carolyn's point of view if she wanted a good-looking, intelligent young barrister with nice manners, an attractive speaking voice, and the usual assortment of social habits and accomplishments, O.K., she probably wouldn't do better than Paul.

I liked him, but he didn't strike any sparks for me. Maybe he didn't, really, for Carolyn; and maybe she preferred it that way; maybe she thought sparks were dangerous.

I got on with Carolyn right from the word "go." In no time at all she was telling me what work at the Topsail Travel Agency was like and we were laughing together at the details of the evasive action she had to take to elude an over-amorous boss.

Carolyn was no angel and her non-angelic moments must have been a lot of fun for the boys concerned; but when I joined the Tammerton Square team Paul was looming large on the horizon and she was trying to take him as seriously as he took himself. After all he had an aunt who was Lady Somebody and he had been to Winchester. He was in the stud book.

I got myself a new job three days after moving into number three.

Percy M.'s bland theory about taking my time to look round for the sort of job I wanted had sounded all right in the Kardomah Café in Fleet Street but I didn't think so much of it three days later. I wanted to get started somewhere and to feel the stuff coming in regularly every Friday.

Carolyn had gone off to her travel agency and Funchi, Vicky's canary, was singing his head off in his cage. I was sitting over a cup of coffee, my first cigarette of the day and the *Daily Mail*.

"Edward West," I read, "Britain's Leading Bookmaker."

I must have seen Edward West advertisements dozens of times before, but I wasn't interested in them so for all practical reasons I *hadn't* seen them. Now I was reading this one and looking at it.

Somebody had made it sound pretty attractive. There was a list of horses running in some race or other (I wasn't interested enough then to notice which) and all you had to do was to name the first three in the correct order to pass the post. If you did this Edward West would pay you anything up to £50,000 according to the odds.

Fifty thousand pounds makes a nice sort of sound in any language but I wasn't interested in that aspect of the advertisement at the moment. Edward West was the only millionaire I had spoken to and I remembered him. I remembered not being able to figure out whether he was a zombie or not: I remembered those remarkable eyes of his; and I remembered his saying if ever Jimmy threw me out I could go to him for a job.

I had an idea that a job with West's might be more interesting than most.

Which didn't seem so likely when I stood in the entrance hall of Westbet House, a narrow dark place with a little glassed-in corner which said "Edward West, Inquiries" and a lift which I didn't propose to take.

It was Friday, 22nd September; eleven-thirty in the morning; and the traffic was swirling round Cambridge Circus outside with an occasional suicidal pedestrian trying to dodge over from the Charing Cross Road to the pavement in front of the Palace Theatre; it was fine and sunny; the midday *Standard* was on sale in the streets; and although it didn't mean a thing to me at the time it was the second day of the Ascot Heath meeting on the flat and there was racing under National Hunt rules at Newton Abbot.

Somebody must have come into the building just behind me because when I reached the first floor landing—there was a mezzanine floor with a window out of which I had seen the swirling circus and the sun—the lift doors were opening.

Edward West stepped out.

"Why didn't you take the lift up?" he asked.

I told him I disliked lifts.

By this time he had remembered me. That man had an extraordinary memory for faces and names.

He smiled. "Hallo, I know you. Jimmy Mancroft. Correct?"

"That's right, Mr. West."

"Don't tell me Jimmy has turned into a betting man and wants you to open an account here?"

"No. I want a job here."

"Good. These betting shops keep drawing my staff away like nobody's business. We train 'em here and the other people come along and snap them up. You'd better come into my room and I'll get hold of Mr. Berry."

I had to keep reminding myself that this man was a double millionaire because the office he took me into ("Edward West, Private" on the door) was as dingy and uncomfortable as could be imagined.

The only pictures on the walls were photographs of horses and (as I found out later) of checks paid out by the firm in settlement of extra large bets with the betting slips attached.

Edward West's own chair looked pretty tatty and the one I had to sit on would have been thrown out of most suburban kitchens. Maybe if you are worth a couple of million you don't have to worry about making visitors comfortable.

"The only thing is, Mr. West," I said, "I don't particularly want a job as a telephonist."

"But you are very good on the telephone. I heard you."

I told him I was good at lots of other things too, and gave the slightly lascivious grin which men expect with that kind of remark. It didn't register with Mr. West. Maybe he had grown out of that sort of thing; or making two million had kept him too busy. I wouldn't know. Anyway he wasn't interested. Suits me, I thought, it will save a lot of trouble.

One odd thing about his desk I noticed, there were absolutely no papers on it. There was a telephone, a desk diary, three buzzer buttons and a small book bound in dark gray which looked as though it might be (but probably wasn't) a Bible.

I thought of the chaos which reigned permanently on Jimmy's desk and was impressed.

He pressed the top one of the three buzzer buttons and a man came in. Thin; quick dark eyes; going bald. It took him six steps to get from the door to the desk and that was enough for those quick dark eyes to take a damned good look at me and for him to wonder (I imagine) what the hell the chief was doing with a girl in his room.

"Mr. Berry, this is Miss Barton."

Mr. Berry smiled and nodded.

"She wants a job here. I suppose you can do with an intelligent young lady?"

Mr. Berry said he certainly could.

"I know she's good on the telephone because I've heard her. But she doesn't want to be a telephonist. She wants something more interesting. What about training her for a settler?"

Berry's eyebrows went up a bit and he took another good look at me. I felt I ought to be up on a rostrum turning round slowly so that the customers could appreciate my good points.

"We *have* had two lady settlers—" Berry admitted. Whatever this settler business might be you could see that he wasn't exactly one hundred percent sold on the idea of letting a woman tackle it.

"And they were damned good," West said, "as good as any of the men."

"I'm bound to agree with you there, Chief."

"How are we off for settlers, hard up, aren't we?"

"Desperately. A day like today we can manage all right. Only two meetings, and there won't be a lot of business at either of them. But tomorrow, for instance, with three meetings on the flat and three under National Hunt rules, well, with staff as it is we shall be stretched to the limit."

"How many have we got in the school?"

"The settlers' school? Only six, Chief."

"We'll take Miss Barton on and make it seven."

"If you say so, Chief. How old is she?"

I didn't know whether to put a bit on my age or not. In the end it seemed simpler to stick to facts. So a bit apprehensively I told them.

"I'm nearly twenty-two."

They looked at one another.

"A shade on the old side to start learning settling," Berry said. "I'd sooner she was seventeen."

Hell's bells, I thought; what sort of job is this settling where a girl's gray-haired when she's still under twenty-two?

"How many days a week do you have them in school? Two?"

"Three now, Chief. We're trying to push them on a bit."

"She can do two days in the typing pool then, which will be useful, I suppose?"

"I'll say it will be useful. We could do with three more whole-time typists straightaway."

"You'd better take charge of Miss Barton then and show her the ropes."

"Just as you say, Chief."

The whole thing was obviously settled. The Great White Chief had spoken and the Head Vizier had agreed.

But there was one small item I hadn't heard about yet. So I piped up with it.

"How much do I get?"

Berry had that one wrapped up O.K.

"You'll be paid a tenner a week while you are in the school and helping with the general typing. Once you're through the school you'll be a settler under supervision for a couple of months and then you'll be on your own. Settlers get a basic wage of fifteen. With overtime at Ascot and Newmarket and any other special days."

"How long shall I be in this school?" I asked.

"Probably a year. You can rarely learn to settle under a year. And lots of 'em can't learn at all. How did the chief come to be interested in you personally, Miss Barton?"

We were outside now, having been dismissed from the presence and walking along a dingy brown corridor with more photographs on the walls of large sums paid out.

1961. The Derby. 1st Aurelius. Edward West Ltd., paid out £92,321 in winnings.

There it was: a photograph of the three horses finishing which to my untutored eye looked like any other three horses finishing any other race. Ninety-two thousand, three hundred and twenty-one pounds sounded like a lot of money to me. If you paid that out and survived how much did you take in? No wonder Edward West was a millionaire.

"We met privately," I said and Berry nodded.

"There'll be a school directly after lunch, two-fifteen. You may as well make a start in that," he said.

"Not that you'll understand a damned thing to begin with," he added.

I had an uncomfortable feeling that he was right.

Vicky didn't show up in Tammerton Square until I had been there a week. By that time I loved the place. I reckoned it was mine.

The oval piece of grass and the little lead cupid throwing up his thin stream of water—I owned the lot. Sometimes I would walk round in the evening, the lights would be on in the houses, you would hear people laughing and perhaps a snatch of music, maybe an L.P. record of *Fascinating Lady* and all around you the hum of London in the air and the light of it in the sky.

"Less than an hour away by taxi is a place called Hansbeck Road," I used to tell myself. Which made me laugh aloud. I didn't believe it.

Vicky arrived early on Tuesday evening. She was due at Pinewood the following morning where she had a small part in a comedy film.

One of her legs, the right, was two inches shorter than the other. How, if you are a girl, do you manage to have that sort of disability and get away with it?

Vicky did. I don't believe it would have mattered if she had lost one of her legs completely, she would still have dominated any company she happened to be in.

There were two bedrooms in the Tammerton Square flat, a double and a single.

Carolyn, who snored, had the small one, so Vicky and I shared the other.

In many ways Vicky was the exact opposite of what you might expect. She was excessively tidy for example. It might be three in the morning before she came in and she might be dog-tired from dancing which she loved, but the room never looked as though a whirlwind had hit it, bra, panties, stockings all over the place, the wardrobe door open and the dress of the evening thrown over a chair which was how I was apt to leave it if I came in late.

And the very first evening Vicky shook me by kneeling down and saying her prayers.

I couldn't believe my eyes. One moment I had been giving her a pretty lurid account of life with Jimmy, to which she had been listening in that interested, amused way which made her such a wonderful companion and then, the next, there she was on her knees, praying.

I didn't get it. I thought only zombies prayed.

She told me about her leg one day, but only because I made her. I dug it out of her, which was a sort of necessity on my part, because I just could not understand anybody deliberately wanting to climb. I simply could not do it.

A man at a party once told me that fear of heights goes with claustrophobia. If you suffer from one you'll suffer from the other. Maybe he was right. Men at parties are right sometimes, let's face it. Anyway it was so in my case. If I see a film of people roped together climbing up a sheer face of rock, on a ledge that a fly would have trouble with and a drop of hundreds of feet below, I just can't look.

"Aren't you scared?" I asked Vicky.

"Yes, very."

"But you still do it?"

"I'm frightened. But I love it. In a way I actually love being frightened. I suppose I get a kick out of it. Some form of perversion, probably."

"What happened when you had your accident?"

"We were on Climp Fell. Doing The Swansneck. It's difficult, but no more. Not one of the real problem climbs. There were three of us. Gaythorn Fender, Tommy Wilson and me. It had been half raining, half snowing during the night. Little scurries, nothing much, hardly enough to lie. And the morning was wonderful. Bright sun and a desperately cold wind and you could see for miles. Up on The Swansneck it was like being in another world. I saw an eagle floating about in the air below us. Gaythorn was leading and I was in the middle. We were roped, of course. Tommy said not to go up the Stairway; but to try the far side for once. He said it was called The Chimney; but personally I don't believe that it had a name, I don't think anybody had ever tried it before. But Tommy's like that. He must have a go, so of course we had to have a go with him. Halfway up, when we seemed to be doing fine, Gaythorn slipped. He always blames himself. I say no one's to blame. An accident is an accident. The foothold isn't as safe as it looks, it crumbles slightly under you and *wham*.

"If things go wrong when you're climbing they can go wrong frightfully quickly.

"One minute you are resting on a ledge; pressed against

the rock face, loving it, loving the hardness of it; something elemental, something you are kin with; something you are fighting; but you respect it and it respects you. The wind is as cold as a steel knife, but you're sweating. Your heart's thumping and the clean cold air is coming right into your lungs. Champagne was never like it.

"One minute you're like that and then, God Almighty, the man above you is shouting, there's a spatter of pebbles and small rocks on your upturned face and before you know what it's all about all three of you have landed up at the bottom of the short crevasse lying muddled up in a heap as awkwardly as possible. And you are staring at a bone you've never seen before sticking straight out of the middle of your leg. What astonished me most was the fact that it didn't hurt at all. Which it didn't. Not then."

Through Vicky I got in touch with the theatrical world again.

Of course I told her very early on not to believe any nonsense she might have heard from Carolyn about my having influence there.

Vicky was the sort of person you wanted to get yourself straight with right from the beginning.

When I first got to know her she was in this comedy film with only a small part; but there were rumors that *The Road to Mandalay* was going to be made as a musical— a sort of second *Cavalcade*—and that she might get one of the lesser leads in it.

I suppose her size, or lack of it, and her leg may have been against her to some extent when casting directors were looking round.

She was very small; almost minute; lovely? No, you couldn't call her lovely. Not exactly pretty, either. A high-cheeked, bold face, steady, level gray eyes that looked at you completely fearlessly; a generous mouth. You felt she had got the world weighed up. "All right, go ahead, drop your bloody bomb," you felt inclined to say. It didn't seem to matter so much with people as decent as that about. She was all wool and a yard wide, that one. The Hon. Victoria Louise Thesiger-Browne. Vicky.

People in, or on the fringe of, the theater world came to see her in the flat. Most of them knew Jimmy, or at any rate knew of him and it was fun talking to them. And I needed someone to talk to.

I needed some relaxation. The settlers' school at Westbet House was damned near killing me.

"The term 'Up and Down. Double Stakes,' sometimes called Double Stakes About (D.S.A.) means that the stake in the A.T.C. (Any to Come) part is twice the initial stake on the selection in the original part . . ."

When you first heard it it sounded like so much Chinese but if you didn't lose your head and listened it gradually sorted itself out. I don't know whether it was the teaching, or whether I had some hidden talent in me I hadn't known anything about, but I actually enjoyed learning the stuff. Certainly it was hard work but when the first week was over and I began to get used to the terms I found myself coming away each evening with something fresh learned, with one more bit of the jigsaw firmly in place. And that was fun. Hard work but fun.

Vicky's Austin Mini was kept in the garage at the far end of Tammerton Square where Peter the Pole seemed to work every hour of every day. Maybe they don't have unions and tea breaks and squabbles about who holds the hammer and who tightens the nut in Poland.

Peter was quite something. Most women agree that Poles can give everybody else ten yards' start in a hundred when it comes to love-making.

Not that Peter ever made love to me. But he would have liked to. He had very talkative eyes.

The Thursday on which Carolyn's engagement to Paul was announced in *The Times* Vicky asked me what I was doing that weekend. I wasn't doing anything. She said why not go home with her. I couldn't think of any reason why not and plenty why.

"Father is always telling me to bring down somebody interesting."

"That lets me out, then. I'm not interesting, Vicky."

"Are you not?" She often spoke like that in an almost stilted way. "Are you not? You're a *femme fatale,* Liz."

Peter the Pole filled up the Austin with petrol before we started out on Friday evening.

"You go away the end of the week?" he asked me.

"Yes. Off for the weekend."

"No boy friend?"

"We're picking them up later," I said, not liking to disappoint him.

"Ah, you come back Monday morning?"

"Sunday night, I expect."

"Plenty tired, eh?"

These Poles have got one-track minds; but it gave us something to laugh about as we fought our way out of London.

Vicky drove fast and well, her small serious face intent over the wheel, her gear changes swift and smooth; she didn't take risks but she never lost an opportunity to get on, never missed a trick.

I don't think that I had ever been in Berkshire before and this was well into the county, high up on bare hills.

"The Berkshire Downs," Vicky said.

The road dipped suddenly and there was a scatter of stone houses.

"Blaydon Village. We used to own most of it."

Then the darkness of trees and we turned in at a gateway. "Blaydons. Where we live. Don't be alarmed at some mild eccentricities on Father's part."

It was Jimmy who had taught me the value of *Who's Who.*

"Before you meet anybody," he used to say, "Look 'em up."

"Thesiger-Browne. The Hon. Victoria Louise, only dau. of the Earl of Linwood (q.v.)," had led me to the L's.

So I knew a potted summary: born 1890; Eton and Balliol; two sons killed in the war; a Lord-Lieutenancy; an honor or two; White's and Brooks's.

There was nobody else there on Friday night, just Vicky and me and Lord and Lady Linwood.

Lady L. was something of a *grande dame*. She remembered the ten indoors servants and eight gardeners period; and as far as she was concerned everything that had happened since was so disastrous that she did her best not to notice it. And I don't know that I blame her.

If I had ever had ten indoor servants and eight gardeners (to say nothing of grooms, keepers, boys and hangers-on generally) I think I should take a dim view of the modern setup.

The old boy was a pet. I didn't see any of the eccentricities Vicky had hinted at unless you call going out of your way to make yourself pleasant eccentric. Maybe it is nowadays. I'll bet he ruffled a few hearts when he was a young man.

When you were talking to him he made you quite certain that nobody else existed. You were the only person in the world and you had his full attention. And moreover nobody in all his seventy-odd years had ever been quite as interesting as he now found you.

I fell for him in a big way.

"I hear you are a woman of the theater, Miss Barton—"

What did I think of this actress; had I seen that play; my views on the modern drama generally; the gentle question, the quiet, attentive listening—anybody can be at her best with a host like that.

"Intensely interesting," he said, "intensely."

"I told you you were a *femme fatale*," Vicky teased me up in her room. "Father's fascinated by you."

"Quite a man, that father of yours," I told her.

"That's the bathroom," she said, explaining the upstairs

geography of the place, "with the loo just beyond it and the chapel at the end of the corridor."

A chapel at the end of the corridor? Shades of Hansbeck Road.

But I thought that maybe this was a different sort of a chapel.

By my bedside there was a satin-covered tin full of biscuits, a water jug and a glass. Waterford, I expect.

Next morning I came out of the bathroom just as Lord Linwood was passing along the corridor. He went into the chapel. So my theory that only zombies prayed got blown sky high once and for all.

"We are asked out to dinner for Saturday night. D.J.'s. So pack something suitable," Vicky had warned me. Which was why I had my yellow evening dress with me. I hadn't had it long. I got it by sheer chance. I was going along Knightsbridge one Saturday morning and I saw it in the window of a shop I didn't know existed until then. The yellow dress and three others. I wouldn't have been seen dead in any of the others. But the yellow dress was me. Yellow's my color, anyway. It does things for me. And if this particular dress had had a notice on it "Reserved for Liz Barton" I couldn't have been more certain that I had to have it.

It was only a formality to try it on. I knew it would fit. It had to. It fitted perfectly and I bought it there and then.

"I'll wear this for the first time on some special occasion," I promised myself. And here it was. The special occasion.

"We're going over to Hollington," Vicky told me. "Some people called Vespar live there. I expect there'll be a party. They're great people for entertaining. He's something to do with tobacco. Oodles of money. I hope you'll like it."

"I know I shall. I'm excited about it."

"It will probably turn out frightfully dull."

"It can't. Not tonight."

We drove over in Vicky's Mini. There was a wind blowing

so that every now and again the clouds were swept away and a burst of moonlight came through. It happened like this when we were going up the drive, one moment you couldn't see much beyond the headlights and then suddenly there the house was, in moonlight. *Childe Roland to the Dark Tower came,* I thought.

The door was opened by a manservant and the moment you were inside it you could smell money.

The unmistakable sweet smell of success.

Whatever else Vespar had done with his spare cash he had certainly bought himself something out of the ordinary in the way of a wife. Italian. Tall and dark and lovely. She looked equally capable of making love to a man and knifing him. Quite a piece.

Vicky and I had come last and the drawing room already had eight people in it. Mostly standing round the huge log fire, or by the drink table.

"Miss Barton would like a glass of sherry, Mike," Mrs. Vespar said, and the man she called Mike turned to hand one to me.

I only just didn't exclaim.

"Don't be alarmed," he said flatly, "you'll get used to it."

I learned later that he was one of the Archie Macindoe guinea pigs. When they dragged him out of the plane he didn't have a face at all so I suppose it was unreasonable to feel shocked at what he looked like now. But just at first you couldn't help it . . . that awful, staring, glassy eye, and the mottled stained skin.

But Mike was good fun, he got me my drink and stayed by me talking.

There were two married couples, one of them Americans, who had just been staying in the Bahamas at the Beach Hotel, and the others from nearby.

And there was a young Englishman in a bad temper standing next to Vespar, who was mixing more drinks.

"Come and be introduced," Mrs. Vespar said.

Johnny didn't welcome the interruption. Well, naturally, he wouldn't. He and Vespar were talking about investments, about money. And money, how to keep his place in the warm comfortable drawing rooms of the rich, was always Johnny's favorite subject.

"Miss Barton; this is Mr. Mannington-Travers."

John Ivor Mannington-Travers.

Ivor, as I found out later, because it was a family name. But Johnny to me. Always Johnny to me.

SIX

Wₑ ɢₒₜ ʙᴀᴄᴋ to Blaydons late. Lady Linwood had gone to bed. Lord Linwood was sitting by the fire reading. The room was in darkness save for the tall standard lamp close to his chair and the firelight. Wantage, an old black Labrador, lying by his chair. A dignified old man at his ease. A sort of complete, collected human being somehow. You could see things making sense with people like him around. He was drinking whisky and soda out of a lovely Irish goblet.

Would the young ladies like anything to drink. The young ladies wouldn't. They had done themselves pretty well over at the Vespars', thank you—

"A pleasant evening?" he asked me. Yes, a pleasant evening, thank you, Lord Linwood, I told him. If that's what you call it when you feel yourself knocked over backwards; picked up and sent flying through the intoxicating air, stunned.

"Isn't it time you were in bed, Father?"

"Presently, presently. If you don't sleep you may as well be awake in front of a good fire reading, as staring up at a dark ceiling worrying."

I thought he had a point there. I wondered what he would worry about? Death duties? Schedule A? Repairs to the roof in the north wing? Vicky? Vicky's odd choice in friends (e.g. me)? Whether Wantage ought to go to the vet or not? His immortal soul?

"Father's a bit of an old pet." (We were up in Vicky's room now.)

"I think he's absolutely sweet."

"He'll sit there reading for another hour yet." It was half past one already.

"I don't suppose he has to get up very early, does he?"

Vicky laughed. "He'll be up before any of us."

She began the preliminaries of undressing and I sat on the end of her bed watching her.

"How lovely Manni Vespar is," she said suddenly.

"I'd give quite a lot to look like her."

"You looked all right yourself, Liz. Don't worry. Yellow suits you."

Well, that was something. Maybe he had noticed, maybe he liked yellow too.

"Did you win any money?"

I emptied my bag on to the bed and began to count.

"Over nine pounds. I've never won so much in my life before."

"Lucky Liz. I lost. I always do at every sort of gamble."

After dinner, when we had got back into the overheated and brilliantly lit drawing room, Harry Vespar produced a roulette board.

"I expect everyone would like a flutter," he said, "and it saves talking."

"How right you are." (Johnny of course.)

Roulette was obviously the routine at the Vespars'.

A pile of magazines (*Life, The New Yorker, Country Life, Elle*) was swept off the table and in no time everything was set; cloth, wheel, beautiful chips out of an expensive-looking box, and Harry Vespar with green eyeshade and croupier's rake.

I wasn't going to say I had never played roulette in my life. Never apologize; never explain; and never say you can't do a thing. Just stick around and watch the others for a bit and you'll get by.

All I knew about the game was what I remembered from

an occasional film-shot of people playing at Monte Carlo and places like that.

The important thing was how much was it going to cost me?

"Chips I sell," Harry Vespar said, "buy what you like. Fifty, twenty-five, ten, five. But more if you like, Miss Barton."

I told him five quids' worth would do for me.

And it would do for me, too, if I lost it. Luckily I had been paid that afternoon at Westbet House. A tenner less P.A.Y.E., National Health Insurance and other deductions, less also what I gave Carolyn each week as my contribution to living in Tammerton Square, left me exactly five pounds two and sixpence.

Of which I now handed five pounds over to Harry Vespar.

"You can always come back for more," he pointed out, "if you run out of these."

"Rather."

Later, counting notes and coins out on Vicky's bed I found that I was nine pounds fifteen and something to the good.

"I'm not surprised, Liz. You're the sort of person who *would* be lucky at gambling."

And in love? I wondered.

Vicky was taking her face off in front of the mirror.

"Did you notice anything odd about that boy John Mannington-Travers?" she asked.

Me notice anything about John Mannington-Travers? I took a deep breath so that my voice wouldn't shake too much when I answered her.

"How do you mean odd? Three legs or something?"

"The way he played roulette. He cheated."

"Vicky, what a frightful thing to say."

"Oh, I don't know. Human beings are human. It's what my father is always telling me. And anyway, maybe I was mistaken."

"I'm sure you must have been."

Which was a pretty good thumping lie because I had spotted what Johnny did; only I was hoping nobody else had.

The men had all been smoking cigars and everybody had a big balloon glass of brandy. Harry was calling out *"Faîtes vos jeux"* and *"Rien ne va plus"* just like they do in the films and, I suppose, at Monte, though I've never been there.

I soon began to get the hang of how to play.

The essence of it was easy. You threw a chip down onto the big cloth that covered the table, the croupier spun the wheel, and if you were lucky you won something; if you weren't you lost.

It was as simple as that.

There were certain complications. Different odds were paid on different parts of the table.

Individual numbers; zero by itself; the dozens; odd or even; red or black, high or low.

I got interested in it right away because of the work I was doing in the settlers' school at Westbet House.

Harry Vespar did the croupier business well. As soon as each spin was finished he called the winning number and all the details about it. For instance. High. Black. Even. Third dozen and so on, and then got busy with his rake, scooping in all the losing chips and pushing out the piles of winnings—if any.

I soon saw that you didn't have to put the whole of your chip on an individual number, which after all was always a thirty-five to one chance against you. What you could do was to "quarter" place your chip in the middle of four numbers so that you had a quarter of it on each. Like backing a horse for a place. It gave you more of a run for your money and I did it most of the time with an occasional go on Pair and Impair for a change.

The Pair and Impair space was close to the edge of the

cloth and more than once there was a little confusion about whether chips which people had piled in front of them were actually staked or not.

The chips were red, blue, yellow and green, which meant £5, £1, 10s. and 5s.

Several people were staking red chips most of the time; but I reckoned yellow was my color so I stuck to that, with frequent excursions into green for economy.

Johnny was on the other side of the table from me, not quite directly opposite but almost so.

But if the entire chorus of the Windmill in the nude had been opposite him I don't think he would have taken any notice of them.

Not that Johnny didn't like things in the nude. But he liked gambling better. Money meant more to him than anything else in the world. Love, honor, decency, integrity —they all went down before money with Johnny.

But I didn't know that then.

I only knew that his dark, handsome, scowling face was four feet from mine across the table and that apart from a quick occasional glance of envy when I won anything I never got a look from him. Not even a scowl.

He was using reds a good deal of the time except on the individual numbers. At one point he had a whole pile of chips in front of him and the scowl had gone, he was smiling away as pleased as Punch. Johnny in winning vein. Johnny with the lick of money on his lips.

Then the table began to run against him and his pile of chips kept diminishing.

"You can always buy more," Harry Vespar told him.

"I think I'll do that very thing," Johnny said, fishing for his notecase. "And what about another brandy, Harry?"

I watched his bets each time before I made my own. He was backing individual numbers mostly and if he put his chip, a red one, on 18, for instance, I would quarter my yellow one on 18 and three touching numbers. Even then

I had a feeling that Johnny was lucky, but not quite so lucky as he thought he was.

He seemed to like eights: 8, 18, 28, and he backed these more often than other numbers.

He won occasionally, of course; everybody won sometimes; but more often he lost, and his pile of chips, in spite of replenishments, was going steadily down.

The maximum on an individual number had been fixed at one blue chip (a pound) and as the odds paid out were thirty-five to one this could be expensive for the bank. Towards the end of the game Johnny said:

"Fiver on a number, Harry?"

"You'll ruin me, Johnny."

"I should say so. Just for luck a red on 28, eh?"

I don't think Harry Vespar was keen about it, but I suppose he didn't like to sound mean; anyway he shrugged his shoulders and said:

"O.K. Just this once."

So Johnny put his red chip carefully and precisely in the middle of square 28. I watched him as he put it there and he was deadly intent about it. I waited till most of the bets were made and then did my usual thing of quartering Johnny's choice with three numbers touching it.

"*Rien ne va plus,*" Harry said and spun the wheel, throwing the ball into it against the spin.

Johnny's chance of winning one hundred and seventy-five pounds had stirred things up a little and there was a good deal more money on the table than usual.

Harry had given an extra flip to the ball as he threw it into the wheel and it shot round, *clicketty, clicketty, clicketty, click, click,* hitting the little lozenges of metal and ricocheting off with everybody watching it in silence.

Sometimes the ball lodges quickly, sometimes it manages to keep out until the wheel has practically stopped spinning. Which is what it did this time until in the end the wheel was turning slowly enough to make out the numbers and still the ball hadn't lodged.

At last it hit the point of the metal division between two numbers, 7 and 28, and for what must have seemed an awful long time to Johnny it stayed there undecided; then it actually began to slip into the 28 slot and I heard someone take in breath quickly and sharply behind me.

But the wheel was still spinning, slowly it is true but fast enough not to let the ball settle, and with one last flick it shot out of 28, where it had almost lodged, hit one more metal lozenge and was finally deflected into 17 where it stayed.

The wheel came to rest and Harry, with considerable relief in his voice, was calling "Seventeen Black. Odd. Low. Second dozen. Bad luck, Johnny old boy."

I was watching Johnny. He was always inclined to be pale, but at that moment he was deadly white.

A hundred and seventy-five pounds had been right in his grasp and slipped out and he could hardly believe it.

I was "quartered" in 17 so I was paid two pounds three and ninepence on my five-shilling stake. I was one of the very few winners on the spin. If he felt anything at all about me at that moment I think it was angry resentment.

Everybody felt that to be the climax of the evening and people began to talk of going.

"Last spin," Harry announced. *"Faîtes vos jeux."*

Everybody had something on the last spin. I was in pocket now. So I decided to go a bust and back a number. I put a green chip on 18. Johnny had two red chips left, but he had bought twenty pounds' worth since his original five pounds' worth so he was losing fifteen pounds.

I watched him trying to make up his mind. I could see that he desperately wanted to put both chips on, but that meant risking the loss of ten pounds in addition to the fifteen that had already gone whistling away and he couldn't quite bring himself to do it.

In the end he put one of his chips on to the Pair space along the edge of the cloth just in front of him.

"All on?" Harry asked. *"Rien ne va plus.* Off we go."

He set the wheel spinning and threw the ball in. Of course I wanted 18 to turn up, but even if it didn't I was still just on the right side so I wasn't worried.

It was a long spin ("a good one for the last, Harry") and the ball seemed as though it would never lodge. While it was click-clicketting round someone behind me was helping himself to a drink. I heard the decanter chinking against the glass and the hiss of the siphon.

Then the ball suddenly stopped its rattle. It had lodged home swiftly and safely but the wheel was still spinning a shade too fast to be sure where.

But it looked like eighteen.

There was a crash behind me, and the crackle of splintering glass.

"Damn the bloody table," a man said and for a moment everybody looked to see what minor disaster had happened.

When I turned to look at the wheel again it had almost stopped moving and now there was no doubt about it, the ball was safely in 18. Good for Miss Barton, I thought, doing a settler's job on the bet and making out that the bank owed me eight pounds fifteen.

Funny how you can see two things at once sometimes.

I saw the good little silver ball nestling as snug as you like in the 18 slot and at the same time I saw Johnny's forearm move forward.

There was still some confusion over the spilled drink and the broken glass behind me and not everybody by any means was looking at the roulette table.

The movement of Johnny's arm was small and swift. If you weren't directly looking at him you wouldn't have noticed it. But I did happen to be looking and I saw it. Now he had two red chips on the Pair space instead of one. And Pair had won.

"Never mind about the mess on the carpet," Harry Vespar was saying. "Eighteen. Red. Low. Second dozen. Even. I pay, and some lucky so-and-so on the number itself."

I was the lucky so-and-so. Eight pounds fifteen. Very nice too. Thank you very much.

Johnny watched me being paid and could scarcely bear it. He must have backed 18 half a dozen times that evening and it had never turned up for him.

"Why the hell didn't I back it?" he said, scowling at me as though it was all my fault.

Harry was settling up all round the table, although as it happened there were not many winners.

"Whose two reds are there on Pair?" he asked.

" 'Fraid they're mine, old man," Johnny told him. "Touched a bit at last."

"Good for you," Harry said, throwing two red chips out from the bank and pushing them together with the two already on the table over to Johnny.

So John Ivor Mannington-Travers managed to cut his losses for the evening and I knew he was a cheat.

Not that it mattered.

I hung about in Vicky's room even after she had got into bed. I wanted her to talk about Johnny but I couldn't bring myself to say his name.

I wanted to say it out loud. To shout it. John Ivor Mannington-Travers. I wanted to find out how well Vicky knew him. I wanted to know about his family. And, since, if the knife is going to cut you, you may as well get it over with, I wanted desperately to learn about Johnny and the other girls.

"You're a menace, Liz, go to bed."

"I'm not sleepy. I never am after a party. I like to talk it over."

"It's a pity Johnny Mannington-Travers cheated."

"Are you sure he did?"

"Absolutely. He pushed a chip forward on to the table

after the wheel had stopped spinning. Didn't you see him?"

"I was too busy thinking about what I had won."

"It's a good job Harry Vespar didn't spot it; there would have been a frightful schemozzle."

"Tranby Croft."

"Practically."

"I suppose he lives round here, does he?"

"Johnny?" Vicky laughed. "No, our Johnny's a town bird. His mother lives in a cottage at Embleton and he comes to see her occasionally. Mostly when he has run short of money, I imagine. Are you interested in him?"

"In John Mannington-Travers? When a fascinating man like Harry Vespar was there?"

"Ah, don't get ideas about Harry. Manni keeps him on a very short lead."

She could keep him in a kennel for all I cared, I thought, when I was finally in bed staring at the chink of moonlight showing between the curtains.

Are you interested in him? Well, yes, you could call it interested, I suppose. I didn't know it would be like this. Love, love, love—a half-witted crooner will mouth the word ten times in one sloppily sentimental chorus. I didn't know it would be like somebody tossing a burning torch into the middle of you. Something eating you up. Something drying and searching, like a hot wind blowing in a desert. Something frightening.

Thank God I enjoyed working at Westbet House. If I hadn't I don't know how I could have coped with the thing that had hit me. But in the settlers' school it just wasn't possible to think of anything else. Mr. Chess had sorted us out by this time into top and bottom halves. Two men and myself in the top; the other four in the bottom.

Chess hadn't said so, but we all thought it meant that the three in the top half would probably make the grade and that the others had already been half decided against.

"It's a flair," was what everybody said about settling. If

you didn't have the flair you would never be able to do it.

"I believe you've got it," Mr. Chess said to me one Wednesday afternoon when the settlers' school was finished, and the rest of them had gone. "I really believe you've got it."

He took a quick look round the room. It was empty except for us two and the door into the passage was half shut. Then he slipped one arm round me, pulled my face up to his with his other hand and kissed me full on the lips.

Well . . . I thought.

Two seconds later he was out of the room, hurrying down the passage. Scared either of himself; me; or Edward West looking in and catching us.

Well, I thought again.

No girl in her senses minds being kissed by a man. And I liked little Arnold Chess. He was frightfully good at ex plaining and he never lost his temper if you were slow in picking a thing up. I just hadn't thought of him as masculine. Until then.

The next settlers' school was on the following Monday morning and Arnold (I had to think of him as Arnold now; a girl can't keep tagging "Mister" onto a man who has kissed her like that) didn't show a thing. Unless you count standing behind me for rather longer than was necessary to see if I was getting my work right. I couldn't altogether blame him. I had rather a low-cut blouse on and standing behind you and looking down a man can get quite a disturbing view.

Well, good luck to him, I thought. Nothing wrong with a bit of cleavage. I was too busy concentrating. Any to come; Round the clock; Up and down; the Patent; the Roundabout; a Rounder and a Yankee—I had mastered the details of all these different bets by now but I was still slow in working some of them out. "The Yankee is a bet on four selections and makes six doubles, four trebles and an accumulator" is the sort of thing I was thinking about in the settlers' school and if Arnold Chess had been walking about the room stark naked I don't think he would have got more than a passing glance from me.

I was in the school for the first three days of the week; on Thursday and Friday I had to go into the typists' pool in the mornings, which I hated, and in the afternoon I was in the low stake betting room which I liked.

"I don't think you enjoy the typists' pool much, do you, Miss Barton?" It was the first time Arnold had spoken directly to me since he had kissed me.

"Not one bit."

"You'd sooner be in the room?"

"Much."

"I'll have a word with Mr. Berry."

The following Thursday I was sent to the room instead of into the pool.

"Thank you very much," I told him when we ran into one another in the corridor that evening.

"I told Mr. Berry you were my best pupil and I wanted you to have all the betting practice you could."

"It was sweet of you."

Rather a pet this Arnold Chess, I thought, with his round chubby face and his sad eyes. Rather a pet.

And a pet was a pleasant relief after the sort of turmoil that went on inside me all the time that I wasn't concentrating on work, and quite a lot of the time that I was.

It was like a buccaneer or a pirate sailing up to a virgin island and planting his flag, *wham*, in the middle of it. He sails away again but his flag's there; and there it will stay till he comes back to claim it. If he ever remembers to. Not that I was any virgin island. Not after a year and a half living with Jimmy. And I was glad I wasn't. Living with Jimmy had been fun. And that was it. Fun that could be rolled up and tossed out of the window and forgotten. Fun that hadn't lasted and didn't hurt.

Johnny was different.

"I don't know if you ever—possibly—sometimes at the weekend—if you're doing nothing, free I mean—" poor little Arnold could hardly get the words out.

"I'd love to," I told him.

I wasn't quite sure what it was I had told him I would love but it didn't matter; and anyway I was grateful to him for getting me out of the pool.

"Next Saturday then after racing?"

"Lovely."

That particular Saturday wasn't a heavy one. There was racing at Doncaster, Sandown Park and a National Hunt meeting at Sedgefield. But even on a comparatively light day it was exciting to work in one of the rooms.

The smallest of them dealt entirely with bets from other bookmakers.

On the floor below, the "alphabet" rooms were side by side.

Sorting out which room a client belonged to was part of the telephone girl's job. A to M in one, N to the end of the alphabet in the other. Every client had a number assigned to him, like the registration number of a car; it might be MQ 4131 for instance and the moment a punter said this over the telephone the girl taking the call knew that his surname began with M (Maynard or Mills or what-have-you) and that his weekly credit was limited to £20. R after the initial would mean a weekly top limit of £30, S £40, and so on up to U which meant £60. V meant "over £60," and in some cases far over it. The vast majority of clients were Q's, or under. If I had thought about betting at all before coming to Westbet House it was when I occasionally saw details in the paper about some huge sum being won and I had got the idea that most people bet in large amounts. Some of them did, sometimes, certainly; but there were very many bets for five pounds or less.

The work was exactly the same in both rooms, of course, but A to M had usually more bets to handle, although on big days—Ascot, Epsom or Aintree for instance—everybody was working to capacity throughout the whole building.

But with only three meetings, and one of those a small one, this particular Saturday was nothing out of the usual.

The only reason I was there was to get practice in settling which meant that I was somewhat in the way and none too popular when things were really busy, although the man I always stood behind to watch, Jack Stranson, never seemed to mind.

I don't think he noticed me. When you're settling you can't think about anything else; you don't know that anything else is there. All the slips are piled by your side and you take each one in turn and look at it.

The winner, the placed horses and the prices have already been declared and you've got them written up in front of you in case you forget:

1.	Abbots Land	100–7
2.	Cherry Pie	3–1
3.	Greenfinch	6–4

The first slip—Naughton NQ 6461—shows £3 each way on Woodpecker so takes less than a second to deal with; a loser; next—Norton NQ 3790—is one of the many which will be backing Greenfinch the favorite, a modest bet this, 10s. each way; in no longer time than it took him to decide that Mr. Naughton had won nothing Jack has marked Mr. Naughton's slip and thrown it on to the pile on his right. Looking over his shoulder I am there almost as quickly as he is. Ten shillings for a place at 6–4 against is three and ninepence. I don't have to work this out. I know it. Ask any ordinary person what seven eights are. He says fifty-six. He doesn't have to start calculating; he knows what seven eights are because he has learned his multiplication tables. That's how settlers have to learn to work. If a horse wins at 13 to 8 against and a punter has two pounds five on it he has won three pounds thirteen and a penny.

Anybody could tell you this ultimately either by working it out or by looking it up in a ready reckoner; and if you tried to run a business like Edward West's by either of these methods you wouldn't last a week. Bets are made in such enormous numbers and settlement must be made so promptly that they have to be dealt with at lightning speed and the trained settler is the answer.

Jack's next slip—Norberry MQ 342—was for a five-pound each way bet on the winner and Jack was writing in the figures (62. 10. 0. for the win; 15. 12. 6. for the place) almost before the slip was flat on the table in front of him.

I stood behind him and tried to work as fast as he did. I couldn't keep up with him all the time and I didn't expect to; he had been at it for three years and more; but I wasn't doing too badly.

That was the first race at Sandown Park, and a boy is already writing up the runners for the two o'clock at Doncaster on one of the three boards. At this stage we aren't interested in the odds. Bets come in and we take them, and the starting prices will be what they will be. *Che sara sara,* as Jimmy used to say to me.

There are four benches of telephonists, sitting like a class full of schoolgirls; Edward West likes his telephonists. He says they give the best service in the world. I believe him. I have looked in at the telephonists' school a couple of times out of interest and believe you me those girls have to learn their job.

The last-minute bets are pouring in now for the two o'clock at Doncaster and each one gets written by the girl who takes it into a separate slip. As soon as the slip is complete a clock boy picks it up and puts it into a time-stamping machine. Part of the Edward West security system, this, to stop any fiddling with times; and fiddling with times can be highly profitable as several big bookmakers have found out to their cost.

"Flag" the boy writes on the board so we know that the starter's flag is up and the off will come any minute.

Jack Stranson has just finished his In slips for the first race at Sandown and is leaning back taking a breather, glancing incuriously at the Doncaster runners. He doesn't care which horse wins. Or at what odds. 5–1, 11–4, 100–9, they are all equally part of the mechanical side of his brain now.

Maybe he does care, though.

Nobody working in Westbet House can have a bet there, but most of the settlers are supposed to bet heavily outside.

So Jack may be interested in Doncaster after all.

He's going slightly bald on top and there's dandruff on his collar. Rumored to drink like a fish and not to take any interest in women. I wouldn't know about that. Certainly he hasn't taken any interest in me. Thank goodness.

"Off," the boy says and draws a line across the board.

"Sorry, sir, they're running," the girl just behind me is saying down the phone and the punter at the other end sounds angry. Even from where I am I can hear him spluttering. I can't distinguish what he is saying but I can guess at it. One of the "do you know who I am?" type. ". . . do you know who I am? This is Sir Peter Coldworthy speaking. I've been betting with Edward West for—"

"I'm sorry, sir, no bets can be taken when they are running—"

"I've a good mind—"

The girl listens politely to what he has a good mind to do, and waits till he has rung off.

"Silly bastard," she says wearily to the girl next to her. "Seems to think I make the bloody rules."

But she says it quietly. Bad language isn't approved of in Westbet House. I have discovered already that there are a lot of things you can get away with in the world outside which you mustn't try in a bookmaker's establishment. Not in Edward West's, anyway.

We are all watching the Doncaster board now. Arnold Chess has come into the room and is standing just behind me. I can't make up my mind whether his slight pressure against me is merely because he is leaning forward to see the board or whether it means anything. I suspect this is because the little man can't make up his mind to mean anything. He probably regards me as a dangerous woman. And Johnny, I wonder—how does he regard me? If he thinks of me at all, that is.

The boy at the board is holding a telephone receiver to his ear with his left hand and in his right he has a pencil with which he taps the board.

The phone is direct from our man on the course; but how the race is going isn't blared out into the room because of the noise.

Several of the settlers, especially those with the "heavy" letters, the B's and the M's for instance, are still working. So the boy doesn't call anything out but as our man at Doncaster (little Paddy Tyke) reads the race to him he taps with his pencil.

No taps to start with, so we reckon they are all away to a good start and are bunched together at the moment; nothing in it.

Tap against Fairy Queen, tap, King's Choice, tap, Moonbeam. Three of them beginning to pull clear. We know from the bets that Moonbeam is the heavily-backed horse and is expected to win. The telephone girls have all relaxed. One of them is looking at a paper, two of them filing their nails. They couldn't care less what wins. Moonbeam, Sunbeam, Starlight—it's all the same to them. It's just a job and they want to get it over with and to be off and away. Shopping; meeting the children from school; ringing up their lovers.

Tap, tap, tap, against King's Choice which must have

come to the front with a rush. King's Choice will be a fair price. Not that price makes any difference to you if you are settling.

Tap, tap, Moonbeam; tap, tap, King's Choice. These two are fighting it out.

Tap, tap, tap, then a line under King's Choice which, subject to weighing in and objections, has won.

Jack picks up his pile of slips and knocks them on the desk into neatness.

Some of the telephonists are getting busy again on the next race; the boy writes up the Doncaster result and the prices (King's Choice, 100–6, Moonbeam, 11–8, Sea Voyage, 4–1) on the board at the side and begins to wipe his main board clear for the two-thirty.

Jack has already jotted down the result and has started . . . "Moonbeam, £4 each way; King's Choice, £1 for a place only . . ."

Another boy is writing up the Sedgefield runners. The supervisor is watching him. "You've spelled Tintinnabulation wrong," he calls out. And personally I'm not surprised. Who the hell wouldn't spell it wrong anyway? But not in Westbet House. There's a pretty high standard there.

I look over Jack's shoulder and try to keep pace with him. He's a good settler and he works quickly. One slip he holds up for me to see. A Mr. Dewley. £20 to win on King's Choice. I can read that one as quickly as Jack can. Three hundred and thirty-three pounds, six shillings and eightpence. Nice work, Mr. Dewley. You lucky so-and-so.

After the three-thirty Arnold Chess touched me on the shoulder.

"I thought, perhaps—"

It was Saturday afternoon and I didn't have to be there at all. I had gone to the room for practice in settling.

I smiled at little Chess and nodded.

"Right-o!"

He had a car tucked away in Lite Street.

"Usually I come by train," he explained, "but on Saturdays parking is easier."

His car was a small black Standard saloon which might have come out of the Royal Mews the way it was kept.

"I like to have things clean and tidy," he said.

The route he took out went quite close to Hansbeck Road, in fact we actually crossed the bottom of the High Street, at the lights.

"I used to live near here once," he told me. I didn't tell him that I used to live there as well. I didn't see that it would interest him; and frankly it didn't interest me any longer.

"But I couldn't stick living in London."

Well, everybody to his choice; but personally I couldn't imagine living out of it.

"I must get out into the country."

"You need the wide open spaces, Arnold."

"If you can call Cotterfield 'wide open spaces'!" He laughed. "But at any rate it's better than Cambridge Circus."

I could see what he meant when we got to Cotterfield. It looked countrified enough to me at first sight, but as he pointed out there were a hell of a lot of houses around.

"Would you—I don't know if you would care to drive round a bit?" he suggested.

"Love to, Arnold."

And I meant it, too. The way that little guy drove you had a chance of seeing things.

We got out at one point and walked through a wood, which he told me was called Cromwell's Copse, to the edge of a hill and looked out over the view.

"You can see the railway over there," he said, pointing. "The old Great Western." It sounded as though "the old Great Western" meant a lot to him, so I said, "Oh, yes," and tried to sound interested, but I couldn't get worked up about it. Men are unwise and curiously planned.

"I don't know if you would care for a cup of tea," he said

in his tentative way. I told him just to try me and see, so we ended up in Heath End Cottage.

I suppose maybe it was at the end of a heath at some time; anyway it's pretty well tucked away on its own even now and inside it was as clean and tidy as a new pin.

He put a match to the fire in the living room and it blazed up brightly.

"I won't be a moment getting the tea," he said.

I couldn't get the form at all. No Mrs. Chess? I had always imagined little Arnold heavily married to a come-here-and-he-cometh, do-this-and-he-doth-it sort of wife.

When he came back carrying the tea tray, I asked:

"Do you live here all on your own, Arnold?"

"Now, yes. And may I call you Liz?"

I looked shocked. "Good heavens, no. Miss Elizabeth Angela Barton to you, sir. In full, every time."

"I'm rather shy about that sort of thing."

"It's a nice change, Arnold, believe you me. You didn't always live alone then?" I could see that the only way to get anything out of the little man was to dig, so I dug.

"No. Not always. I was married you see and—"

"What happened?"

"She went off. With somebody else."

"Oh, dear. What was her name?"

"Sandra."

The only other Sandra I had known in my life was a three-dimensional, one hundred and two percent copper-bottomed bitch. No reason why all Sandras should be the same, of course, but I couldn't persuade myself that a Sandra was the right sort of person for little Arnold.

"Not that I blame her," he was saying.

"No?"

"You see—pour the tea out, would you mind, Liz?"

I poured out and saw that he had what he wanted to eat and generally mothered him. He was pathetically grateful.

It must have been quite a time since anybody did anything for him in Heath End Cottage.

"So Sandra went off and left you?"

"I'm not saying it was her fault—"

"Never mind about whose fault it was, just tell me."

"She should never have married a schoolmaster."

"You were a schoolmaster, then?"

"Oh, yes." He seemed surprised I didn't know. "I taught mathematics. I took a mathematical degree, you know. That's how I came into Edward West's in the end."

"I see." Which was more or less true. "And what about Sandra? Were you very much in love with her, Arnold?"

The poor little man was nearly in tears and I could see that it would do him all the good in the world if he had a real good cry.

"Yes, I was," he said, bending forward and fiddling about with the fire. "Very, very, very much. But, of course, I can quite see she shouldn't have married me."

"How come she shouldn't?"

"I was flying too high. You know, she was here, there and everywhere. Always out at parties and things, having a good time. Not the sort of thing I was much good at, really. But I plucked up courage and thought if other men could go about with her why shouldn't I?"

"Good for you."

"I don't think she ever forgave me about the headmaster-ship."

"You were a headmaster somewhere, Arnold?"

"I was going to be. At the grammar school. It was prac-tically settled. At least I thought so. There was a short list of three and we were interviewed and the list was reduced to two; myself and another man. I had another interview with the governors and they told me I was going to get the job. It couldn't be for six months, not till the beginning of the new school term and in the meantime there were certain formalities, but I needn't worry. I would get the job.

"I told Sandra that evening and I asked her to marry me. Asked her again, I mean. I had asked her before. When I told her about the headmastership she agreed. We got married in May. Early in August the school governors sent for me again. Which was what I expected as the new term would start September the fourteenth.

"They made it sound as nice as they could, but there it was, the other man had got the job and I hadn't."

"But hadn't they told you you were going to get it?"

"If words mean anything and if people mean what they say, yes, they had."

"But you didn't have anything in writing?"

"I never thought it was necessary—"

Of course he wouldn't think it necessary. He was one of those men, poor boobs, who are never likely to win in any fight. And on the whole women find them infuriating. Capture me and clothe me. Rape me and bring me home a leopard skin. Any woman understands those tactics. The cave-man stuff still goes down in a big way. But Arnold was no cave man. Eventually he found out by devious grapevines what had gone wrong. The chairman of the board of governors had a wife (another Sandra probably) and she fairly gave him hell when he came back with his nonsense about appointing Arnold Chess.

The other candidate was a cousin of the Bishop of Dumchester and the Bishop of Dumchester was an Honourable as well as a Right Reverend, so what the devil did this poor fish of a chairman of the school governors think he was doing throwing away social chances like that? Just like a man to mess the whole thing up. His wife had to get busy at once putting things right. Still, she had some months to work in, and she was an energetic social-climbing bitch (God bless her, which of us isn't?) and by the time August came along she had got it all sewed up.

That ridiculous little Arnold Chess was out on his ear.

Not the right type at all, my dear. Not one of us. Just newly married too; which was too bad.

Especially as his wife, who had really married the head-mastership and all that she hoped would go with it, never forgave him.

Failure, if you keep on letting your man know you think him a failure day in and day out, by direct statement and by innuendo, by open word and by glance or gesture, it begins to get him down.

Or so little Arnold Chess told me; and I believed him.

He ought to have turned her over in bed and beaten her bottom black and blue with a slipper. Only it was no good telling him that. For one thing it was too late; and he didn't belong to the bottom-beating school anyway.

And in any case bed hadn't been too happy a place for him either apparently.

By this time all his inhibitions were gone; we were sitting side by side on the sofa and he was telling me everything. Even if I had wanted to stop him I couldn't have.

Sandra began to tell him that he was a failure in bed. Not satisfactory enough for her, anyway. Which depressed him still further.

"Impotent, impotent," is a nasty thing to have chanted at you all over the house, he said.

So after two and a half years which he didn't enjoy much, the thing came to an end (jolly lucky for you, I thought); the manager of the local garage, who was going to Wimbledon to take on a bigger and better job there, took Sandra with him. A husky sort of man, Arnold said, with a big mustache, ex-R.A.F.

It was just another instance of what Percy M. called the human situation. Why the hell can't human beings manage their situations better and be happy together, I wondered.

"And since then I've never looked at another woman till you came to Westbet House," little Arnold said.

Oh, lord . . . I didn't want to play it that way.

Interest, pity, mild affection, I could feel all these for the little man. But you don't go to bed with a man because of mild affection. By this time he was trying to get his arms round me and to kiss me. All in the nicest, most tentative way possible. And who the hell wants tentative kisses, anyway?

"Look, Arnold," I said, "let's take it gently."

"It was too marvelous you saying you would come out with me like this."

"I've enjoyed it, I really have."

"I—I'm afraid I've begun to behave very badly."

I had got his hands under control now and was holding them in my own.

"Good or bad doesn't come into it. But it's no good getting tied up in things which aren't really going to work out for either of us. Is it?"

"I suppose not. And I'm afraid you're offended now."

I kissed him in the middle of his forehead just to show that I wasn't offended.

"Let's go and wash up the tea things," I said.

He wanted to motor me back to London but of course I wouldn't let him, so he took me to Cotterfield station and I traveled back to Baker Street huddled in a corner seat and a glow of virtue—the Girl who Refused an Affair.

Only you couldn't really call little Arnold Chess an affair; it could be, I thought, that his wife was right when she taunted him for not being any good to her. Or it could be that he just needed some encouragement and sympathy. Like most of us do in life about one thing or another.

Vicky was in at Tammerton Square, which was unexpected. At the weekend she usually went home to Blaydons, or if she stayed in town she was nearly always out.

"Oh, what a pity," she said when I walked in. "You ought to have been here an hour earlier."

"I was busy defending my virtue."

"Successfully?"

"It was never in much danger actually. What happened an hour ago?"

"John Mannington-Travers called."

"For me?"

"He seemed quite cross you weren't here. Just like Johnny."

I didn't know whether to throw myself into a corner and weep or to burst into full-throated song; in the end when the room finished contracting and expanding and the furniture came to roost again I managed to push out some ordinary-sounding words.

"Did he say he would ring or anything?"

"Not a thing. Trust Johnny. If he can't get what he wants at once he's away."

"Oh, well—"

"He'll probably give you a ring tomorrow."

"I doubt it. Most likely he found himself with nothing to do unexpectedly and called in here on the spur of the moment."

The only reason I said that was because I didn't want to believe it. Saying it myself, putting it out bluntly like that in so many words seemed to take some of the sting out of it somehow. Sort of witch-doctor stuff.

"He won't ring," I went on, smiling at Vicky in a womanly sort of way, and all the time my heart was crying, *Johnny, Johnny, oh Johnny, why couldn't you have come an hour later, why couldn't you?*

He didn't ring, of course. The witch-doctor stuff hadn't worked. Saying the evil thing hadn't averted it. The phone was in the hall in Tammerton Square and we had a working arrangement with Mrs. Nagelson in the ground-floor flat; if she went out in the evening we looked after Sibelius and she took telephone messages for us during the day. Mrs.

Nagelson, heavy costume-jewelry earrings and always made up as though she was about to go on as the Gypsy Queen in the local carnival. That woman must have smoked a hundred cigarettes a day. Vicky said she was a witch and went out to the local coven and that's why we had to look after Sibelius, "and we had better treat him properly or he'll report us and old Mrs. N. will put a spell on us."

"Nobody rang me up, I suppose, Mrs. Nagelson?" I asked airily every time I came in.

"Nobody, my dear."

"Good show," I would say brightly; but I didn't fool her. If I had the courage I'd have asked her if she brewed love potions.

At Westbet House poor little Arnold Chess was tied up with embarrassment. Anybody would have thought that he had torn all his clothes off in Heath End Cottage and run naked round the place screaming out four-letter words at me.

I did my best to let him see that I hadn't been upset and that everything was O.K. "Life's too short to worry, Arnold," I wanted to tell him, although in a way it was a hell of a sight too short not to worry. . . . "Nobody rang me up, I suppose?" "Nobody." The days went by and the telephone call didn't come.

Less than a week after the Heath End Cottage business Mr. Berry had me into his office.

Berry was a big potato in Westbet House and I respected him because he knew his job.

"Miss Barton, I understand that you are doing very well in the settlers' school. You like the work, don't you?"

"Yes, I do."

"You sound surprised."

I told him I was surprised. If anybody had told me at high school that I would take up a job where mathematics were everything I would have advised them to get their head examined.

He laughed. "You're not the first settler we've had here who had no idea he had a flair for it. How long have you been there now?"

"In the school? Ten months."

"I'm pulling you out this week and starting you in the 'N to the end' room under supervision. Frankly, it's sooner than I like, but Mr. Chess tells me how well you've got on and we are very short as you know."

"What about money, Mr. Berry?"

He thought for a moment and then said, "You can come on to the basic settler's money straight away. Fifteen. How's that?"

"Fair enough, Mr. Berry."

"It's Westbet House policy; if it's worth it, pay for it."

As the actress said to the bishop, I thought. Only I didn't say it aloud. Probably Mr. Berry was just as much interested at heart as any other man in the various things the actress told the bish. But he and I weren't on those terms. His next words astonished me.

"And Miss Barton—"

I turned back from the door.

"Arnold Chess—"

I tried to look totally surprised.

"He's a first-rate teacher in the settlers' school—"

"He's wonderful."

"But he's a bit of a babe outside. Let him down gently."

He nodded and I was on my way out.

Well, well, I thought, you never knew how much people notice in life.

On the way back to Tammerton Square I bought a bottle of wine to celebrate. After all, a girl doesn't get bumped up from ten to fifteen quid a week every week.

Vicky had been at the B.B.C. all day hanging about and rehearsing and wasting time over a five-line part she had in the third episode of a serial.

She was tired and her leg was hurting her so she was glad of the wine.

We two had it between us because Carolyn had been married to Paul in the summer and although we talked almost daily about getting somebody in to take her place we hadn't done anything about it. And now with an extra fiver a week coming in it wouldn't matter so much.

"That was good," she said, draining her first glass. "Just what I needed."

"Nobody seems to ring us up these days."

"Nobody. But you've got one boy friend, Liz."

"I have?"

I hoped, but I wouldn't let myself hope; I thought, but I refused to think, that she might be going to say something about Johnny.

"Father. He wants me to take you down to Blaydons again. What about the weekend?"

If I said yes and went would Johnny be in town, at a loose end, and come round to the flat on an off chance again? If he did and found me out a second time it would probably be the end of it. . . . "Liz Barton, Tammerton Square? She's no good. Never there." Cross her off the list and try somebody else. If I didn't go; stayed in town; moped in the flat waiting for the call, the ring at the door, that never came, would he be choosing that very weekend to visit his mother at, where was it, Embleton? Would he be hard up and be down at the Embleton cottage on a borrowing expedition? I could find out where this Embleton place was somehow and do a must-have-some-fresh-air-after-being-cooped-up-in-London-all-the-week act. Go for a long walk. Hearty as they come Liz, that's me. A lane leading to Embleton and I'm striding along it, suddenly out of a drive entrance steps Johnny. "Fancy seeing you here," etc., etc. Only of course it wouldn't happen. Forget it, Liz Barton.

Vicky's steady gray eyes were watching me.

"Would you like to come, Liz?"

"Love to."

Peter the Pole filled the Mini up with petrol.

"The young ladies are off again for the weekending?" he said.

"Never a dull moment."

"Some boy friends you make very happy, yes?"

"You bet."

"I like to be these boy friends very much."

"Peter, you're sweet."

"Strong, too. Polish men very strong. Very good for ladies."

"Goodbye, Peter."

When we got to Blaydons there was another guest already there. A thin man with a stoop and very deep lines on his face. But he had extraordinary eyes and he could see the joke; he had a sense of humor. "Monsignor Lucas," I was told he was. I wasn't entirely sure what a monsignor was; a sort of high-powered priest I imagined and for a moment wondered what they would think of me in Hansbeck Road, hobnobbing with monsignors!

It happened that he and I were alone in the drawing room for a few minutes before dinner that evening. He asked me if I would like a glass of sherry and poured one out for me.

I couldn't help noticing those eyes of his. I wanted to turn round all the time and look at the things they were seeing behind me.

He held his glass up to the light.

"Good stuff, sherry."

I agreed. I said I loved it.

"Any idea how it's made?"

Made? Sherry was wine—or was it? And wasn't wine made by people jumping up and down on grapes? A bit off-putting if you thought about it, but no worse than looking at a waiter's hand and imagining what happens to your food in restaurant kitchens.

But it seemed that I was way off beam. Things weren't as simple as that and there was a lot more to the making of sherry.

"The point is," Monsignor Lucas went on, "that you can enjoy it without understanding it. Like life."

"Well, that's a comfort."

"That's what I thought," he smiled. "When people see a priest they are apt to imagine that he has got some sort of specialized knowledge about what makes the world tick; that if they ask the questions he can supply all the answers."

That shook me a little because it was precisely what I had been thinking when I was looking at those deep brown go-right-through-you eyes of his. Here's somebody who knows the form, I thought.

"Can't he?" I asked. "Or aren't there any answers?"

"There isn't much wisdom. There is an immense amount of knowledge. If you go to the reading room of the British Museum you can command hundreds of thousands of books packed with knowledge about any conceivable subject. You couldn't possibly read them all—a tenth of them, if you gave up your life to it.

"But if you want the wisdom of the world, why, it's all contained in three or four books. Almost in three or four sentences."

"Must be handy to know them."

"Except that there's a difference between knowing and understanding. You know that the television picture comes on when you turn the switch, but do you understand how it does?"

"Do *you* understand? I don't mean about the telly, but the whole bag of tricks?"

"I've learned one bit of wisdom that there are a number of things in the world which are just not understandable, by us at any rate. An hour before the San Francisco earthquake thousands of butterflies suddenly appeared in the sunshine and copulated. Last year in France, Professor Rimel took a section of an ants' nest away from the parent part and kept it under glass. The ants thrived and did well but when he killed the queen ant in the main part of the nest at that very moment all the ants in the removed section twenty feet away showed signs of intense distress and died too. Do you understand these things?"

What I didn't understand was the sort of person he himself was.

"Don't you ever talk about sin and going to church and the jumble sale in the parish room next Thursday evening at eight?" I asked him.

Which made him laugh.

"Not to be happy is to waste life," he said, "and that is the real sin."

We all went to bed pretty early and Vicky and I sat talking up in her room.

"I told you Father had fallen for you," she teased. "Just look at the way you monopolized him during dinner."

Of course it wasn't true, but equally of course I didn't mind her saying it.

"The Aged Parent is frightfully simple in many ways; he regards you as the epitome of the modern young world; which is why you fascinate him."

"Is Monsignor Lucas a priest?"

"A priest? Yes, of course, he's a priest."

"Does that mean he'll—well, you know, never go with women?"

"Of course he won't. He's taken a vow of celibacy."

"He seems to understand such a lot."

"He's probably a saint."

I would have laughed at that if I hadn't caught sight of Vicky's face. But I still felt like laughing. Even I knew that a saint didn't offer you a glass of sherry and sit opposite you at dinner.

Or did he, I wondered.

"One thing you ought to know about him, he's dying of cancer."

"He's *what?*"

"He saw the specialists about a month ago and he has got it in one lung. They told him he can't possibly live for more than three months."

"Good God!"

"That's exactly what he said when he heard the news, but I'm not sure that he meant it in the same way."

That shook me, I must say; and I didn't feel like a spate of girlish chat afterwards. When I had said good night and was going out through the door Vicky called after me:

"Oh, by the way, good news too, Mother has asked two young men in for drinks tomorrow night. A boy called Tony van der Maast and John Mannington-Travers."

I was back in that room like a flash.

"Johnny is coming here?"

"Tomorrow night."

She looked at me in that half-serious, half-comical way of hers and then asked:

"Pleased?"

"I can think of things I would like less."

"Have a care, Liz."

"You sound like Mrs. Nagelson croaking a warning."

"Maybe you ought to have a word with Mother N. and hear what she says."

"I've had a word with Monsignor Lucas—"

"About Johnny?"

"About lots of things. Butterflies copulating, ants dying. And I've heard what he has to say."

"What was that?"

"He said not to be happy is to waste life and that is the real sin."

Vicky began to brush her hair. Short lovely hair (which

I always envied her); a heavy silver-backed brush with a monogram on it.

"And you think you can be happy with Johnny?" she asked.

"I can't be happy without him, Vick."

"You've only seen him once."

"It was enough."

She laughed gently and said:

"By our first strange and fatal interview."

"What's that? Where does that come from?"

"A line of poetry. Donne, I think."

I knew nothing about anybody called Donne. Jimmy Mancroft had put me on to Browning but he hadn't said anything about this Donne character. I could see that I should have to look him up.

Meanwhile I had got this bit tucked away all right. "By our first strange and fatal interview" rang a bell. It went alongside my others: "When I was a windy boy and a bit," and "Childe Roland to the Dark Tower came."

I said it over to myself in bed, the last thing before going to sleep.

By our first strange and fatal interview . . .

Lady Linwood had laid on a sherry party for next day, which was Sunday. Only a very few people. There was a woman who looked exactly like a camel I saw in one of Cliff Michelmore's programs on TV. Her husband had been in India for a long time; retired now; seventy if he was a day; but still with a pretty active libido I would guess from the way he hung about me. Maybe his libido didn't get much chance at home. He was a born mauler if ever I saw one; give him half a chance and his hands would be all over you. His wife didn't go much on me. There were the Three Weird Sisters. The Misses Somebody. I never got their name; one of them was called Angela and she seemed to be the local authority on gardening. Every remark her sisters made began with "Angela says." Angela said that if you didn't do something or other in the herbaceous border at once you'd be too late; Angela said that *jollica pollyanica* (that's what it sounded like) simply love lime; Angela said . . . I was fed up hearing what Angela said. As far as I was concerned Angela could go and get stuffed. Not that that looked very likely I was bound to admit. There were two young marrieds and there were the two young men.

Tony van der Maast, who very probably conformed to all the proper standards, clean behind the ears and wearing the right tie and making the right noises, I just wouldn't know. He was there and my eyes didn't see him; he spoke and my ears didn't hear.

Johnny was there. Dark, handsome and on this particular evening smiling Johnny. Not a scowl.

I thought perhaps he wouldn't notice me. I thought perhaps he didn't know anything about strange and fatal interviews.

"Weren't you at Harry Vespar's a week or two back?"

I nodded.

"Playing roulette?"

I nodded again.

"You cleared up quite a bit, didn't you?"

"I was lucky on the very last spin. How did you come out?"

"I won a bit on the last spin too."

"I noticed."

"You share with Vicky in Tammerton Square, don't you?"

I nodded again.

"I called there one Saturday but you were out."

"I'll try to be in next time, Johnny."

"You do. I prefer it."

"And what you prefer you always get, eh?"

"Usually."

"Highly convenient, I must say."

He took a long leisurely look at me. God Almighty, Johnny, I thought, don't look like that at me. You're giving me aches all over.

"Are you motoring back with Vicky this evening?"

"No. Vicky's staying down here for a week. She's running me to the station about half past eight or nine."

"I'll pick you up here at eight-thirty and take you up to town. O.K.?"

"Lovely; if it's not too much trouble for you."

"I wouldn't do it if it were."

He was only half an hour late, which really wasn't late at all for Johnny as I was to discover.

"Goodbye, Miss Barton," Lord Linwood said.

"Goodbye," said Monsignor Lucas who was dying fast of cancer and who didn't seem particularly disturbed about it. "God bless you."

"Drive carefully," Vicky told Johnny. "Can't have you smashing my Liz up."

Less than a quarter of a mile from the house we were doing over sixty and I was wondering at each bend whether we would make it or not.

"I hate people telling me to do things carefully," Johnny said. "You O.K.?"

"Drive how the hell you like," I shouted at him.

After a quarter of an hour he calmed down a little, and in any case we had run into some pretty thick traffic.

"Who were all those people at the drink party?" he asked.

I told him I didn't know any of them from a crow.

"Those three ghastly sisters! But it's always the same at Blaydons. If you go there you're in grave danger of meeting worthy people."

"Does that include me?"

"We shall have to find that out, shan't we?"

"Monsignor Lucas—"

"The pie-in-the-sky merchant?"

"He's got cancer; he'll be dead in three months."

"Tough," Johnny admitted. "But after all what's he got to grumble about? He can afford to die. You and I can't. We're too interested in living."

In Tammerton Square he stopped the Sunbeam Rapier outside the flat and said, "Here you are. Home and dry. What are they bleating about 'drive carefully' for? Didn't I drive you well?"

"You drove like an angel, Johnny."

"And you'll be in next time I call?"

"Why not give me a ring first?"

"I can never remember telephone numbers."

"Try Flaxman 72729. Say it over and over to yourself in bed, Johnny."

"I've other things to do in bed."

"72729."

"All right; don't keep on about it. Hop out."

When I was on the pavement he suddenly called, "Liz."

"Yes?"

"Seeing that you cleaned up so usefully at Harry's the other night, can you lend me a fiver?"

Thank God for increased money at Westbet House, I thought. I had a fiver and some loose silver in my bag.

"Thanks a lot, Liz," Johnny said, folding it away in his pocket. "I shall invest this in a highly profitable manner during the week and take you out to dinner some time on the result."

After the Sunbeam (CAT 333—three 3's were lucky, I hoped) had roared away I didn't go into the flat at once but walked slowly round T.S. The four big lights were shining onto the garden and the little cupid was holding up his lily out of which the thin stream of water played. It sparkled in the light of London's night. Fat, chubby little god of love. I felt an affection for him. If there were gods at all there should most certainly be one of love.

SEVEN

JOHNNY WAS SHOUTING angrily into the telephone. I was sitting curled up on the settee. A highly convenient piece of furniture that broad comfortable settee with its half dozen cushions. As Johnny used to say, grinning, "Every active bachelor gentleman should have one in his rooms."

"I waited fifteen minutes in The Yorker, *fifteen minutes* and you never showed up."

I couldn't hear what the girl at the other end was trying to say by way of excuse but Johnny was certainly lambasting her.

"I don't give a damn if you couldn't get away from the B.B.C. I'm not interested. Not-inter-es-ted. Get it? I won't be kept waiting by anybody . . . I should damn well think you were sorry. Don't let it happen again." The receiver went down bang.

"The great chief has spoken," I said, rolling onto my back and looking up at the ceiling. "Now clap your hands and have a slave or two beheaded."

He grinned. "I wish I could. I'd like that."

"What a bad-tempered bastard you are, J."

"They like it. You like it."

I took a good look at him.

"I put up with it. I'm not saying I like it."

He sat on the settee and ran his hands over me.

"It's worth putting up with, Liz, isn't it?"

"How conceited can a man get?"

"Stupid little bitch with her B.B.C. appointment. What the devil do I care about the B.B.C.?"

"All right. Relax. You've said all that once. Who was she, anyway?"

"One of Rupert's little bosomy pals."

"Don't tell me you don't like them bosomy any more, and anyway, keep off everybody else you lousy so-and-so."

"If you talk to me like that do you know what I shall do to you?"

"Haven't a clue," I lied.

He bent over me to show me.

This was just after six o'clock, nearly four months after Johnny had motored me back from the country to Tammerton Square.

A hell of a lot can happen in four months. One hell of a lot. I was still living with Vicky in Tammerton Square, but only just, as you might say.

Johnny had managed to remember the number that mattered. He must have said it over to himself once or twice. Possibly even in bed. 72729. He had phoned me the Monday evening after the weekend at Blaydons.

"Some excitable young gentleman for you," Mrs. Nagelson said, calling up the stairs. "He seems in rather a bad temper." She was never much good on the telephone.

"Is that you at last, Liz? Who was that moron bleating down the phone at me? Is she totally deaf as well as gaga? Hop into a cab and come over. I want to see you."

"I'm not quite sure—"

"For God's sake. Don't start stalling. I'm bored. I want to do something. Didn't you say ring up Flaxman 72729? Here I am ringing it and so far all I've got is a half-wit landlady and you stalling—"

"I'm coming, Johnny."

"I should bloody well think so."

"Hadn't you better tell me where to?"

"Don't you even know that? Lovell Street. Fourteen. The top flat."

I borrowed the taxi fare from Vicky and made my first

journey to Lovell Street. Johnny tried to borrow another fiver from me which I hadn't got to lend him so he had to take me out to a restaurant where he could sign the bill. Afterwards we went back to Lovell Street and after he had pointed out the advantages of the settee to me with a practical demonstration I didn't get home to Tammerton Square till nearly two.

Vicky woke when I went into the room. She was always a very light sleeper.

"O.K.?" she said sleepily.

"O.K.," I told her. Well, that was one way of putting it.

"Had a good time?"

"Oh, marvelous."

And that set the pattern of it. If anybody wanted to see a first-rate action picture of a girl taking a flying leap into the deep end and not giving a damn whether she swam or sank they only had to watch me. I lived to hear the phone ring; and if Johnny whispered down it or crooked his little finger I went running to him.

If he had said move in here and we'll set up establishment together, Tammerton Square, much as I liked it, wouldn't have seen me for dust.

But he never did that. His story was that the woman who owned 14 Lovell Street and let it out in flats (a Mrs. Wallington, the widow of a brigadier) wouldn't stand for it. Which may have been true. But Johnny was such a liar that you never knew which of his tales to believe. Although in the heart of me I knew what the truth was. And the truth is nearly always either humiliating or frightening. This particular truth was that Johnny hadn't got it as badly as I had. He didn't want me in the way I wanted him. We got on wonderfully together. Even when he was bloody-minded and we were quarreling we both knew we would sooner be doing that with one another than acquiesce with anybody else; and when we weren't quarreling, when we were locked in the act of love, it was marvelous. Johnny felt that. I know he did. To have me on hand, Flax. 72729, whenever he wanted me as lover or companion suited him fine. But he didn't want to be tied.

At half past six one evening the bell rang.

"See who it is," Johnny said. "I'm not in unless it's somebody very rich or very sexy."

Actually it was two men. One behind the other, echoing him as it were. The one in front tall and not bad looking.

The smell of riches didn't come out from him and as far as I was concerned he certainly wasn't sexy. But then I was prejudiced about things like that.

He was tremendously polite and he wanted to know if Mr. J. I. Mannington-Travers (*a*) lived there and (*b*) was in.

In spite of Johnny's fiat I thought this needed a bit of looking into so in my best watchdog-for-the-boss-and-keeper-of-the-outer-office manner, I said:

"Who is it who wishes to speak to him, please?"

The man said his name was Gledhill, which didn't mean a thing to me. "Detective Sergeant Gledhill," he added, "of the Special Branch."

He pulled an identification card out of his pocket just to prove it. Well, I thought, what do you know? Why pay eight and sixpence for a seat at the pictures when it can all happen on your doorstep?

I didn't quite know what to do, and while I was trying to work it out Detective Sergeant Gledhill slid into the hall and his shadow after him. It seemed to me that as he was in the house he might as well come upstairs. Which, come to think of it, is probably all part of the technique.

Upstairs I told Johnny who his visitor was and it was clear that he hadn't a clue what it was all about. He was the sort of pig-headed bastard who always reacted stupidly to the Law. Show him any kind of uniform and Johnny wanted to know at once who the hell they thought they were ordering about.

So the moment he heard the words "Detective Sergeant" he went in off the deep end.

"CAT 333," he said. "A Sunbeam Rapier. All right, I've parked it somewhere where I shouldn't have parked it according to your bloody gestapo outfit. Well, where *am* I going to park it? Tell me that. Or is it a legal offense to own a car at all? And if it is why does the flaming Government take twelve pounds ten a year off us for doing it? To pay your wages, I suppose."

How to make friends with the Law, I thought, listening to this typical bit of Johnnyese. But the Law didn't seem to mind. The Law actually smiled slightly and said he was afraid there was some misunderstanding but it wasn't anything to do with a motor car; he was hoping Johnny would be good enough to help him with the answers to a few questions and might he sit down.

"For God's sake sit, lie, climb up the lamp. Do what you like."

The Law looked politely toward me.

"Don't mind about her," Johnny reassured him. "Miss Barton, my mistress. Doesn't live here but whirls in whenever the mood takes her. Which I am glad to say it frequently does. They get like that. Are you married, Sergeant?"

Sergeant Gledhill said no, he wasn't married yet. He looked slightly embarrassed which was the effect that Johnny's bad manners had on lots of people.

"You're missing something. But no doubt you get all you want on the side. What was it you wanted to see me about?"

"I believe you are acquainted with a Mr. Rupert Cahill, sir." (This was the same Rupert who specialized in the bosomy little pals.)

"Rupert Cahill? Certainly I am. Is that an indictable offense or something?"

"That's the Mr. Cahill who is the managing director of Raymond Development Properties, sir. Correct?"

"And half a dozen other swindles too."

"Is R.D.P. a swindle, sir?"

"Not more than anything else I should think. Or is that just what you're trying to find out? Has old Rupert embezzled the cash?"

"I take it you put some money into R.D.P., sir?"

"A bit. When I was flush. And that doesn't happen very often, I can tell you."

"Are you actually a partner in the company, sir?"

"A partner? I suppose I am. I'm not sure. I left all the legal side of it to Rupert."

"A shareholder anyway?"

"Yes. I told you I put some money into it, so I must be a shareholder, mustn't I?"

"Did you put much money into it, sir?"

"What is this? A bloody third degree or something? I know I'm behind with my income tax. So are fifty thousand other poor bastards who are being harassed to death by the blue-arsed baboons from Whitehall. So would you be most likely if they didn't knock it off you in P.A.Y.E. before you get the chance of spending it."

"I'm not concerned with income tax, Mr. Mannington-Travers. I'm trying to find out something about Raymond Development Properties Limited. No doubt they've got offices somewhere?"

"Offices? I haven't the vaguest idea. Mr. Cahill looks after the office part. All I did was to put some money into it."

"What about staff?"

"Look, Sherlock Holmes, I know nothing about R.D.P. except that Rupert Cahill said, Put some money in and you'll soon be pulling a heck of a lot out."

"Have you in fact pulled anything out, sir?"

"I have in fact pulled something out, sir. Bits and pieces.

Nothing to get excited about. Is it an offense now to draw a dividend?"

"I wonder if you know where Mr. Cahill is, sir? Is he in this country at the moment?"

"Probably not, if he has embezzled the funds. Most likely he has flipped over to Brussels."

"Brussels? He's in the habit of going to Brussels, is he?"

"Brussels, Paris, Amsterdam. Mr. Cahill, Sergeant, is an adult male with healthy instincts. He wants his greens regularly and he's in the habit of going anywhere where the greens are good. And the best of luck to him."

"But you can't tell me where he is at the present moment?"

"And I certainly wouldn't, if I could."

"Well, thank you, sir, very much," the Law said, adding that that seemed to be about all and he was sorry to have troubled us and he wished us a very good evening.

"What the hell do you suppose all that was in aid of?" Johnny asked when we were alone again.

He picked up the telephone and dialed Rupert Cahill's number and didn't get any reply. When I told him that this was hardly surprising he got angry.

"What's in the wind, Johnny?" I asked. "Are you in some sort of swindle with Rupert Cahill?"

"Don't you start, for God's sake."

"I suppose I'm entitled to know something about it"— which was a silly thing to say. With Johnny you weren't entitled to anything, you just got what he liked to dish out. Which he now proved to me by catching my arm and doubling it up behind my back.

I didn't want to call out, but I had to. He twisted harder.

"Johnny . . . *Johnny!* . . ."

"Say, I'm a silly interfering little bitch."

"Johnny . . . for God's sake."

"Go on, say it."

"You'll break my arm."

"Say it."

"I'm a silly interfering little bitch."

"Good. And again. Slowly this time."

"I am a silly interfering little bitch."

He let go of my arm and smiled. He was quite good tempered now and thoroughly pleased with himself.

I took a swing at him but he saw it coming and caught my wrist.

"Temper!"

I tried with my other hand and he caught that too.

"I could kick you somewhere where it would hurt you very much indeed," I told him.

"That would be a very short-sighted policy on your part," he pointed out.

Which made me laugh. I was furious and my arm was still hurting, but I laughed. With Johnny it was always like that.

"Fix the drinks, Liz."

You had to be careful with Johnny's whisky. Never soda; water and just the right amount of water and of course no ice.

"Good girl. Just how I like it. What do you keep looking at the clock for? Don't start any nonsense about having to fly off somewhere. I owe you money, Liz, and I am about to take you out to a really good dinner—"

"Johnny—"

"If you say you can't come I'll never ask you again."

"I—"

"You've got something fixed up?"

"Yes. As a matter of fact I have. More or less."

"Well, unfix it. Go ahead. There's the telephone. He's on the telephone, I presume."

"More or less" was a lie because it was quite definite. Vicky had said, "The thing starts at eight-fifteen, so we'll all meet in the Vaudeville just after eight." It was to be a

party of six and after the show we were all going on somewhere for supper.

I dialed Flaxman 72729 wondering just how much of a
heel it was possible to be.

"Vicky, I—I can't make it."

"Oh—"

"It won't matter, will it? I mean there'll be five of you
anyway—"

"Everything's fixed."

"I can't come, Vicky."

"Where are you speaking from?"

"Lovell Street. Vicky—"

"Skip it, skip it. Look after yourself."

"Vicky—"

But she had rung off.

Johnny was smiling at me. "You'll have to be mighty
nice to me to make up for the things you make me do," I
told him.

"Not to worry."

"Have you ever been to the Casse Croûte?" Johnny asked
me when we were ready to go out. Yes, I told him. I had;
but I didn't mind going there again. I had better not mind,
he said, restored to explosive good humor, because that's
where we were going.

So the Casse Croûte it was. It seemed a very long time
since the first evening I had been there with that little so-
and-so Sonia; and Tubby (the Leicestershire Bartons); and
Jimmy Mancroft.

"I suppose your previous boy friend used to bring you
here," Johnny said.

"Sometimes."

"What was he like?"

I took time to think that one out. Then I came up with,
"As a matter of fact he wasn't unlike you in some ways."

Johnny was interested. Talk about himself always interested him.

"Such as?"

"He was capable of being rude and appallingly bad tempered."

Johnny stared at me. I think he was genuinely hurt. The evening was now going along splendidly for him. He felt O.K. with the world; why the hell couldn't the world feel O.K. with him?

"You don't really think I'm bad tempered, do you?"

I laughed.

"It's just that there are such a lot of bloody fools about."

I held out my glass. "Fill it up, Johnny. I like Nuits St. George. I liked it the first time I came here."

I spent the night in Lovell Street. I kept some makeup things permanently there now, a sort of second toilet table and that was all I needed. As Johnny used to say, a night-dress was only a waste of time anyway.

At ten o'clock next morning I was getting some coffee and Johnny came out naked from the bathroom.

"Don't you work on Saturdays?" he asked.

"Only every other one." It amused me that he had never yet bothered to find out exactly where I did work. I suppose he wasn't much interested in my working life. I did some sort of secretarial job, and that was that as far as he was concerned.

He took a good look at me and seemed satisfied.

"You'll do," he said, "just as you are."

Which was more than could be said for him, as I pointed out.

"Depends what you are thinking of."

"Not at ten o'clock in the morning."

"I'm talking about racing. Towcester. Ever been to a race-meeting?"

I laughed. It was a funny thing, but I never had been to a race-meeting. Towcester. Of course there was a meeting at Towcester. I could have reeled off the day's fixtures without any trouble: Newmarket, Stockton on the flat; Chepstow, Kelso, Towcester and Woore under Rules. I knew a lot about racing now, but I had never been to a meeting.

"What's so funny?" Johnny asked.

"You. Why don't you get some clothes on?"

"We'll leave about eleven and pick up some lunch somewhere on the way."

"O.K., Johnny. Lovely."

We left not later than eleven thirty-five, because, as I was to find out, when Johnny went racing it was a serious matter. Racing meant betting. And betting meant the possibility of making money. And what could be more serious than that?

"Somewhere on the way" turned out to be a pub called The True Lovers' Knot at Sandyridge.

There were three local characters in the bar who looked mildly surprised but who didn't object when Johnny did a squire-bountiful act and insisted on everybody in the place having a drink with him.

For once in a way he seemed to have plenty of money. Which was just as well, I thought, if he was going to throw it about.

I wasn't so sure what was the best drink to go racing on but I settled for brandy and ginger ale which seemed to be working out all right.

As we were driving into the car park at Towcester, Johnny said:

"We are sure to run into some of the lads and lassies on the town so try not to sound a complete boob about racing even if you never have been to a meeting before."

"I'll try, Johnny."

He bought two badges for the enclosure and handed me one. "How much money do I owe you, Liz?"

He owed me seven pounds twelve and six to be precise.

"I don't know," I told him, "I've never totted it up."

"I should bloody well think not. I hate totter-uppers. Here, how's this for settling up?"

He pushed a five-pound note at me and I took it.

"Suits me, Johnny."

"You don't know how lucky you are to get it. Let's get cracking on the first race."

I knew from conversation on the way that Johnny's great hope of the day was a horse called Halfpenny Green, running in the 3:45, but of course he intended to have a bet in all the other races as well.

There were twelve runners in the first race and naturally I hadn't a clue about what was going to win. Back in the "N to end room" at Westbet House you didn't care what won. Hot favorite or rank outsider, it was all the same as far as the settler was concerned. Whatever odds the winner came in at you worked out the slips accordingly and that was that.

I thought of the rooms now. The telephone girls busy taking calls. The clock boys time-stamping the slips. Toni, the board boy, making sure he had got the runners written up right. Jack Stranson sitting doing nothing, waiting for his share of settlement slips after the result was out.

"Any hunches for the first race, Liz?"

I looked down the list on the card.

"Not that you need bother," Johnny went on. "Pigsticker will walk this. Only he won't be any price."

The only name that suggested anything to me in the list was Badminton Club. And that suggested Hansbeck Road and Nancy and the row with Father about Mr. Armstrong and the beginning of everything as far as I was concerned.

"Badminton Club," I said.

Johnny laughed. "You can get twenty-eight to one on it from the bookies and anything you like on the tote. If Badminton Club wins, I'll walk home."

"It's just a hunch. You asked me if I had any."

"You're obviously not as good at racing as you are at a few other things, my pet."

Badminton Club won fairly easily with Blue Flame second and poor Pigsticker only third.

I wasn't certain what Johnny had lost on Pigsticker, but it was at least five pounds and he was gloomy about such a bad start.

"Pity you didn't back your hunch," he said.

"But I did. On the tote. The first bet I have ever made in my life."

"How much did you put on?"

"Ten shillings each way."

"My God, you'll pick up a fortune." He was furious.

I didn't pick up a fortune exactly, but I didn't call thirteen pounds fifteen and sixpence bad all the same.

Johnny was explaining all this to the party we had by this time attached ourselves to. It took me some time to sort them out. Except the girl.

Tessa Franklyn. The daughter, as I learned during the course of the afternoon, of Admiral Franklyn, whoever he might be; but I suppose if you are the daughter of an admiral it counts for something, even in these days. And if you've got tweeds like Tessa had and could wear them like she did it certainly counted for a hell of a lot.

I liked Tessa even though I could see from the word go that she had Johnny-itis almost as badly as I had.

In spite of her good tweeds and her smart talk she wasn't much more than a kid. You could almost hear the clash of Roedean hocky sticks behind her. She was vulnerable.

She seemed to be swimming about with a tall character called Charles who was dressed as Johnny was in a bowler and a light brown overcoat with race glasses slung over one shoulder; and they had another young couple with them.

Johnny told them all about my win on Badminton Club.

"Not that she knows a damn thing about racing," he explained. "Just virgin luck. And come to think of it that's stretching the term a bit."

Charles made a face at me . . . *our Johnny, we all know what he is, not to worry* . . . The girls laughed.

Charles had backed Pigsticker before coming to the meeting.

"Not that there'll be much," he said. "I only put a quid on each way and what that will be for a place at eleven to eight, God only knows."

"You'll win six and tenpence for the place, so you'll be thirteen and twopence to the good."

Everybody stared at me.

"If you're right," Charles said, "I shall regard you as a mathematical genius. Which will upset one of my most cherished illusions. I didn't know a pretty girl could ever be any good at math."

The admiral's daughter would have liked to hang around Johnny but the rest of the party whisked her away.

"See you after the next race, Johnny?" she said.

"I expect. I'll be knocking about."

When they were gone Johnny said:

"Six and tenpence. I wonder if that's actually right?"

"Of course it's right. The 11 to 8 odds are easy. One pound makes one seven six for a win, six and tenpence for a place."

He was staring at me incredulously.

"And suppose I had had a fiver on it?"

"To win?"

"Each way."

"Six seventeen six for your win; one fourteen four for your place."

"Good God, you must be a senior wrangler or something. How on earth do you do it?"

I gave a hoot of laughter. "It's just that I'm doing it all day."

"I thought you had some sort of secretarial job."

"You never even asked what I do."

"I knew you were in an office. I imagined you did office work. Whatever that is."

"I am in an office. Edward West's."

"The bookmaker?"

"Westbet House."

"But you said the bet you just made was the first you have ever had."

"So it was. And I won. Virgin luck like you said, Johnny. And do you have to go telling everybody in words of one syllable that we are sleeping together?"

"But what do you do in Westbet House?"

"Settle. I'm a settler. I work out a bet. It goes down on a slip and after the race the settlers go through the slips and work them out. Well, you don't actually work them out. You just do it automatically, like multiplication tables."

"And what do you imagine is going to win the next race?"

I hadn't a clue what was going to win the next race. Which Johnny found it difficult to believe. He couldn't get rid of the idea that a girl who worked in Edward West's office and who could rattle off winnings and place money for various odds must have some sort of information about the horses.

And of course being an average sort of stupid sucker, I couldn't get rid of the idea that having got one hunch right meant others coming up as well.

I looked through the list of runners and said I thought Dark Tower would win.

Johnny put his glasses on to a bookmaker's board to see what odds were being offered.

"They've made it second favorite at the moment. Six to one. Did you hear anything about it at Edward West's?"

"Not a thing. You don't care what wins there. They are just names and prices; and that's all you bother about."

"What makes you pick it out then?"

"Childe Roland to the Dark Tower came."

"What the hell does that mean?"

"I don't know. It probably doesn't mean anything. It suggests something. It starts you thinking."

"Where did you get all that from?"

"A man."

"What else did he teach you, Liz?"

"Nothing compared to what I've learned from you, Johnny. Oh, nothing, nothing."

"Sure?"

"Absolutely sure."

I slipped my arm into his, which was a mistake. He always hated anything like that in public.

"For God's sake," he grumbled, "let's go and put something on this hot tip of yours."

I didn't want him to. Who the hell said it was a hot tip anyway? "Childe Roland to the Dark Tower came." "When I was a windy boy and a bit." "By our first strange and fatal interview." My three bits of poetry. Maybe at the end of your life, I thought, you'll be able to sum it all up by turning out half a dozen separate lines like that.

I didn't want Johnny to back Dark Tower. It would lose and then he'd be furious. With me, of course.

We ran into Charles and Tessa Franklyn on the way to Johnny's bookmaker and they joined us.

"Six and tenpence," Charles said. "I've been on the phone to my bookie to find out. You were absolutely right. Marvelous."

"She's Edward West's private secretary. Not so marvelous after all."

Tessa's eyes were fixed on me. She didn't mind whose private secretary I was; so long as I wasn't Johnny's mistress.

"And she knows what's going to win this race! Dark Tower," Johnny said, pulling out his wallet and saying to the bookie, "A fiver each way Dark Tower."

I didn't want him to lose ten pounds on the horse I had said would win and then to be furious with me about it.

"Not five pounds each way," I said. "For heaven's sake. It's only a sort of hunch."

I ought to have known better. Check Johnny about what

money he was spending at any time, but especially in front of anybody else, and he took it as a personal insult.

From the way he looked at me I knew I was going to hear about it after.

"Make it ten each way," he said to the bookie.

"Ten win, ten place, at sixes."

The other two backed it as well.

"And for God's sake don't start lecturing me on what size bets I'm to make."

"Sorry, Johnny."

"I should bloody well think so."

Tessa Franklyn watched us, fascinated.

I prayed harder than I had ever done before in my life that Providence, or whatever it is who organizes the show, would let Dark Tower win.

It was obviously being well backed because the price shortened and just before the "off" I noticed that it was being offered at nine to two. So we hadn't done badly to get sixes on it. Provided that it performed the necessary formality of winning.

It looked like winning, too, for two thirds of the race, then it just faded away and tailed off right to the end.

Providence either didn't like my brand of prayer or wasn't interested in horse racing.

"My God, what a hunch."

"I told you not to, Joh—"

"Don't tell me. Either what to do or what not to do. I don't like being told. It doesn't amuse me."

Which pretty well set the note for the rest of the afternoon.

Johnny lost on every race and the more he lost the more he gambled. Even Halfpenny Green was beaten by a short head in the three forty-five.

It looked a certain winner until ten yards from the post and I saw Johnny's face when this other thing came up from nowhere and flashed by to win.

I saw his face, but I wasn't risking the explosion there'd be if I tried to give him any more advice about betting.

"Men are unwise and curiously planned"; I thought the chap who wrote *Hassan* had certainly got something there.

Of course I got hell in front of everybody. Part of the technique. If you're feeling fed up with everything in general take a good kick at the dog. Especially if you know the dog is fool enough not to bite. Not even growl much. I could tell from the way Charles looked at me that he would have said something if he hadn't thought (quite rightly) that it would only make matters worse. And the admiral's daughter was fascinated. Probably she was wondering how she would make out in the role and envying me. That's the way a woman's mind works. When she's in love. Which I was, God help me.

I didn't enjoy the afternoon much.

When we got back to town I said:

"Take me to Tammerton Square." I didn't know whether Vicky would be in or what arrangements, if any, had been made for an evening meal. And I didn't care.

But Johnny had done one of his lightning change acts. The bad temper had blown out of him and he was suddenly gay.

"Nonsense. You won thirteen quid on that first hunch of yours. You can afford to take me out to dinner—"

"Of course—"

"And then we'll go back to Lovell Street afterwards and you can stay the night—unless you have any marked objection to doing that, Liz?"

"Not very marked, actually. No, I haven't."

Before we went into the Gay Fusilier he said:

"You had better hand me the money, Liz. You don't imagine I want a girl to pay for me in public, do you?"

I handed him two five-pound notes. If there had been fifty of them in my bag I would have given them to him.

In the instant he was lively and amusing. When Johnny

172

wanted he could be the best company in the world. The best.

"You mysterious creature," he said. "Not telling me anything about your job in Edward West's."

"I didn't mean to be mysterious, Johnny."

"I like mysterious women."

"I'll be a maze of mystery."

"Can people come and see over Westbet House? See how the thing is worked?"

"Yes. There's a P.R.O., he brings people over occasionally."

"I'll fix something up with him. I'd like to see how the punter's money gets swallowed up."

I felt like telling him that if he didn't punt it wouldn't get swallowed up. But I had the sense not to.

He paid the bill and added a lordly tip and put the change in his pocket. Goodbye to my ten pounds. Not that I minded. I didn't mind anything as long as Johnny was nice to me.

A long time later the only light in the room was the glow from the cigarette he had just lit. He was lying on his back looking up into the dark.

"Shift your head a bit, you're giving my arm cramp," he said.

I moved so that my head was on his bare chest.

"What was that bit you said about the dark tower?"

"Childe Roland to the Dark Tower came."

"What made you think of that this afternoon?"

"It just blew into my head."

"And what are you thinking about at this precise moment—now?"

"Nothing. Happiness."

"*Are* you happy, Liz?"

"Now? Yes."

"I'm not sure that I am entirely. I lost over fifty pounds today."

I wanted to say, "Johnny, Johnny, forget it." I wanted to tell him not to think of money all the time. I felt suddenly that I ought to say to him, "Don't come to Westbet House, Johnny."

But I didn't do any of those things. I turned my head and bit him very gently close to his breast.

"Little devil," he said quietly; but I didn't know whether he was really thinking of me or not.

EIGHT

Vicky was too bighearted to be really angry with me, as she should have been, over the theater business. We didn't often discuss Johnny, but she knew exactly what was happening to me. I expect a woman can always tell when another is sunk, head over heels, lost without trace.

"Take care of yourself, Liz," she said once. "Mind you don't get hurt."

I was happy that day. I had been with Johnny the night before and he had been in one of his best moods. I was riding high, wide and handsome. Why the hell should I get hurt?

She laughed with me; but she didn't believe it quite.

"Johnny's a dangerous sort of man," she said.

"Maybe that's why I like him."

"You're too loyal, Liz; and loyal people get hurt."

"Loyalty's the only thing worthwhile in life"; but by loyalty I meant love and by love I meant Johnny.

By this time I was getting on well in Westbet House. There was only one slight snag about working in the "N to end" room, and that was that Arnold Chess had been put in there permanently as a supervisor. He didn't make any passes at me, or anything like that; but all the same I couldn't help being aware that he was there, behind me. I suppose the little man must have gone over that teatime in Heath End Cottage a dozen times and called himself all the names under the sun because he hadn't been more forceful. No woman minds a man having lascivious thoughts about her; but I didn't want little Arnold's to bubble up to the point of becoming a nuisance again.

So I just bent over my slips—I was working in T—and stuck to it—Kingsway won the third race at Bath at the nice price of 100–8 and Mrs. Tomlinson (TQ 9222) had seventeen and six each way on it.

Don't ask me why seventeen and six. By this time I was completely used to the oddities of people who bet and of the bets they made. I don't give a thought to seventeen and six. I mark £10. 18. 9 for the win, £2. 14. 8 for the place and initial the slip.

Arnold Chess reaches over my shoulder and picks the slip up.

"TQ 9222 is on the Q.L.," he says. "That's the ninth successive winning bet she's had in three weeks."

That's his concern as supervisor. Not mine. In the settlers' school we had been given a talk about the various rackets that people have tried to get money out of bookmakers. Lots of them were stupidly obvious and never stood a chance from the start; but some were fantastically clever. Where they all came unstuck (we were told) was in being too greedy.

If a punter thought up a dodge by which he could rig the result he always overplayed his hand. He didn't have the sense to lose occasionally; he must go on winning all the time. With the result that one of the standing rules among the security boys in Westbet House was that any punter who began to have an uncanny sequence of winning bets came under suspicion. He went on the Q.L. The query list.

The argument was that in the nature of things nobody won so often and so consistently as that; hence there must be a catch in it somewhere; and it was up to the security people to find out the catch before it did too much harm.

After his discovery of where I worked and his talk about being interested in seeing over a bookmaker's office Johnny hadn't mentioned the subject again, so I got the surprise of my life when one afternoon the door of the small bets room opened and he came in with Captain Fender, our P.R.O.

The second race from Ripon was just coming through on the phone and being tapped out by Toni on the board. Swan Song was going to win it and from the way the bets had been coming in I guessed it would be a hot favorite.

Johnny was wearing a new suit and looked, as he always did, very smart. For a man who never had anything in his bank except an overdraft he always managed to look astonishingly prosperous.

I had been with him two evenings but not a word had his lordship said about coming to Westbet House. However I was due to go round to Lovell Street when I left work that afternoon so I reckoned I would hear what it was all about.

When I caught his eye there wasn't a flicker of recognition in it. Why he wanted to play it that way I couldn't guess; but if you went against Johnny in one of his whims you only risked an almighty flare-up. So I looked down again and began to get my slips in a tidy pile waiting for the result and the prices to come through . . .

"*Swan Song. Evens.*"

You didn't have to be a particularly good settler to work that one out. Which was just as well because the P.R.O. and Johnny were standing directly behind me now and while listening intently to what Fender was saying about the way the clock boys time-stamped the slips Johnny managed to get a piece of my back between his fingers and thumb and to give me a most almighty pinch. Just for the hell of it. I only just managed not to call out. I rather enjoyed it, really, of course. *You wait, you sadistic so-and-so, till I get hold of you tonight,* I thought.

". . . each slip is time-stamped as it comes from the telephonist who takes the bet and then it goes straight to the settler . . ."

"Jolly interesting."

"And the settlers work alphabetically. B is the biggest

letter. More names start with B than with anything else. M's and S's are big too. And there are always plenty of W's."

"You've never tried any of these computers?"

"You can't beat a good settler. You'd be astonished at how quickly they can work."

"I'm sure I should."

"You'd be astonished at how quickly I can work," I told Johnny when I got into his flat that evening.

He grinned.

"I've got a bruise the size of a half crown where you pinched me."

"Don't worry. I'll make it better."

"You might have warned me you were coming."

"It was just a sudden idea."

"Why the great incognito act? Aren't I supposed to know you in public now?"

"I didn't want to embarrass you in any way."

"John Ivor Mannington-Travers, you can say that after some of the things you've done to me!"

"Who was that small thin character snooping about at the back of the room all the time?"

"The supervisor. Arnold Chess."

"What's his job?"

"A supervisor supervises. But he's quite harmless."

"He looks it."

"He made a pass at me once—well, almost."

"Have a heart, Liz, you'd kill him."

"He's not a bad little man."

"As I understand it the girl who takes the bet over the telephone hands the slip to the clock boy who shoves it in one of these time-stamping machines straightaway? Truth?"

"That's it. Mr. West wanted me to be a telephonist but I jibbed at it."

"You know Edward West personally?"

"I know him—yes."

"How well *do* you know him, Liz?"

"I should think he has completely forgotten my existence by now."

The telephone rang and Johnny reached across me.

"I'll take it. You're not my bloody secretary, you know."

I knew who it was without knowing. Which is a definition of intuition, I suppose.

Johnny said: Of course not; don't be silly; why should she think that; come off it, pet; that's better; *of course* he hadn't forgotten; seven thirty; in the little entrance place; *et toi aussi* . . .

French now, I thought.

"Why don't you dance a hornpipe for the bloody admiral's daughter?" I asked him when he put the phone down.

The front-door bell rang and Johnny said, "Go and see who it is."

I reminded him that I wasn't his secretary and only just managed to dodge the book he threw at me.

By this time in my relations with Johnny I had seen Rupert Cahill a couple of times so of course I recognized him. Not my ideal type of manhood.

Just under forty-five. Getting a paunch. Going bald, with side bits of hair that stuck out over his ears. Podgy fingers and thick lips. A voice that had Eton, Oxford, Guards Club, Stock Exchange and the rest of the racket stamped all over it. Probably a homo, though I wouldn't know about that.

"Is Johnny in?"

He seemed agitated.

Johnny wasn't expecting him, I was pretty certain of that; but he was in a good mood in spite of my remark about dancing a hornpipe so he reached out for the bottle of Vat 69 and said:

"Hallo, Rupert, what news on the Rialto?"

"Water and very little of it," Rupert said.

Johnny poured the drinks and if Rupert's hand wasn't actually trembling it was close to it.

"Has all that nonsense blown over?" Johnny asked. "Everything O.K. again now?"

"I'm on my way to London Airport."

"Lucky you."

"I'm flying to Paris."

"It's lovely in Paris—but then, of course, as the girl said, it's lovely anywhere."

"I'm not coming back, Johnny."

Johnny took a long swig at his drink—so did Rupert.

"How do you mean, you aren't coming back?"

"Things have become too complicated here."

"Complicated?"

"Tax-wise. Inland Revenue-wise."

"Scotland Yard Special Branch-wise?"

"Well, if you put it like that—"

"What's gone wrong, Rupert? What's the form?"

"Everything has gone wrong, Johnny. Every conceivable bloody thing. Christ, what hasn't gone wrong. R.D.P. has had a jinx on it from the word go. And it never should have had. Half a dozen times it's been on the verge, but on the verge, I tell you, of getting right away. Into really big money. And every time—just not. Something has slipped up just at the last moment. Is that clock of yours right?"

"Within a minute or two. Is this what that Sergeant Gledhill type came poking his nose in about?"

"I suppose so."

"You told me there wasn't anything to worry about—"

"There wasn't. Not if the merger came off. If the merger with Wilson and Anstruther had come off, God, you and I would be rolling in it, rolling in it."

"Was that the Wilson who shot himself?"

"And there you have it. What the hell can you do when

a man shoots himself? It upsets people. They think there's something fishy. They start ferreting about. If that silly bastard hadn't blown his brains out—on the golf course, too, what a place to choose—R.D.P. would be right away in the clear!"

"And as it is?" Johnny asked slowly.

"As it is, Johnny, I'm off to Paris, supposing no interfering son of a Special Branch bitch stops me at London Airport, and I'm not coming back. Not for a hell of a long time, anyway. Not healthy enough."

"What about me?"

"They can't touch you, Johnny. They can't pin one solitary thing on to you. I fixed that. Christ, you don't think I'd run away and leave you in the muck, do you?"

From the expression on Johnny's face I guessed that this was precisely what he had been thinking.

"What about the money?" he asked.

"The money—ah, well." Rupert spread his hands. "That's another question, isn't it? R.D.P. has been in the red for two years. There isn't any."

"What about all the money I put into the show?"

Rupert spread his hands again.

"But, Christ Almighty, I can't lose all that."

"You show me a way to save any of it, old boy."

"But *two thousand quid.*"

"Look, Johnny, you put in two thousand and did sweet Fanny Adams. I put in a sight more than that and I've worked like a black. We both thought we were backing a winner. And we both made a mistake. Can I help it if things turned out like that?"

"But—"

Rupert got up, one eye still on the clock.

"If it's just a matter of bankruptcy," Johnny asked, "why are the Special Branch people interested?"

"When the ship is sinking any sensible mariner is apt to

pull bits off the furniture to try to stop up the holes. If the narks come here asking questions don't let on you know where I've gone to, Johnny."

"Am I likely to?"

"Christ knows. I've reached the stage when I don't know what anyone is likely to do. I've had my bellyful of this country."

When he had gone all Johnny said was, "And that's how two thousand quid takes a jump out of the window."

If I'd been wearing one, I would have taken my hat off to him for the way he took it.

Obviously he was shaken. Well, who wouldn't be? "For one thing I borrowed half that two thousand and that's got to be found now," as he told me when we were discussing it.

"Did you know there was some sort of swindle going on in R.D.P.?" I asked.

"Swindle? What a perfectly bloody bourgeois mind you've got. I'll bet you were brought up singing hymns and going to chapel and tying reef knots in the Brownies," (which wasn't a bad guess, seeing that I had never said a word to him about Hansbeck Road). "Mergers, amalgamations, take-overs, they are all swindles if it comes to that. Somebody does well, somebody does badly. The chap who does badly thinks it's a swindle. The chap who does well puts on his white tie and stands up after dinner and talks about the glorious tradition of the great city of London.

"Anyway, I left it to Rupert. He said R.D.P. would make a fortune for anyone who could put in a couple of thou. quickly. I backed a loser, that's all. What I've got to do now is to back some winners quickly. And meanwhile strict economy."

Which was why an hour later we were sitting on two tall stools at the Capri bar in The Golden Horseshoe.

Opposite us were about three hundred miniature liqueur bottles hanging from string on the wall. Quite a collection.

And Antonio, who looked as though he had at least three brothers in the Mafia.

The place wasn't as full as normal. There was a smarty-tarty party being noisy at one end, and an old gentleman with a fancy waistcoat and a white mustache getting quietly sozzled in a corner.

He kept eyeing me, the two slinky girls in the noisy brigade and a picture of a nude sitting astride a champagne bottle. He looked like an Edwardian regretting the fact that it wasn't any use to him any more.

"Two more," said Johnny. *"Due ancòra."* For a man who had just kissed goodbye to a couple of thousand, half of which wasn't his, anyway, he was astonishingly cheerful. I couldn't make it out.

The ex-Mafia type grinned. He enjoyed mixing champagne cocktails, apparently. And I must say he did it well. And I was in a position to know, I had had two already.

"I shall have a frightful head tomorrow morning, Johnny."

"You won't wake up till late. You'll be too tired."

"Is that a promise?"

"You like-a also something to eat? Is good to eat, eh?"

"Si, si, mangiare."

"The *signor* spika the Italian very good. *Eccellentissimo.*"

"What have you got, Antonio?"

Antonio surveyed his kingdom.

"We have-a the smoked salmon. Is very good-a the smoked salmon. Is expensive."

"Don't bloody well tell me what I can afford and what I can't. Two large plates of smoked salmon. *Subito, pronto* and every other word ending in *o.*"

"Si, si, signor. Subito, pronto."

"There isn't any better food than smoked salmon," Johnny said a bit later.

If my mouth hadn't been full of the stuff at the moment I would have told him that I couldn't agree more.

"Of course to get it," Johnny pointed out, "you've first of all got to have the salmon and then it's got to be smoked."

It didn't seem too obvious to me at the time; it sounded more like a profound statement of truth.

The Edwardian gentleman, who now seemed to be squeezing the whisky out of the ends of his really very magnificent mustache, shifted his position so that he could get a better view of my legs perched up on the high stool at the bar.

Not that I minded. Let the old boy have his bit of fun.

"It's the human situation," I told Johnny.

"What the hell are you talking about. What is?"

"I don't know. Everything."

"You're getting plastered."

"Not really. Not very."

"Can't have you getting tight, Liz," he said, signaling the Mafia chief to mix two more.

"You mustn't be late for work in the morning."

"I shan't be. Don't worry."

"What I want to know is, suppose you were a telephone girl, why you can't time-stamp one of the slips yourself?"

"They used to. Several years ago. When the place was much smaller. Each girl used to time-stamp the slips as she entered them up over the phone."

"Why can't she do it now?"

"She's just not allowed to, that's all. There's a clock boy standing in front of every three telephonists and as a slip is entered he picks it up and gets a time stamp on it in the machine. The girls aren't allowed to use the machine at all."

"Bloody suspicious lot you must have up there."

"In any case, Johnny, I'm not a telephonist."

"You could be."

"Of course I couldn't. Not now."

"Couldn't that little supervisor snoop fix it for you? I'll bet if you got him in a dark corner you could talk him into anything."

"Not into putting me on phones. I'm a trained settler now."

"What about letter bets?"

"The postmark has got to show a time prior to the 'off' of the race."

"Suppose whoever was opening the letters lost an envelope and made up a slip and put it in with the rest?"

"Johnny, they aren't mugs up there. Not all of them. You just can't mess about with the letter bets."

"Why not? Why can't you lose an envelope? One in how many, thousands I suppose."

"Because every morning the letter bets are opened, the bet is pinned to the envelope and both are photographed."

"Photographed?"

"Photographed. Every single letter. So that the time on the postmark is showing. And if the time is smudged or there are two postmarks and any fishy business at all, the stake is sent back, the bet goes into the N & V file and the photograph is waiting to show to the client if he turns nasty."

"N & V?"

"Null and void. In any case I don't open the letters."

"Of course you don't. You're a settler."

"That's right."

"You work out what's owing on the slips after the race."

"Or not owing. Mostly not owing. Edward West is worth two million pounds. All made out of suckers—sorry, punters. And in any case we don't work things out. We just settle —like that."

"Just like that."

"Just like that."

"What's five quid at eleven to eight on, then?"

"The answer is," I said, speaking very slowly and hitching my skirt up a bit higher which put a dangerous strain on the Edwardian gentleman's blood pressure, "the answer is . . ."

Champagne cocktails and settling didn't seem to mix very well; where the hell was my 11 to 8 table? It ought to be in a particular place in my brain. I ought to be able to see it there. I could, if it would only keep still. Half a minute, though, 11 to 8 *on*. Quite a cunning question. Come to think of it, Johnny was quite a cunning bastard. Johnny, Johnny, Johnny, Johnny, what are you trying to make me do!

By our first strange and fatal interview. Odds on, now let's get this thing straight. And it's all for the pride of the thing anyway because John Ivor Mannington-Travers, sitting on a high stool in the Capri bar of The Golden Horseshoe, reasonably full at the moment with champagne cocktails and smoked salmon (is-a plenty bloody expensive) certainly won't know whether the answer is right or not. Which is partly why, just for the hell of it, I made an effort to catch sight of the fast-disappearing table in the foggy corner of my brain and tell him.

"Three pounds twelve shillings and ninepence."

"I'll check it tomorrow and if it's right I shall regard you as a bloody genius. Which you are already at some things. One anyway."

"Don't speak so loud, you're giving the old gentleman in the corner ideas."

"About all he can get by the look of him, poor old sod. Is that what you call the human situation, Liz?"

"Could be. Part of it. It's a part I never want to suffer from."

"Ni moi non plus."

"Don't speak French to me, Johnny. Not to *me*."

"O.K., O.K. And you won't be suffering from that particular worry for some time, I wouldn't think."

"Let's go back to Lovell Street, Johnny. Take me back."

"We're going. We'll end up there all right. Don't worry. How many bets does Edward West lose a day, pay out on?"

"How many does he pay out on? God knows. Thousands. Must be."

"There you are. Thousands a day. What's one extra in that lot?"

"You can't work it, Johnny. It can't be worked."

"No? O.K. It can't be worked. I dare say it can't. So no harm in talking about it. But suppose it *could* be worked?"

"It can't. The only way you can work anything is for the bet to be made after the race is won. When the result is known; and then, somehow to get the slip stamped with a time previous to that. Which you can't do. They've got it all sewn up, believe you me."

"And Edward West is worth two million smackers?"

"Every bit of it. So they say."

"Is a man worth two millions going to miss say five hundred, a thousand, even five thousand that I'm lucky enough to win?"

"Go ahead and win it, Johnny."

"Why shouldn't we?"

"Johnny—"

He put a hand on my thigh and pinched hard.

"For Christ's sake stop tying knots for the Brownies. What the hell do you mean 'the human situation,' Liz? Aren't we all in it? Isn't the human situation that we've all got to live? Have you found out how to do that without money? Have you? Have you found out how to have four champagne cocktails and two plates of smoked salmon each without money? Have you?"

"This Mafia type's deadly interested," I said.

"Eff off," Johnny told Antonio.

Antonio effed off to the other end of the bar and looked hurt.

"Money's not everything, Johnny."

"Only when you've got plenty it isn't. God, you don't think I'd be talking to *any* girl like this, do you, Liz? You're somebody. A man can trust you. You'd do things for a man —or wouldn't you?"

"Oh, Johnny, anything, anything."

"I'm up against it, Liz. You saw what happened this evening. Rupert Cahill. The bastard. Well, I don't even say that. I don't say it was his fault. But there it is. The human situ-bloody-ation if you like. I was relying on R.D.P. to get me in the clear again. Now Christ only knows what sized hole I'm in, or how I'm going to get out. I've got to have some winning bets, Liz."

"Johnny, I've told you. You can't work it."

"Maybe not. But do you believe in fate, destiny, what have you?"

> *I was meant for you*
> *You were meant for me,*

the oldest of square tunes. Destiny. People were dancing to it before Johnny and I were born even. I don't know where I had heard it sung. But I had. And it had stuck. God, yes, Johnny, I believed in destiny. The way things go. They wrap themselves round you and you can't get out. By our first strange and fatal interview. Johnny, Johnny, Johnny boy, I believed in destiny. And why the hell couldn't you leave me alone, and why couldn't I turn round and walk away from you, slap away from the Capri bar, Antonio, the picture of the nude astride the champagne bottle and the old gentleman fumbling with his flies, the lot?

So with all that boiling up inside me and and in the certain knowledge that it's one of the most stupid questions I have ever asked in my life I say, just like a fifth former at the end of French lesson or, come to that, like a Brownie at a knot-tying session:

"Why, Johnny?"

"Because, Liz, look, listen. This is the perfect setup. Me on the outside, just an ordinary silly punter, like any other. Only a bit different. Because I've got you on the inside. You're there, right in the middle of it. Don't tell me it isn't possible to work out something between us."

"Everybody who has tried to work something has come unstuck."

"How do they know that? The security people can only tell there's a swindle on when they rumble it. For all they know someone is diddling them out of a regular fifty a week at this moment. You only know about the rackets you find out."

It sounded as though there might be something in that. Up to a point.

"Not a regular fifty a week," I said. "Not every week."

"Why not?"

"That's where all the clever boys go wrong. Too greedy. They work their system so that they win every time and no punter wins every time."

"That's pretty profound, my pet. We shall have to arrange an occasional artistic loss."

"You'll have your work cut out to arrange an occasional artistic win."

"Between us we shall be clever enough to arrange that," he said. "Believe you me."

"Johnny, leave me out of it."

"Don't be ridiculous, the whole thing will depend on you."

"What if I don't want to have anything to do with it?" He rose and held out his hand.

"Upsadaisy," he said. "Off that chair, my pet. We will now go through the inclement London night back to Lovell Street where I shall demonstrate to our united satisfaction that you will always be delighted to do exactly what I tell you to."

NINE

For the next two weeks I took particular notice in West-bet House about the chances of working a swindle. And very thankfully I came to the conclusion that it just wasn't on.

As the telephone girls sat there entering up the bets on to the slips they were faced by the clock boys.

As soon as a slip was written a boy picked it up and clocked it. The time-printing clock was on a table behind him so that it was impossible for one of the telephone girls even to approach it without getting up out of her seat and making something of a fuss and commotion.

Once the time stamp was on the slip the bet was "good," but of course the timing clock was never operated after the "off."

In order to time-stamp a slip after the result of the race was known you would have to get a telephone girl, a clock boy and the supervisor (Arnold Chess!) all working in a swindle together, and even then it would almost certainly be spotted by somebody else in the room.

So I didn't think Johnny was going to have much joy in his scheme for putting a fast one over on Edward West. And I was glad. I knew that if he wanted me to do anything, I would probably do it; but I also knew, I felt quite certain inside me, that it would all end up disastrously.

But all the same Johnny's fever about money had got hold of me to some extent. When you go about a lot with somebody who is talking about money all the time, how much he has made and what his plans are for making more and how desperately hard up he is for it, you begin to think along the same lines yourself. Not that any human being I ever met needed much encouragement to think of money.

Some of the slips that came up to be settled made it look pretty easy to help yourself to a sizable chunk of the stuff, too.

There was one, a fortnight after Johnny had been questioning me about the telephone girls and the timing. I remember it now because it was the biggest I had settled up to that time. A Mr. Tilson of Bromsgrove made the bet. A straightforward five-pound win treble on three horses running at Newcastle. Sea Fever in the two o'clock, Sand Pit in the three-thirty and Sebastopol in the four-fifteen. I remember noticing that all three horses had names beginning with S. Perhaps that was why Mr. Tilson backed them. The telephone girls say that they get used to all sorts of queer reasons for backing horses; one punter regularly backs any horse with Blue in its name and another always follows horses called after birds.

Anyway Mr. Tilson of Bromsgrove had a win treble on those three whose names began with S and they all came up. So I had his slip to settle.

The odds were eight to one, four to one and twenty to one, so he won £4725, less his original stake of £5 (which is the way you work this type of bet) leaving him £4720 for his £5 invested.

Not a difficult slip to settle and I entered the amount, initialed it and threw it into the "settled" heap in a shorter time than it takes to tell about it.

But I couldn't help thinking: nearly five thousand pounds for a fiver! If Johnny could only pick winners like that! Because that was the way I thought about things now, the way I looked at life. Everything that came along only had meaning because of the way it might affect Johnny, because of what he would think about it.

Since that evening in The Golden Horseshoe I hadn't in

fact seen much of him. Knowing Johnny was like that. Every now and again he would suddenly withdraw himself from circulation; not a word of warning that you weren't going to see him and not a word of explanation, of course, when he picked you up again and expected to find things just as they had been.

Which he always did with me. There's no sucker like a sucker in love.

Whenever we saw one another we went on just from where we had left off. It suited Johnny and I managed to do it. I managed not to ask him if he had been dancing any hornpipes lately and how the admiral's daughter was getting on. Just managed. I had looked the admiral up in the *Who's Who* in our P.R.O.'s office. Rear Admiral Sir Cecil Clifford Franklyn, K.B.E., A.D.C. to the Queen. Half the ships in the Navy and three West End clubs. One dau.

A nice wicket for Johnny, I used to torment myself by thinking, if he can get his foot in there. And keep his nose clean.

The day I settled the five thousand pound treble at Newcastle, Sergeant Wingram stopped me on the way out. Winnie was the commissionaire in Westbet House, he lived in a little glassed-in box in the entrance hall and what we should all have done without him I can't imagine. He knew all there was to know about everybody and could always get you anything you wanted from a safety pin to a taxicab at no notice at all.

As I was going past he put his head out and winked.

"Message for you, miss."

Nobody was supposed to ring us up privately at Westbet House and theoretically he wasn't allowed to take any messages. Actually I think he only did it if he had a soft spot for you.

"Golden Horseshoe at eight o'clock. O.K., miss?"

O.K.? Certainly it was O.K. I had been planning to go with another girl from Westbet House to see the film at the

Carlton. But she could be stood up. It was very much O.K.

"Who was it from?" I asked, which must rank as one of the most stupid questions of all time.

"Gentleman said you would know who it was," Winnie said grinning.

I told him I thought I could guess.

When I got to The Horseshoe Johnny was already there sitting at a table well away from the Mafia expert at the bar.

It was so unusual for him to be on time, let alone early, for any appointment that I glanced at the clock. Five to eight.

"I'm early for once," Johnny said. "Couldn't wait to see you."

He bought me a drink and we sat at our table.

"What news from Punter's Paradise?"

"The suckers keep losing money."

"None of them making any?"

"Here and there. I settled a slip for nearly five thousand this afternoon. A win treble."

"Ah, trebles are somewhat ambitious. I'll be satisfied with something much simpler. Five thousand, eh? Nice work if you can get it."

"There's always somebody who's lucky."

"*J'en suis sûr.*"

"Don't talk French to me, Johnny. I don't like it."

"You're a jealous little cat, aren't you?"

"Horribly."

"No need to be."

"No?"

"Liz, I've been thinking over what we were talking about the other night—"

"Two weeks ago."

"All right, two weeks ago. I don't believe it can be worked."

"Neither do I, Johnny."

"For one thing you're not a telephone girl."

"And never will be now, either."

"What letter do you work on, settling?"

"T."

"A nice sensible sort of letter."

"There's nothing wrong with it."

"Do you always stick to the same letter?"

"Once we've started on them, yes."

"That's lucky. I shall be starting an account with Edward West tomorrow as John Travers."

I stared at him, trying to figure it out.

"I thought you were rather proud of the Mannington-hyphen business."

Johnny signaled the Mafia to bring over supplies. "So I am. And the Ivor. A family name, Ivor. Did I ever tell you that?"

"About twenty times. What's the idea of your opening an account with Edward West, Johnny?"

"But to make money, my dear. Why else should punters punt?"

By this time the Mafia had made the supply-drop and retreated to its mountain fastness again.

"But why under T, Johnny? I can't help you. You know that. We've just been talking about it."

"We've just been talking a bit of circular nonsense. There are more ways of getting into a house than breaking the front door down." He bent across the table and lowered his voice a little. "Liz, I'm on to something. I've got something here. I've got a winner. I've had a brainwave."

He pulled a late *Evening Standard* out of his pocket and laid it on the table.

"There was racing at Newcastle today—"

"I know there was."

"Do you happen to remember how many runners there were in the three-thirty?"

The three-thirty had been Sand Pit's race. If I closed

my eyes for a second I could see the runners on the board written up in Toni's bold, clear writing.

"Seven. Place betting only on the first two past the post."

"To hell with place betting. Seven runners. Right. Suppose Mr. Travers rings up at various times before the race and makes seven separate bets. A fiver to win on every horse in the race—"

"You'd have lost twenty pounds."

"Do you think so?"

"Johnny, for God's sake. Only one horse wins any race. You would have lost your stake on six horses which puts you thirty quid to the bad; you win on Sand Pit at two to one against, which saves ten for you. Thirty less ten is twenty. Minus twenty for you, that is. Plus twenty for Edward West. No wonder he's worth a lot of money when there are b.f.'s like you about."

He slid his hand across the table, got hold of my little finger and gave it one of his playful twists. I yelped so loud the Mafia looked over at us probably under the impression that a secret war of some kind was starting. And maybe he wasn't too far wrong at that, either.

"Stop being so bloody clever for Christ's sake. I'm not playing some half-baked parlor game, Liz. I've got a plan here. A winner. And I want your help, if we play this right we can make money. In the end a lot of money."

"Johnny, we've been into all the business about the timing clock."

"Forget the timing clock. Everybody in Westbet House has got their eye fixed on the clock because that's where they think a swindle must come from. Excellent. Let them watch the bloody thing till their eyes drop out. Let everybody do the obvious thing, sit in a ring watching the front door while we see if there isn't another way into the building.

"Let's get back to the two o'clock at Newcastle.

"When the race is over and the winner goes up—"

"Sand Pit."

"What the hell does it matter what it was. Don't interrupt. Sand Pit, O.K. When the result goes up you start settling. Right?"

"Yes, at once. If there isn't an objection."

"And you'll be dealing with all the T slips. Right, again?"

"Yes."

"So in the course of time all my seven slips will be dealt with by you?"

"And six of them will be losing bets."

He leaned back. "Will they?"

"Only one horse—"

"You can't be as stupid as all that surely, Liz. I don't like girls who are stupid anyway. They bore me. Shake yourself up. You get seven bets from me to deal with. One of them is a winner which you naturally keep. Six of them are losers which you naturally get rid of. Right?"

I stared at him, thinking hard.

I was beginning to see that it was possible.

The telephone girls were watched by the clock boys all the time, but once the settlers had started working on their piles of slips nobody paid much attention to them. They were left to get on with it for the ten or fifteen minutes of intensely concentrated work that they had to get through before the next race.

Arnold Chess walked about the room, certainly; but he couldn't be everywhere at once and there were six settlers (the experienced ones did two letters each, some three; I was the only one on a single letter and probably I should soon be doing U as well).

Besides, as Johnny had said, if people were thinking about a swindle at all they were automatically thinking of the timing business, not of anything after that. If you were careful and quick it would be possible to get rid of some unwanted slips.

"It's possible, isn't it?"

"I—"

"Keep the winner and get rid of the losers. It can be done. Truth?"

"You would only have won ten pounds."

"Because Sand Pit was only two to one. Four to one and I should have won twenty. Twenty to one and I should have won a hundred. Average it at threes. Twice a week. Not every day. Let's be modest. Just twice a week. Thirty quid a week free of tax. I shan't object to that at all and I'm quite sure it won't hurt Edward West."

"If you win every time you bet you won't last three months."

"I shan't win every time I bet. I'll remember your useful little lecture on the subject. Moderation in all things. An occasional judicial loss, like we said. But a lot of useful wins as well."

Exactly a week later I handled the first John Travers slip.

It was directly after the result of the three o'clock at Birmingham had been declared. There had been eight runners and betting was tight. Evens about the favorite, then two horses at two to one against and the rest at fives.

The favorite was beaten into second place and a horse called Featherbed won at five to one.

As it happened Johnny's first slip was the Featherbed one. Five pounds to win. So I marked it £25 in the "You win" column and knew that there would be seven more "Travers" slips which I would have to get rid of.

During the last week I had been thinking over this problem and the damnable part of it was I could see it wasn't going to be difficult. If only I had been on telephones the thing would have been out—impossible; but Johnny, trust him, had hit on the weak spot. His idea could be worked. I realized that as I thought it over.

And, although he couldn't know this, of course, it was easier for me than for any other of the settlers.

I worked at the end of the line so it was only from my left-hand side that I could be observed, and there wasn't a great deal of danger of that because when you are settling you are concentrating much too hard to notice what's happening next to you.

My table had a drawer in it where I kept my bag and a spare handkerchief and a box of face tissues and by the time I had finished settling for the three o'clock at Birmingham that afternoon it had seven losing slips of Mr. John Travers in it as well.

It had turned out to be too easy to slide them in there while I leaned across the table pretending to arrange the pile of slips I had just dealt with.

Arnold Chess came along collecting our settled slips.

"All finished?"

He wasn't allowed to come round too soon because one of Edward West's principles was "never hurry the settlers."

I smiled at little Arnold and handed up my slips.

"Not many on that race."

"You never get really heavy betting on a small field. You'll have plenty to do on the three forty-five."

"I expect I'll manage."

He walked away as I picked up the paper on the floor beside me and pretended to be reading it.

I hadn't realized working a swindle would be as simple as that and I still didn't quite believe it. I was still scared. Somebody, surely, would tap me on the shoulder in a moment and say, "Excuse me but just what was it I saw you stuffing away in your drawer?"

In two days' time Johnny would get a check for twenty-five pounds. I only hoped the so-and-so would be grateful.

He was. Grateful enough to take me out for the evening on the proceeds, anyway.

"Didn't I tell you it would work, Liz? Wasn't I right?"

"You're always right, Johnny." I almost meant it too.

"Was it tricky?"

"Not very."

"Isn't it quite an idea?"

"Don't overplay it, Johnny."

He had the sense not to. He didn't bet again for a week. And the odd thing was that I was looking for his slips all the time and as much disappointed as anything else that they didn't turn up.

Then it was Chepstow, the last race of the day, nine runners this time and the winner came in at the useful price of six to one. Johnny's usual luck because there was an odds-on favorite that wasn't even placed. Doped, possibly. In Westbet House you didn't care whether a horse had been doped or whether its jockey had committed suicide. All that concerned you was the ratified list of first, second and third. And the odds.

Nine runners meant eight losing slips to get rid of. But slips are small things on thin paper and presently I was looking across the room smiling at Arnold Chess and nodding when he raised his eyebrows which meant, "Are you finished? Can I come and collect your slips?"

$5 \times 6 = 30.$

Thirty quid for John Ivor Mannington-Travers, alias John Travers, alias my occasional lover; alias also perhaps the lover of the admiral's daughter.

I didn't know about that. I did my best not to think about it. Johnny never mentioned her and I told myself that all the times when he didn't want to see me and was "doing something else" he was out with the boys at his club playing poker.

Not that I believed myself entirely; but a little self-deception is very comforting at times.

I used to take the losing slips away in my bag and get rid of them in the flat.

Vicky saw them one day and casually asked what they were.

"Odd bits of paper from the office."

"Bets?"

"Canceled ones. No good."

One had fallen to the floor and she picked it up before I could stop her. Foolishly I made a half move forward; she noticed it and it must have surprised her slightly.

"John Travers?" she said. "Is that Johnny?"

I nodded. "He bets with Edward West now. It just happens his slip was one of the spoiled ones." I hoped to God she wasn't going to look at the others.

"Does that mean he has lost his bet?"

"It means that particular slip is no good."

"He'll be cross about that."

"Very likely. Johnny takes money seriously."

"Liz, are things working out all right between you and Johnny? Are you happy with what you get out of it?"

When Vicky asked you things you wanted to give her the right answers.

Well, I could answer that one.

"When I'm happy I am frightfully happy. Shaken with it. And even when he makes me miserable I'd sooner be that way with him than anything else."

She smiled at me. Honest-to-God Vicky, straight as a sword blade.

"You really are in love with him, aren't you?"

"Desperately, Vicky, desperately."

"I've never loved like that yet."

"You're lucky," I told her.

Not that I meant it, not that I meant it. Or did I? When you're in love you put on spectacles. You see a lot of things more clearly. I used to think back to the zombies sometimes. Think back and realize that the poor pathetic stupid little zombies were right in a way.

"God is Love," they used to tell one another in the chapel in Hansbeck Road, and by God they meant some non-sexual, teetotal thou-shalt-notter, who had a nice hot hell ready for anybody who showed any signs of enjoyment. Some God. I had discovered that Love is God. I was prepared to believe that. In the moments of ecstasy I could believe that I was part of the whole act of loving in the world. I thought the world was revolving round Johnny and me on a bed at the center of it. Even when there wasn't any ecstasy. Even when he hadn't bothered to see me or ring me up for three or four days together, even then I was more alive in my hurt than I had been before I knew him. I was in love. And Love was God.

"Is Johnny's betting with Edward West a good thing for you?"

It was a funny question; but Vicky had a habit of asking funny (and disconcerting) questions. When people are as honest as she was they have a trick of seeing into the heart of a matter without realizing it.

I shrugged my shoulders. I smiled. I had got the rest of the slips safely under control now.

"It doesn't matter to me," I said. "If Johnny wins, good show; if he loses that's just too bad."

And he was having the sense to lose occasionally. Every now and again he made just one bet on a race choosing a horse which didn't stand an earthly, but on an average he was doing very nicely thank you, biting Edward West in the ear to the tune of about twenty pounds a week.

At the end of a month of this I went round to Lovell Street one evening with a streaming cold. Which annoyed Johnny. Not that he was afraid of catching my cold but simply that he had no use for you if you were feeling blue or miserable in any way. You had to be on top of the world all the time to please Johnny.

"What do you want to get a cold for?" he demanded.

Which made me laugh.

"Give me a good whisky and I'll forget about it."

The bottle of Vat 69 was empty. He held it up to show me. I stuck my toes in at that. With what he was making out of Edward West Johnny could afford to have full bottles, not empty ones. And I told him so.

For once he was unexpectedly docile.

"O.K., O.K. I'll go down to the pub on the corner and get one."

"Don't be long."

"I'll be as long as I bloody well like, Liz" (which sounded more like a return to form).

"Meanwhile what about my cold?"

"You can get sozzled when I come back."

So I turned on the telly, sat close in front of the electric fire and wondered just how subhuman it was possible to feel.

When the bell rang I thought it was possible that the silly clot had forgotten his key and had locked himself out.

Not a bit of it.

When I opened the door there was the admiral's daughter; and if I wasn't particularly pleased at the sight of her I could see that she was even more shaken to see me.

"Oo-oh," she said.

Well, there you are, I thought; the human situation. Only probably she doesn't know about the human situation much. It's not a thing you can learn about at Roedean. You learn about it by coming up against it. I felt sorry for her. A bit.

"Johnny's just gone out," I said.

"O-oh."

"He won't be long. He's gone to get a bottle of Scotch. I've got a foul cold. Are you scared of catching it?"

"N-no. Not a bit, actually. I never catch things."

"Well, come along in then and wait."

All right; you tell me what else I could have said. "Don't hang about there. Pack up and—off. I'm his mistress and I hate the sight of you."

Maybe she realized that that was what I really meant. Maybe she was too dumb for that even. But I don't think so. I think she was like me. Any sort of contact with Johnny was better than none at all.

When we got upstairs I switched off the television and

treated her to a detailed, fully documented account of my cold.

"I expect it's all this wet weather," she said.

"I dare say. I don't seem to have been dry for weeks."

"I've got a message to give him from my father and I was just motoring by so I thought I'd look in."

"Good idea. He won't be long. Unless he finds some character in the pub to talk racing to."

"He's awfully fond of racing, isn't he?"

"Mad about it."

"Do—do you go to many meetings with him?"

"I've only been once. When we all met. At Towcester."

"Oh," she smiled. She could beat me. And she couldn't resist saying so. "I've been quite a number of times with him."

"I hope you enjoyed it."

"My father used to own some racehorses."

"The admiral?"

"You don't expect it from a sailor, do you? But we were all mad about riding. Do you do any?"

No, I told her; it was the Leicestershire Bartons who did all the riding.

"Oh." I could see she didn't like the sound of the Leicestershire Bartons. Maybe I wasn't just a passionate little piece from nowhere after all. Maybe I was more dangerous than she had been thinking.

"It's the human situation," I told her.

"Sorry?"

"Not to worry. Nothing. Things work out."

"I suppose you're frightfully fond of him?"

Frightfully fond. Well, I suppose you could call it that if you liked. I nodded.

"So am I," she said

"And is he frightfully fond of you?"

She looked at me steadily and said, "I hope so. I think so!"

When Johnny came back, which he did at that moment accompanied by a bottle of Vat 69 and a hearty character whom he had taken a liking to in the local, it was difficult to be certain that he was frightfully fond of either of us.

I could see it from his point of view. He had probably gone to a considerable amount of trouble to keep us apart during the last few weeks and when he returns on a good-will mission bearing a bottle of Scotch there we both were as cozy as could be. Just two simple girls together, letting our hair down and having a nice confidential chat.

Men quite rightly feel uneasy when women get together and talk. That's how palace conspiracies start and the reigning king naturally doesn't like it.

It was lucky that Johnny had brought this character from the local in with him. He was a great big bouncing happy Boy Scout aged about twenty-eight. When he wasn't drinking he was laughing. And he did a good deal of each.

I found myself hoping that he had paid for half the bottle of Vat 69 because that's about what he drank out of it.

Still, there was one thing—as long as he was there the conversation (if you can call it that) never got a chance of flagging.

When he decided to go the admiral's daughter went too.

She had delivered the message from her father and it must have looked to her as though I was there for keeps. So she beat it. No staying power, some of these debby types.

"Why didn't you go with them?" Johnny demanded as soon as we were alone.

"I'm much too fond of you."

"Don't be funny, Liz. There's no point in shouting out to the world how things are."

It was the first time I had known him bother much about what the world would think, and I said so.

"Who minds what anybody thinks? It's just—oh, what the hell? Let's have another drink."

"If your newly found chum has left any."

He had. A little.

"Everything all right at Westbet House?" he asked.

"You ought to know. You're getting your check every week."

"I told you it would work, Liz."

"You're always right, Johnny."

He lit a cigarette and threw his leg over the arm of his chair; his favorite way of sitting. Dark, handsome Johnny.

"She's only a kid, Johnny."

"Then don't worry about her."

"Or has she grown up a bit since meeting you?"

"Chuck over the *Radio Times* and stop nattering."

"Are you by any chance fancying yourself as an admiral's son-in-law?"

"Mind your own business."

"Wouldn't it be my business, at any rate a little, Johnny?"

"Can you see me getting married, Liz?"

"I can see that you might be getting a very comfortable niche ready for yourself."

"And leave my little Liz in the lurch?"

"I expect that's where they've all been left before, isn't it?"

"Chuck over the *Radio Times*."

"Or am I different, Johnny? Just a bit different?"

He looked across at me and said:

"You ought to know, Liz; you ought to know."

TEN

Vicky was happy these days because she got fixed up with a contract to play in the Coventry Rep. They were going to do a short season of Shaw, starting off with one called *Pygmalion.*

"Not bloody likely," Vicky said.

I didn't get it. I thought it was all fixed. And I said so.

"It's a quote from the play. It's one of my lines. It made *Pygmalion* famous."

"That one line?"

"The use of the word 'bloody.'"

I thought she must be joking; but apparently not. It seems that because this girl Liza in the play when asked whether she was going to do something or other said, "Not bloody likely," the whole of England talked about it for weeks.

Well, I often wondered what they did talk about in those days. Now, apparently, I knew.

I very seldom discussed Johnny with Vicky. I knew that fundamentally she didn't like him and when you are in love with somebody you can't bear it if your friends aren't enthusiastic.

At Westbet House we ran into trouble. A wave of flu hit the place and at one point thirty of our telephone girls were away and what was even worse, three settlers. Everybody was working under pressure and people got very edgy.

I remember that we were just beginning to get over the worst of it when Vicky was due to go up to Coventry to start a week's rehearsals.

It was a Tuesday morning. I was eating breakfast and Vicky was sitting in her dressing gown reading *The Times*. She was going to motor up to Coventry immediately after lunch.

The post had just come. One letter for Vicky; nothing for me. I was thinking of Johnny, wondering what the chances were of ever getting a letter from him.

Vicky gave a little exclamation as though she had just seen something that startled her.

"What's up?"

She hesitated a moment and then said, "Johnny's engagement is in the paper. Did you know?"

I was buttering a piece of toast at the time and I just went on scraping away with the knife without realizing what I was doing. I felt sick. I felt as though something had exploded in my stomach. *Did I know?*

Christ Almighty, of course I didn't know—or had I known all the time and not allowed myself to know? Had I been living in a fool's paradise with my eyes tight shut, afraid to open them? Johnny, Johnny . . .

"I was wondering when it was going to appear," I said. "Can I see?"

Vicky handed *The Times* over.

". . . Mr. John Ivor Mannington-Travers . . . Miss Teresa ('Tessa') Franklyn only daughter of Rear Admiral"— and all the rest of it.

I read it two or three times. I suppose if a man gets his death sentence handed to him the poor so-and-so reads it through a couple of times just to make sure there's no mistake.

Vicky was watching me.

"Liz—"

I smiled at her. A thin performance but there it was, a smile.

"I hope it keeps fine for them," I said.

Vicky didn't say I told you so. She had warned me that

I should get hurt. Here I was getting hurt and she had the sense not to rub it in.

"If you would like to go to Blaydons this weekend," she said, "I could lay it all on and I know that Father would love to have you there."

"Vicky, it's kind of you—I'll think it over—"

I got out of the room without going to bits. But only just. And when I was out of the flat I walked slowly round the square to get hold of myself a little.

It was a clear, fresh morning and some children were already pedaling tricycles about on the oval piece of grass. The little leaden cupid was throwing his jet of water up into the sunlight and the noise of London rumbled all round us.

Darling T.S. The nicest square in London. I told myself I was a very lucky girl to be living in it. I told myself I was a bloody fool. How can a girl be lucky when someone has taken her heart out and broken it for her . . .

Oh, Johnny, Johnny, Johnny, why at least couldn't you have told me face to face?

"Why couldn't you have told me face to face, Johnny?" I asked him that evening in Lovell Street.

It was half past six, there was a large whisky and water on the mantelpiece; through the open door of the bedroom I could see his dinner suit and a white shirt laid out ready on the bed.

John Ivor Mannington-Travers was in great good form. Looking forward to his evening with the admiral's daughter. Going to be introduced and shown off to one of her aunts up from Bath I shouldn't wonder. Also he was a bit scared. Of me. Which is why he meant to play it all as high-handed as be damned. Johnny's way.

"How could I tell you?"

"It's exactly a fortnight today that I asked you if this was going to happen and whether I wasn't a bit different from all the rest and you said yes, I was, and we ended up in there on the bed. Remember?"

"So what have you got to grumble about?"

"You couldn't have told me then?"

"Listen, these things aren't always shouted out from the housetops. Or didn't you learn that down in Balham or Tooting or wherever it was—"

"Hansbeck Road."

"Hansbeck Road. What a place to live in. People don't always want these things made public till they are made public. God knows, I don't care. But Tessa's got a family. The admiral, aunts, uncles, Christ knows what. She said let's keep it dark till we put it in *The Times,* from everybody."

"Including me."

"Anyway, I'm not sure that I knew about it that last time you were here."

"No?"

"I may not have made up my mind then."

"The great dictator."

"My God, you can be a bore at times. Mix me another drink and have one yourself, for Pete's sake."

I mixed a Scotch-and-water and handed it to him.

"Oh, Johnny, Johnny, if only you had said something to me."

"Now be reasonable. A man can't always ride the race the way he wants to himself. He has got other people to consider—"

That made me laugh. If I hadn't laughed I would have burst into tears. So I laughed instead. It wasn't all that hearty though. Other people to consider? Hadn't you got me, Johnny, hadn't you got me?

"Didn't you have me, Johnny?" I asked him. "Didn't you have me, haven't you got me now, body and soul, fool that I am?"

"The only reason you've got to gripe is that I didn't tell you anything. Didn't I put the bloody thing in *The Times* this morning? And if that isn't telling everybody I don't know what is. Or perhaps you can't read? This isn't the end of everything, Liz. Why should it be? You're still in Westbet House. I'm still here in Lovell Street. We needn't be enemies. For God's sake. There's enough cribbing and quarreling in the world, surely. And now I've got to start getting dressed. I'm going out."

"Dance a good hornpipe."

Just for a minute I thought he was going to hit me. Johnny got sudden gusts of anger that took hold of him like that.

But he held his hand back and smiled.

"I'm not going out immediately, Liz. You can have another drink and watch me change if you like."

I didn't like. But only just didn't.

"Not bloody likely," I said, "and that's a quotation, in case you don't know. It's funny; frightfully, frightfully funny."

I went back to Tammerton Square and the flat was empty —thank God—because Vicky was up in Coventry, so I didn't have to pretend.

I lay on my bed in my clothes and the room was dark and cold. I couldn't be bothered to switch on the light or to light the gas fire or to undress. I was dark and cold inside myself, with the darkness and the coldness of misery.

The next morning I felt ghastly and when I got to Westbet House the senior settler said:

"Hallo, it won't be long before you're packing off to bed, by the looks of it."

I told him it was all right, I'd carry on; and I've no doubt he was relieved to hear it, as we were still short-handed.

There were two meetings (Birmingham and Lewes) and business was fairly heavy. I had learned already that some meetings always attract a lot of betting, and Birmingham was one of these.

As I plugged away through the afternoon I thought, Thank God most of this is automatic because I couldn't have got through it otherwise.

The same thing was going round and round in my mind; or maybe my mind was going round and round the same thing at the center of it. I was finished with Johnny. And that wasn't true either. He was finished with me. I didn't really dislike that little hazel-eyed deb of an admiral's daughter but I was jealous enough to have killed her. I was eaten up with a thing like a clawing animal inside me. Consumed by it. I thought, Christ, if this is what jealousy does to you I'm going to suffer all right.

In spite of feeling rotten and having a blinding headache I didn't want the afternoon in the office to come to an end because when it did I should have to go back to Tammerton Square. Vicky wouldn't be there and I could see myself having a riotous time sitting there alone wondering just how Johnny and the admiral's daughter were getting on together.

When I was settling for the last race at Birmingham about the tenth slip in my pile was a Mr. J. Travers one. On the winner too. A horse that came in at two to one. I marked it, initialed it and passed it to one side while I was still arguing inside myself whether to go on with Johnny's swindle or to throw the whole lot out of the window.

But having passed his winning slip I had to do something about the others. There were seven of them (only eight runners altogether) and I got them away into the drawer of my table without any trouble and as usual without anybody noticing.

The last Lewes race had the flag up and was off and Toni was tapping it out on the board. Lucky Lucy, tap for Administrator, tap tap for Lucky Lucy, tap tap tap for Naval Occasion. I didn't want Naval Occasion to win. I didn't want anything or anybody connected with the Navy ever to win anything.

"Your nose is bleeding, Liz," the settler next to me said. So it was. Great heavy sploshes of blood falling down on to my table.

I was glad of it. I don't often get a nose bleed, but then I don't often have a splitting headache, and I thought that the one might cure the other.

"I'll be back to settle," I said, and hurried out to the ladies' room.

At the doorway I bumped into Arnold Chess. Maybe I looked a good deal worse than I was (the handkerchief I was holding to my nose was certainly a pretty gory mess by now), maybe he couldn't stand the sight of blood—anyway he got into a panic and insisted on sending one of the telephone girls in with me.

"This often happen with you?" she asked.

"Hardly ever."

"Like me to put a key down your back or any of that nonsense?"

"May as well just let it bleed. It's got to stop sometime."

"I'd certainly call you full-blooded. You got a happy sex life?"

"Not very. At the moment. Sorry about all the mess."

"What we want is a box of tissues."

And at that moment Arnold Chess very daringly for him knocked at the door and poked his head in, with a box of tissues in his hand.

"Thanks so much, Mr. Chess," the girl said. "You're brilliant. It's just what we wanted."

"You ought to be one of these blood donors," the telephone girl said. "You've certainly got plenty to spare."

But it stopped at last, and sure enough my headache stopped with it.

I mopped up and said I had better be getting back. As

I was going through the door something hit me and I couldn't stop myself saying, "God Almighty—"

"You O.K.?" the girl asked.

Yes, I told her, just a sudden sort of pain, nothing . . .

She looked a bit worried.

And that made two of us. Only I wasn't worried. I was desperate. I had suddenly realized about the box of tissues.

Arnold Chess must have got it out of the drawer of my table and that meant that he could have spotted Johnny's losing slips.

If he had opened the drawer and got out the box of tissues from it he must have seen them.

The winners and prices for the last race at Lewes were just going up when I got back into the room.

"Sure you can manage?" the settler next to me asked. "I could do yours if you want."

I said no thanks very much I'd be all right. I took a quick look round the room. Chess wasn't in it.

Naval Occasion	4–1
Flash By	2–1
Controversial	18–1

the board said.

The girl on my left had started work so I pulled open the drawer and had a quick look. My bag was in there and nothing else. Johnny's seven losing slips were gone.

I did my settling automatically . . . thirty shillings each way on Naval Occasion. I couldn't have cared less what the details were. I hardly cared whether I got them right. Before I had worked through my slips I looked in the drawer again. Twice. There was nothing there except my bag.

I kept expecting, and even hoping, that Arnold Chess would come back. At least I would know the worst when he came up and spoke to me.

But he didn't come.

We finished settling for the last race and people began to get ready for leaving. Some of the telephone girls would stay on, of course, but the settlers were always free to go after they had finished work on the last race of the day.

Although I was scared of meeting Arnold Chess I didn't want to go now until I had done so.

I hung about after the other settlers had gone and then I got into a panic in case the telephone girls were wondering what I was hanging about for so I got my things together and went.

I waited in the corridors outside but there was no sign of Chess so eventually I went slowly downstairs.

"Seen Mr. Chess about?" I asked Sergeant Wingram.

"Not since he came in after lunch," he told me. "You all right, miss?"

"Yes, perfectly. My nose bled a bit. Nothing to worry about. I'm perfectly all right."

And if "perfectly all right" was the definition of the sort of mess I was in, then God help me, I thought.

I began to walk up Shaftesbury Avenue thinking; and when I saw an espresso coffee place I went in and ordered a cup.

When I came out I walked down to the bus stop at the end of the avenue and got onto a bus for Lovell Street.

I had made up my mind about one thing—I must see Johnny.

He was in and I couldn't see any indications that he was going out later. Perhaps he wasn't dancing any hornpipes tonight, I thought.

He was in one of his boisterous moods, the sort of mood which had always ended up on the settee or the bed. And I didn't think that a little thing like an engagement would prevent him suggesting that we end up that way again.

I thought he might as well get shock treatment so as

214

soon as I was inside I said without wrapping it up in any way:

"Johnny, we're rumbled. Someone has found out."

He stared at me; and I nodded and said again:

"Someone has found out."

He took a quick look round the hall. We were the only people in it.

Then he said:

"Come upstairs and tell me about it."

Up in his room he kicked the door to and turned on me.

"Now then, what's all this?"

I could almost have laughed. You would have thought from the way he spoke that he was having me on the carpet for having done something wrong.

I told him pretty well in words of one syllable what had happened and he never took his eyes off me while I was talking.

When I had finished he said:

"Do you mean to say that you have actually been putting the losing slips into a drawer in the table you work at?"

"Where do you expect me to put them?"

"Couldn't you get rid of them, destroy them?"

"In the middle of a room with thirty people in it and a supervisor walking about?"

"Was it the supervisor who found them?"

"I imagine so. It must have been."

"That thin little man I saw?"

"Arnold Chess."

"What will he do about it?"

"Report it to Mr. Berry presumably and *he*'ll take it to Edward West."

"What's he likely to do?"

"Make a case of it."

"You mean prosecute me?"

"Yes. They always do. If anyone is found out in any sort of swindle they get taken into court. The security people

215

rubbed that into us from the start. So I shall be prosecuted
with you."

"And a hell of a lot of good that will do me."

I told him I didn't suppose I should get much joy out of
it either.

"But it's different. This is going to mess up my whole
life. You don't know Tessa's father. The admiral. He's an
A.D.C. to the Queen. If I get taken into court over a betting racket you don't suppose he'll let me marry Tessa, do
you?"

I said that was his worry. He crossed the room and got
hold of my arm and doubled it up behind my back till it
hurt like hell.

"I believe you're just trying to be funny," he said. "You're
telling me all this with some crazy idea of scaring me out
of marrying Tessa. My God, if that's what you're doing
I'll beat you up so you won't know yourself."

I only just managed not to cry out because of the way
he was hurting my arm. I shook my head and he watched
me closely all the time I was speaking and in the end he
knew I wasn't playing the fool.

"You can disbelieve me if you like, Johnny; but that
won't stop Edward West from taking you into court. Taking
us both into court."

"Didn't you say you knew West?"

"As it happens I have met him, yes."

"Can't you do anything?"

"Edward West isn't interested in me in the way you are—
or were. He's interested in getting a good settler. If the
settler starts swindling Edward West pounces and that's all
there is to it."

"And my marriage with Tessa goes west."

"She's over twenty-one, surely?"

"Of course she's over twenty-one."

"She can tell the admiral to stuff his spinnaker then, and
go off with you any time she likes."

"And what do we live on if her father doesn't make her the two thousand a year allowance he has promised?"

"Tough, Johnny."

"God, I could murder you for making a hash of this."

I shook my head. "I haven't made a hash of anything. I would much sooner not have started the thing at all. But it's too late to say that now. I did start it, because you wanted me to; and that's that. But don't blame me for making a hash of it. If my nose hadn't started to bleed everything would still be O.K. Can anybody help it if their nose bleeds? Can you?"

"What's this Chess character like?"

"Conscientious, I would say."

"That means he'll go blabbing off to the people above him to West?"

"He's sure to. He must."

"Absolutely must?"

I suppose there was something in my voice that made Johnny catch at a straw of hope. By that time in our relationship there wasn't much I could hide from him. And I couldn't make out why nothing had been said to me at Westbet House. If Arnold Chess had reported the business straightaway to Mr. Berry the obvious thing, surely, would have been to have me up for questioning at once, before I left the building.

At the back of my mind I could see it just a possibility that little Arnold, horrified at finding me caught up in anything, had taken the slips home with him and was having a miserable evening wondering what to do.

"What else is Chess like besides being conscientious?"

"He's a decent little man."

"Has he got any money?"

"Money? Only what he gets from his job, I imagine."

"Well, that might be a beginning," Johnny said, throwing himself into the comfortable chair and flinging his leg over the arm.

"I wouldn't try anything with Arnold Chess, Johnny."

"Don't start being virtuous, Liz. It's too late in the day for you. If Chess had reported what he found straightaway surely you would have heard something? Somebody would have said something already. Wouldn't they?"

"I suppose so."

"Perhaps he's scared."

"What of?"

"Maybe he hasn't handled a swindle before? Or maybe he isn't scared. Just soft-hearted. Maybe he has rolled an eye at you. Didn't you say he made a pass at you once? Is that it? Has he, Liz?"

"Go to hell, Johnny."

I wasn't telling him anything about Arnold Chess and me, particularly as there wasn't anything to tell; which he wouldn't have believed anyway, once I had started.

"Do you think it possible he has taken the whole thing home to sleep on it? That he won't make up his mind to do anything till tomorrow?"

I shrugged my shoulders.

"Where does this Chess character live?"

"How do I know where he lives?"

But it's very difficult to lie to a man who knows you as well as Johnny knew me.

He caught hold of my arm again.

"Liz, I think you're being rather a silly girl about all this, aren't you?"

"Look, Johnny," I told him, "I swear to high heaven that if you start any of your rough stuff you won't get a damn thing out of me. Not one damn thing. I'll scream the flat down."

"All right, all right. But can't you see what this means to me? If what we are guessing about this man Chess is right and I can get hold of him this evening before he has made up his mind I may be able to persuade him not to say anything. I'll pitch him the most marvelous sob story he has ever heard. You've got to give me the chance of doing that, Liz."

"Don't bring me into it, that's all."

"You are in it."

"I don't want Arnold Chess to think I sent you to him."

"Just tell me his address, that's all."

"He lives at a place called Cotterfield."

"Bucks?"

I shook my head. I hadn't the vaguest idea. Bucks, Berks, Herts; they were all the same to me.

"What part of Cotterfield?"

"Heath End Cottage."

ELEVEN

I WOULD HAVE given a great deal to have had Vicky in Tammerton Square that evening. I would have told her everything and if she had looked at me with those steady gray eyes of hers and told me (as I think she would have done) that it served me right for getting mixed up in a swindle to start with, O.K., I'd have taken it from her.

She'd have been right, of course; but it wouldn't have helped me much except that to have a talk with anybody would have been a help.

I felt this so much that I actually rang up Western 91421, a thing I had often thought of doing but never got around to. After all Jimmy and I had been great friends and I always felt that he understood me better than anybody else I had ever known. How he would react to a voice calling out of the past, I didn't know. And I didn't get a chance of finding out, either.

"This is Mrs. James Mancroft speaking."

It was bikini Betty, sounding very much in charge of the situation, very much in the saddle.

"Is Mr. Mancroft there, please?"

"I'm afraid he isn't. Who is calling, please?"

"The Indoor Fun and Games Society," I said and rang off, hoping it wouldn't get Jimmy into trouble.

If there was nobody to talk to I would just have to manage on my own. And in any case I didn't really need anyone to tell me just how much of a b.f. I had been. I knew all about that for myself. But I also knew that the ordinary rules don't apply when you are in love. When you are head over heels, hopelessly infatuated with a man, you can talk yourself into thinking that the most God-awful silly things are sensible.

I half thought that Johnny might ring me up late that same evening; but no, no phone call; and in my heart of hearts I wasn't altogether surprised. Johnny went his own sweet way, and it would never occur to him to go to the trouble of making a call just to give somebody else peace of mind.

The next morning was so bright and fresh that I couldn't believe things would turn out quite as badly as I had been thinking.

Settlers have different hours from ordinary staff and I wasn't due at Westbet House till half past ten. The clock showed five and twenty past as I turned into the dark and narrow entrance hall.

Sergeant Wingram put his head out of his office.

"Nice morning, Miss Barton. Message for you from Mr. Berry. Would you please to go up to his office straight-away?"

That knocked the niceness right out of the morning.

This was it.

Clearly Johnny's persuasive tongue hadn't been persuasive enough last night down in Heath End Cottage and little Arnold Chess had done what his conscience told him to do.

I wasn't surprised; I had never really thought that there would be any other way out of it.

"Thanks, Wingram," I said.

"You all right this morning, miss—that nose bleed of yours?"

"I'm O.K.," I told him. "More or less."

Mr. Berry seemed pretty busy. His desk was covered in paper work and Jenny, his secretary, was hammering away on a typewriter in the corner.

I felt slightly sick. I didn't think this was going to be at all enjoyable.

Mr. Berry looked up, smiled, and spoke quickly.

"Ah, Miss Barton, I want you to help me if you would. We are frightfully behind-hand in the pool. Two girls have been away for more than a week and one still is. I don't like to ask you because you are doing so well at settling but to-day and tomorrow won't be particularly busy in the rooms, there's only Leicester today and Ripon tomorrow, so would you mind doing the next two days and possibly even the rest of this week helping out in the typists' pool?"

I must have gawped a bit, but I nodded and said:

"No. That will be all right, Mr. Berry."

"Good girl. Thank you very much. I'll get you back on to settling just as soon as I can."

"Is that all, Mr. Berry?"

"If you wouldn't mind going along to the pool straight-away. Miss Carter will show you what they want a hand with most."

So the mine hadn't blown up yet, I thought, as I walked along the corridor toward the pool.

It was decent of Mr. Berry to ask me if I would mind switching for a few days. He could have switched me with-out asking, and then on the whole the treatment was decent in Westbet House and it was certainly their policy to look after their settlers.

I can't say I felt any better. When you are sitting in the dentist's waiting room there is a great deal to be said for being the next on the list so that you can go in and get it over with. I wasn't going to appreciate this cat-and-mouse business.

Lesly Carter, the head of the pool, wasn't a particular chum of mine. I always felt that she thought I had ideas above my station. Which was true. But she was glad enough to see me that morning and I was quite happy to be given a pile of stuff and told to get on with it.

There was a special circular going out to some of the firm's clients and a typewritten correction slip had to be enclosed with each one, so it was entirely repetitive work and normally would have been pretty tedious. But for my mood that morning it was just right.

"The attention of clients is drawn to the fact that para. 4 should read 'two days' and not 'two hours.'"

Must get the time business right or somebody will try to start a swindle. And a swindle of any kind is the one thing up with which Westbet House will not put; as they say. So I whisk out the notices in the pool as fast as I can, waiting for the door to open and Mr. Berry to look in and say, "Oh, Miss Barton, there was one little matter I forgot. Kindly step along with me to Mr. West's office and you'll shortly find yourself in one hell of a jam."

Which explains why I am not particularly interested in the apparently endless conversation that is being kept up between Lesly, one of the girls, and her great buddy, Sis. About men, of course.

Any protracted conversation in any gaggle of girls is either about clothes (". . . it's caught up a little on the shoulder and then it sort of sweeps away . . .") or about men.

Lesly had apparently got herself an enthusiastic lover. Just meeting her casually before, I hadn't imagined that she was the type. Which, of course, is a stupid thing to say. Isn't she a woman? And aren't all women the type? Hasn't each one of us got somewhere a man who has only got to crook his finger and we move? Or if we haven't got him, don't we wish we had?

Lesly evidently loved it. "My dear, do you know last night . . . can you imagine?"

And Sis loved hearing about it. *He never! Lesly!*

"We're making Liz Barton blush."

"I'll survive," I told them, and every time the door opened I wondered just how much longer I should survive for.

But lunch time came and nothing had happened and by now I was allowing myself to begin to think that nothing was going to happen. Looking at it from Arnold Chess's point of view delay didn't make sense. If he found something fishy going on and didn't report it straightaway, he would pretty soon be in trouble himself. "You're a supervisor, Mr. Chess, why didn't you let us know at once that you had discovered—" That sort of thing. If by hook or crook Johnny had managed to talk little Arnold into delay, then the odds were that we might scrape out of the mess altogether. And when he wanted, Johnny could be very pleasant and very persuasive. I could imagine him pitching a yarn to Arnold which would take a lot of withstanding. Of course the swindle would stop and probably I would have to leave Westbet House. I didn't mind that. Get me out of this, I said to whoever it is we do say prayers to when we are in a jam, and there won't be any more swindles for me.

All of us from the pool lunched in the canteen and Lesly's saga was still going strong. Some performer this boy friend of hers, evidently. And a bit of a wit, too.

"Do you know what he said to me then, when he had finished?"

Sis said she didn't know. . . . I lit a cigarette and tried to make a sort of timetable. If nothing had happened by five, which was the end of the day for the pool, I would go up to Mr. Berry's office and ask him if he would like me to put in an hour in the small bets room in case the settlers were behind.

That would give him a chance to say something if he was going to.

If he didn't say anything, I would get onto a bus as soon as I left Westbet House and go straight down to Lovell Street and find out what had happened from Johnny.

"Have you succeeded," I would ask him, "in saving that

handy little allowance of two thousand a year which you had talked yourself into?"

I wasn't feeling very amiable toward Johnny at that moment.

It was a relief to have some sort of definite program mapped out; but a relief which wasn't going to last long.

We hadn't been back in the pool ten minutes after lunch before Mr. Berry came in.

I knew then that the balloon must have gone up. In the normal office working he would never come down to the typists' pool, and on top of that he looked upset. Something had evidently jolted him.

So, as I say, I knew the balloon had gone up.

But I couldn't guess what balloon . . .

"Miss Carter—"

We all stopped work and I automatically reached for my bag.

Mr. Berry looked positively white in the doorway . . . *Hell,* I thought, *everyone is going to take it as badly as they can;* and I began to realize just how much of a heel I had been.

"Miss Carter, I am sorry to interrupt the work here, but I'm afraid I have bad news for you all."

He paused and looked round the room. He almost seemed scared. It seemed to me an odd way of putting it and all I wanted now was for him to get on with it. I wasn't particularly anxious to be stared at and whispered over by Lesly and company.

"I'm afraid it will shock you," Mr. Berry went on. "It shocked me. I have to tell you that during the lunch hour we heard from the police that Mr. Chess is dead. He was found killed in his home this morning."

TWELVE

THANK GOD that Vicky was away up in Coventry. There wasn't much to be thankful for; but there was that. If Vicky had been at the flat she would have seen the state I was in and I think in the end that I wouldn't have been able to stop telling her all about everything.

As it was I could sit by myself in the room in Tammerton Square with the light out, staring into the fire, and I didn't have to pretend to anybody.

But even if anyone had been there and had said, "A penny for your thoughts, Liz," I would have had a job to answer at times.

Sometimes I used to step back and take a look at myself as it were and wonder what in God's name I was thinking about, what in God's name I was going to do.

He killed him.

I kept saying it over and over to myself. I knew it must be true and yet I couldn't believe it. Couldn't realize it, I mean.

I thought of the papers. How almost every day for the past I don't know how many years, ever since I started to read newspapers, I had seen accounts of people being found killed; flashlight photographs of murderers; interviews with murderers' wives and girl friends—and it had all meant nothing. It had been a sort of show. Something to read about. Turn the knob of the telly and the first thing you see when the picture comes on is one plug-ugly in a bar pumping lead into another. Just something to while away the time before "Double Your Money" is due to start.

But now, God Almighty, it was different.

Now every time I heard the front-door bell ring I jerked my head up and listened. A man from Scotland Yard come to have a word with me, I wondered.

Or Johnny come to tell me.

To tell me what?

At the office it wasn't as bad in one way because the news about little Arnold Chess upset everybody and although I must have looked pretty ghastly I managed to get by with the rest.

Three days went by without my hearing from Johnny in any way. He didn't come round; he didn't ring up; he didn't write.

I had my hand halfway to the telephone a dozen times to ring him. But I didn't do it.

I imagined that he was desperately trying to play it safe. Maybe he was being watched and if any connection could be found between him and Westbet House it might be fatal.

And fatal is a nasty word when it means that they are going to take the man you are infatuated with and put a rope round his neck at nine o'clock one morning. Kick the world away from under his feet. . . .

You don't sleep much when you are thinking about that sort of thing.

"You don't look yourself at all, dear," Mrs. Nagelson said. "Is it a touch of this terrible flu or something?"

"Or something," I told her, doing my best to smile.

There wasn't much in the papers about Arnold Chess. Of course I got them all and read them from first page to last. On the day he was discovered ten thousand pounds had been taken from a post-office van and the car the bandits got away in had been chased by the police and trapped right outside Buckingham Palace. This was naturally front-page headline stuff, and even on the first day Arnold Chess didn't rate higher than a short paragraph at the bottom of a column.

Oddly enough Vicky saw it and wrote to me from Coventry.

". . . I saw an *Evening Standard* yesterday and there was a paragraph about an Arnold Chess being found killed. Wasn't there an Arnold Chess at the place where you work? And can it possibly be the same man? How perfectly horrible for you if it is. They are simply loving *Pygmalion* up here and the famous line goes down splendidly . . ."

I couldn't remember for a long time what the famous line was. But I got it in the end. "Not bloody likely." I only wished that my life was uncomplicated enough for me to have got a kick out of a joke like that.

On the evening of the fourth day the front-door bell rang in Tammerton Square just after eight and Mrs. Nagelson came up to say I had a visitor.

"A young man, dear; that'll cheer you up, won't it?"

Johnny came in hard on her heels, and as soon as she had gone he jerked his head back toward the door.

"Does that old windbag listen outside?"

"No. She goes down to the basement and tells fortunes."

"Fortunes, Christ."

"Johnny, what's happened? What's been going on? I've been going through hell these last four days."

"What do you think I've been doing?"

"What about Arnold Chess, what happened to him?"

"You can't read, presumably?"

I told him that I didn't feel like being smart and wise-cracking at one another and that I doubted if we could afford to do it anyway.

He changed his tone suddenly. He could do that in a flash, could Johnny. One moment bloody-minded and awkward, needling you; the next a different person, quiet and confidential, somebody who wanted you to help him and by God you were only too ready to.

He sat down and faced me.

"You're quite right, Liz, we can't. We've got to play this

thing carefully. Otherwise it can all go wrong. It's one of those fantastic situations that you read about and don't believe can ever really exist. Much less happen to you, yourself."

"What *did* happen?"

He lit a cigarette, blew the match out through his nostrils (a favorite trick of his) and flicked it into the grate.

He looked across at me seriously and soberly like a man about to say something very solemn and important. You bloody liar, I thought, even before he started. And I thought, For God's sake, Johnny, play the man here, play this honestly or where are we all going to be?

"You saw what it said in the papers . . ." he started like somebody giving a lesson at school to a pack of half-wits who couldn't understand words of more than two syllables and who were going to lap everything they heard anyway.

". . . how this Chess character was found in the living room of that cottage of his with his head cracked in—well, that's just exactly how it was. *I* found him."

"You did?"

"When I got his address from you that Tuesday evening I went straight down to Cotterfield, as it happens I used to know some people there so it wasn't difficult to find the way. I stopped at a pub on the way down and worked out what I was going to say to Chess.

"I reckoned that if he had said anything to the bosses at Westbet House you would have been pulled in already for questioning. You hadn't been, so he had kept his mouth shut so far.

"The only reason I could see for this was that he didn't want to get you into trouble. So he looked like a soft-hearted little bastard and the way to tackle him would be to play on that.

"I was going to tell him—"

"Johnny, never mind what lies you were going to tell him, what happened?"

"When I got to Heath End Cottage there was a light on in the downstairs room and I could hear a radio playing. I knocked on the door and waited. Nothing happened. I knocked again. Still nothing. The radio was pretty loud and I thought he just couldn't hear me. So I tried the door.

"It was unlocked and I let myself into the hall.

"I stood there a moment with the radio coming a lot louder now from the living room.

"Then I opened the door of the living room and looked in.

"Chess was on the floor by the fireplace in a sort of sprawly heap; I went over to have a look at him, but actually I had known from the doorway that he was dead. Somebody had hit the side of his head and there was a bit of blood about, not much."

"And what did you do?"

"What a damn fool question. What do you think I did? I went out, got into my Sunbeam and drove back to Lovell Street like a bat out of hell."

We took a long steady look at one another.

"Well, that's all right then," I said at length. "You tell the police that and you've nothing to worry about, have you?"

He didn't like the word "police."

"I'm telling them nothing," he said. "I'm telling them that I've never seen Arnold Chess in my life and that I've never been near Heath End Cottage. And it's quite impossible for anybody to prove I have."

I gave a sort of groan. Reading about Arnold Chess's murder and then the four days bottling everything up inside myself and not hearing a word from Johnny had been too much for me, I suppose. I felt sick. I thought my nose might be going to bleed again.

I wanted to believe Johnny. God knows, I wanted to believe him . . . "one of those fantastic situations that you don't believe can ever happen to yourself," he had said. But they *did* exist; and they *did* happen to you even though you didn't think they could . . .

I kept telling myself this but it never got below the surface. It bounced off all the time. I knew it didn't mean anything. You can know things in your heart without having them proved to you inside your head first.

Johnny was my man and I knew the smell of him when he was lying. He was lying now.

He was watching me closely; not full face but out of the corners of his eyes as he was drinking.

I gave a sort of gulp. I was beginning to feel at the end of my tether. I leaned forward with my elbows on my knees.

"Johnny," I said, "don't you think you owe me something?

"No—" I said when I saw a look come into his eyes. "Not *money*. More than that. You've *got* me. You know that. Body and soul if we've got any souls. Whatever you tell anybody else about this thing you've got to tell me the truth. That's what you owe me."

He didn't answer at once. He sat there working it out. I realized a little later just what he was working out.

He needed my help—was he more likely to get it if I knew just how bad a jam he was in? I suppose he must have come to the conclusion that he was.

"All right, Liz. You want the truth. And this *is* the truth, mind you. I'm not flanneling anything here.

"I got to Heath End Cottage like I said. It's perfectly true that the light was on in the downstairs room and that there was a radio playing. But when I knocked Chess heard me.

"He switched off the radio and opened the door to me.

"He asked, 'Who is it?' and I said, 'We've seen one another before in Edward West's place; can I come in and have a talk with you about some bets I've been making?'

"He asked me what my name was and when I told him

he hesitated a moment or two and then said, 'Perhaps you had better come in then.'

"Well, that was all right, so far. That was just what I wanted. I was going to tell him that you and I thought this scheme up between us; that I had only made a few pounds out of it and I was quite willing to pay it all back to Edward West's if only he wouldn't say anything about it and that if he *did* say anything he would cook my goose completely for me. All my plans with Tessa would be off and I should be in one hell of a mess.

"I never got a chance.

"Just as soon as we were in that room of his the silly little so-and-so went for me. All about you. It must have been me who talked you into it. I had led you astray. I would be responsible for you losing your job and being prosecuted. God, he was like a ranting preacher. Did everything but foam at the mouth.

"I told him for God's sake to calm down and take it easy, if we all kept our heads it surely wasn't necessary for anybody to be prosecuted.

"I might just as well have been talking to the wall. I don't know what you did to the little fool but he certainly had you on the brain. After a minute or two he pulled some bits of paper out of his pocket and started waving them at me."

"My betting slips."

"The losers. The ones he had found in your drawer.

"He kept waving them in front of me, practically slapping my face with them and jabbering about the wickedness of what I had done to you all the time.

" 'You silly little sod,' I thought, 'if I can only get hold of those slips you won't have a shred of evidence left and I can clear out of this madhouse and go home.'

"I grabbed at his hand as he was waving the things about and half caught him.

"He spun round and we both fell, well, stumbled. The

slips were all over the floor and I was on one knee for a moment. We had cannoned into a table and knocked it onto the log basket by the side of the fire and the logs were all over the place.

"I reached out to start picking up the slips before he could and the stupid little bastard trod on my fingers.

"God, I thought he had broken one of them. It hurt like hell. I went wild. I grabbed the first thing that came to hand, one of the logs on the floor. I was getting up off my knees and he was beside me, not quite upright, stooping a little and half turned away.

"He was asking for it and he got it. I hit at him; he moved his head as I hit and I caught him just about over the ear.

"Christ knows, I wasn't thinking of killing him. I was mad at him for being such a bloody little fool and when he stamped on my fingers the pain made me berserk for the moment.

"And anyway, I didn't kill him. Not straight out. He went down like a ninepin and there was a bit of blood, not much. The wood broke the skin and he bled a little. He certainly wasn't dead at once.

"I scrabbled about and got the betting slips together and then had another look at him.

"He didn't look too good.

"I looked round the place for a drink. If I'd seen a bottle of whisky anywhere I might have poured myself a drink and waited a bit to see how he made out.

"But of course there wasn't anything. There wouldn't be in a dump like that.

"So I thought, 'Well, you silly little man, I never wanted it to turn out like this. I wanted to talk you into seeing sense and you started to play it up rough and now you've bought it.'

"I chucked the log I had hit him with onto the fire and went out.

"And whether you believe it or not that's exactly what happened."

I did believe it. I could see it all happening exactly like that. I could see Arnold Chess being morally indignant and Johnny losing his temper.

I stared at Johnny for half a minute, thinking of all this, seeing the thing like a film sequence in my brain.

"So now you've killed a man," I said at last.

He stared back at me. He looked a bit white and he was worried. But he was telling the world to take a running jump for itself. Just the same Johnny as ever. They win Battles of Britain and get into the dock at the Old Bailey and play hell with women, that sort.

"All right. I killed him. He must have a hell of a thin skull. I didn't know you could do it so easily. So am I any different from what I was before?"

"Why didn't I have a word of any sort from you for four days, Johnny?"

"I didn't want to involve you in anything."

I almost believed him. One detail was puzzling me, at the back of my mind.

"You knew Cotterfield already?" I asked him.

"I used to go there for weekends at one time. Sir Philip and Lady Egerton."

"Out of my social class I expect."

"Don't be a silly inverted snob."

"But how did you know where Heath End Cottage was?"

He nodded as though acknowledging that I had hit on something. "I had to ask the way, of course. But I was lucky. I pulled up outside a pub on the edge of the place. I was going pretty fast and the pub was on a corner so I shot a few yards past it before stopping the car. I got out and began to walk back toward it.

"I hadn't gone twenty yards before one of the doors opened and a character came out, to go round the corner, I suppose, and let some of the beer out.

"There were a couple of coaches in the car park and a pretty good noise going on inside so I imagine there was a darts match or something of the sort.

"I called out to this chap and asked him if he knew where Heath End Cottage was and he did."

"Which wasn't all that surprising. I suppose he was a local."

"He told me how to get there—it was pretty straight-forward anyway—and I said thanks and he rolled off round the corner to have his pee."

"So somebody knows you were going there?"

"No. No, they don't. I've thought this one out pretty carefully, believe you me. That chap had a good deal of beer on board already for one thing and he might not remember being asked. Even supposing he does he couldn't possibly swear to what the person looked like who asked him. I was standing, oh, a good fifteen yards from him and I was in the dark. He had just come out of the lighted inside of the pub. If they get onto him at all, all he can tell them is that *somebody* asked the way to Heath End Cottage. He certainly couldn't say what I looked like and thank God he couldn't see the Sunbeam as it was round the corner. No, I'm not scared of that."

But he was scared of something.

"What are you scared of, Johnny?" I asked him softly.

"How many runners were there on that last race at Lewes?"

"Eight."

"So I had seven losing slips?"

I nodded.

"That's what I thought. And I *had* seven, too, at Chess's cottage. But when I got back to Lovell Street I only had six."

"What did you do with them?"

"Burned them and next morning chucked the ashes onto a bomb site half a mile away. They're all right."

"What happened to the seventh slip? Don't you know where it is?"

"Oh, yes, I know where it is all right. That's why I've come round to see you, Liz. You've got to be involved in this now. A man called Masters called round to see me this morning with the seventh slip in his hand."

"Masters? Who's he?"

"A detective inspector from Scotland Yard."

"Johnny—"

"For Christ's sake don't start panicking. How do you imagine I feel?"

"What happened?"

"I don't know exactly. These police bastards don't tell you more than they've got to. But it's pretty obvious that I must have dropped this particular slip on my way out of the cottage to the car and they found it. But it took them three days to do it, so presumably it had blown away into the garden."

"So they know you were there?"

"Of course they don't. I *wasn't* there. I was here in London; all the time. If we stick to that they can't shake me. Nobody can.

" 'Is this betting slip anything to do with you?' the detective inspector asked me. I told him as it had my name and address on it it was pretty obvious that it had to do with me.

"Could I tell him anything about it?

"I told him it was a loser and that unless he was even a bigger mug than most policemen he would do well to give betting a miss.

"Was Edward West my bookmaker?

"I suggested that he looked at the slip. It was an Edward West slip, therefore Edward West was my bookmaker. I thought even he could detect that much.

"Did I know a Mr. Arnold Chess?

"I said I had never heard of anybody called Arnold Chess.

"Did I know that Mr. Chess had been found murdered in his cottage three days ago?

"No, I didn't. Owing to the inefficiency of the police, people were being murdered pretty well every day and the ordinary law-abiding citizen just couldn't keep up with it."

"You must be bloody-minded and smart at all costs, mustn't you, Johnny?" I said.

"Can't let these bastards have it all their own way. All they know is that Chess had a slip of mine down at his cottage. That doesn't prove that I was there. They also know that the slip has got some bloodstains on it. When he went down after I hit him he must have fallen on it. That may give them ideas but it still doesn't prove anything. What it does mean, though, is that they are looking my way. It looks as though this slip is the only one they've got. So obviously the gestapo are going to be questioning me pretty hard. What they are very anxious to find out is where I was and what I was doing on the Tuesday night that Chess got himself killed."

"What are you going to tell them?"

"I have told them already."

"What, Johnny?"

"I took the inspector into my confidence. I said: 'Look, Masters, you are a man of the world, and you will understand. This puts me in a bit of a jam. I'm engaged to the daughter of Admiral Sir Cecil Franklyn who is an A.D.C. to the Queen. I don't want any scandal there, do I? You can understand that. On that particular Tuesday night it happens that I was saying goodbye to an old girl friend of mine and it took us the whole evening together in her rooms to do it. Now, I am not anxious for this lady's name to be made public, nor for any mention of it to come out at all.' "

I stared at him.

"So I may be expecting your Mr. Masters to be calling on me soon, I suppose?"

"Not yet. Because I haven't told him your name. I said I was very loath to let a lady be mixed up in anything like this."

"And that's why you've come round to see me now?"

"Of course."

"So I'm involved after all?"

"For Christ's sake be your age, Liz. You were in the swindle too, weren't you?"

"What did I get out of it?"

"Dinners, drinks, shows—where do you think I got the money from to take you about these last months?"

"I didn't have anything to do with—with the Arnold Chess business."

"Do you think I went down there meaning to kill him?"

"But you did kill him, Johnny."

"So you want me to hang for it. Is that it?"

"Oh, Johnny, Johnny."

"And these police bastards are after me. Don't make any mistake about that. The only clue they've got involves me and it's me they are going to hammer away at. I've told them I've got a cast-iron alibi. Vicky's away, isn't she?"

"Up in Coventry."

"That's what I remembered. Were you in on Tuesday evening?"

"Yes, I was."

"All the evening?"

"If I'm not out with you I'm not out with anybody, Johnny."

"Forget the romantic stuff for the moment." He grinned suddenly. "Or better, don't forget it. I was here, with you, in this room all Tuesday evening. Owing to the romantic nature of our session I didn't leave till nearly midnight. I enjoyed myself thoroughly. So did you."

"Is that what you want me to swear to?"

238

"It's a cast-iron alibi. If I was having fun and games with you in Tammerton Square I couldn't be down in Heath End Cottage hitting that stupid little moralist over the head. They may have suspicions but there's nothing positive they can bring against it. If you give me the alibi, Liz, I'm safe. I shan't hear any more about this."

"And what about Arnold Chess?"

THIRTEEN

And what about Arnold Chess?

I am sitting in the flat in Tammerton Square. Alone. But not to be alone for long. The time is six-fifteen, coming up to sixteen as I watch the clock face, which I have been doing pretty constantly. Twenty-two hours since Johnny called here yesterday evening.

In fourteen minutes, if he is punctual, I am to have a visitor. Detecive Inspector Gibson. I expect he'll be punctual. The police are usually businesslike.

He rang up an hour ago. He thought there was a matter in which I might be of assistance to him. . . . Would it be convenient?

Not much good saying it wouldn't. So I said it would. It would be convenient. *Convenient,* what a word. Would it be convenient if I take your heart out and wring the life out of it? Well, not really, not exactly convenient. But go on, have a go.

"What about Arnold Chess?" I asked Johnny last night.

He lit another cigarette, blew down his nostrils to put out the match and leaned back against the fireplace. He seemed as though he was going to talk reasonably. He spread his hands slightly in a gesture.

"Liz, Arnold Chess is out of it. He's dead."

"And that's all?"

"Well, isn't it? Or are you one of these people who go on with the ghastly farce of keeping a dead person's room just as it was and a place laid at the table and so on? When your time comes, Liz, don't you agree that you'll be dead, finished, or will you expect me to go around in perpetual mourning?"

I told him I wouldn't expect that.

"You can't do anything for people when they aren't here any more."

"But we *owe* people something—oh, not money, not money," I went on, as I saw the reaction on his face to the word "owe."

" 'Not money, not money,' " he mimicked me. "Oh, no, of course not. You're too bloody high-minded to bother about money. But how you propose to live without it I wouldn't know. As far as I am concerned money *is* living. I went down to Chess's cottage to talk money to him. I hadn't the slightest intention of—of even hurting him. I've explained all that to you. If the silly little sod hadn't started almost slapping me in the face with those betting slips nothing like a roughhouse would ever have begun. Then when he stamped on my fingers I saw red for a moment. I've told you how it happened. Don't you believe it?"

"Yes, Johnny, I think I do believe it."

"Well, then."

"You can tell that, all about how it happened to—to any one who asks you, can't you?"

"You mean the police?"

I stared at him.

"—and twelve good honest moralizing morons and true in the jury box? Christ, Liz, be your age. Can't you hear the case being piled up? 'This young profligate, knowing that the deceased had some of his losing slips in his possession and afraid that his betting irregularities would come to light—' that's the way they'll talk. If ever they get me into court I shall be 'guilty' before the tapes go up. I thought you'd do this for me, Liz, I thought you would."

"Johnny, Johnny, I'd do anything for you. Anything!"

"It begins to look like it."

"Since I've been going with you I've never looked at any other man. You know that."

He shrugged his shoulders.

I wondered if he did know it. I wondered if any man ever knows how completely a woman can be emptied out in loving him. The humiliating times waiting for the telephone to ring; the barren small hours when you can't sleep because that evening at the party he smiled at someone else. . . .

"Johnny, you've had all of me, all of me, these last months. You know that. If you had whistled I'd have run a mile; but this—this is different."

"How? How do you mean it's different? You only talk like that because of some mumbo jumbo when you were brought up. This is living, Liz. Life. I'm in a jam and if you help me, I needn't be. That's all there is to it. It's as simple as that."

"It *isn't* as simple as that. This is different, I tell you. Different. This is a man's life—"

"Certainly it is. Mine. Chess is dead, gone, finished. You can be as moral as you like and you can't do him any good. All you can do by your bloody morality now is to make sure that I join him."

"Can't you see how I feel about it?"

"You're scared."

"What of?"

"The police, I suppose. You just don't want to get mixed up in anything. You want to keep yourself nice and tidily out of it while they put a rope round my neck. 'Johnny Mannington-Travers? I used to know him once and then he went and got himself hanged; wasn't it too bad?' "

"Don't, Johnny, don't. I'm not scared."

"No?"

"This isn't me or you or Arnold Chess even, it's something bigger—"

"For God's sake, are we to have sermons?"

I knew I couldn't express it; and I suppose I knew that he wouldn't have understood me even if I had managed to put it into words. Vicky, I thought, might have been able to do it for me and Monsignor Lucas almost certainly. But he was dead of cancer of the lung; and dead men don't know the answers to anything—or do they? Somewhere at the heart of things there was a sort of decency surely, something you couldn't go against without sort of committing suicide. . . .

"Or did this Chess character mean something to you? Were you hopping into bed with him all the times you weren't with me here?"

"Oh, Johnny, Johnny, it wasn't like that. You ought to know that."

"And anyway what right have you got to go all moral, Liz? You started sleeping with your first boss the moment you met him and as soon as he turned you out because his wife came back you came to me. That's no hallelujah chorus whichever way you look at it."

"Johnny, I'm not being moral, or preaching or anything like that. I'm no zombie. But with anybody, everybody, even a person like me, there are some things, one or two right in the middle of you, that you feel different about."

"This is because a man is dead?"

"I suppose that's it, yes."

"Liz, we've had this over and over. One man is dead. O.K., he's dead. Whether that's good or bad you can't alter it. Now, apparently, you want another one to be dead as well. Does that help any? Does it make sense?"

"No."

"Well, then—"

"Well, then," he said when we finally stopped talking, "I'm going to do the only thing I can do. As far as the police are concerned I didn't know Arnold Chess and have never been to his cottage. On Tuesday evening I came round to see you—and for Christ's sake let's get the details right and stick to the same story. I came round to see you here at seven. You let me in. You cooked an omelet for us both up here and we had a bottle of red wine with it. I didn't leave till just after midnight. They can fill in the details as to how we spent the time for themselves, we are too modest to tell them. That's my story and they can't shake it. You're going to back it up and then the bastards really can't shake it."

I couldn't answer him as he went out because I was in tears. I wasn't much use to him; what good to a man is a woman crumpled up in a chair sobbing her stupid heart out?

Next day at Westbet House I gave notice.

I had to see Mr. Berry to do it and he didn't want to let me go.

"Not just when we've trained you and you're beginning to be useful," he said.

I told him I felt a bit of a heel but there it was.

"Is it the money? I dare say we could arrange something about that?"

No, it wasn't the money.

"Well, couldn't you reconsider it then?"

"Mr. Berry, I can't stay on here. I can't. I'm upset about Mr. Chess—"

Well, that was one way of putting it, I suppose. Upset about Arnold Chess. It was true enough. God knows; God knows it was true enough.

I was back early from Westbet House. There were three meetings (Edinburgh, Folkstone and Nottingham) but betting wasn't particularly heavy and I must have looked about as rotten as I felt because the girl next to me said she could easily settle the T slips for the last race if I wanted to get off, and was it true I was leaving?

Don't ask me how the grapevine works; but there it is, it does.

Yes, I said, it was true.

She said she was sorry; she liked working alongside me; and she didn't want to interfere of course, she was only just asking, but was I leaving by any chance because I was going to get married?

No, I told her. I didn't think that was very likely to happen.

"Oh, well," she said smiling suddenly. "Jolly good luck. Keep your chin up."

I walked some of the way back to Tammerton Square. I can think best when I am walking. But it didn't help me much today and I got in just in time to answer the telephone.

"Detective Inspector Walter Gibson of the Buckinghamshire Constabulary. Would it be convenient . . . ?"

A nice voice. And, yes, I told him, trying to stop my own voice shaking, it would be convenient . . . at half past six. . . .

It's twenty-five past now and here I am with my problem.

"What right have you to go all moral?" Johnny asked me last night. None, Johnny, none at all. Back in Hansbeck Road I used to think the people who preached morals at you were all zombies. Come to that I still think so, that particular lot. Not that I've been anything much to shout about myself. First there was all the business with Nancy, saying we were going to the badminton club, when we weren't; then there was Jimmy and then, oh, then, came Johnny.

"I thought you would do anything for me, Liz," Johnny said.

So I would Johnny, so I would. Only "anything" is a tricky word, isn't it? One of the catchwords.

Anything means everyday anything, ninety-nine point nine percent anything. This is different. I tried to tell you that. Tried to make you see it. This is *me*, Johnny, the very middle and essence of me.

And yet isn't it true that Johnny is that too? What is going to be left in my heart if he goes out of it, if I push him out of it?

I read a phrase the other day, "the fool of love," and I know it was for me. My fourth. It closes up the pattern. "When I was a windy boy and a bit"; "Childe Roland to the Dark Tower came"; "by our first strange and fatal interview" and now my fourth, "the fool of love."

Twenty-eight past now.

As soon as I knew the police were coming I got into a panic and tried to speak to Vicky. I got a call through to the theater at Coventry but she wasn't there. She wouldn't be till half an hour before the evening performance. No, they didn't know if her digs were on the telephone. They didn't think so.

So that was no good.

Maybe it was just as well. If anybody could have helped me it would have been Vicky, but as I see it there are some problems in life where no one can help you.

You have to make your own decision.

Half past exactly by my clock and the front-door bell is ringing. Punctual people the police.

You have to make your own decision.

FOURTEEN

"Two COFFEES," Walter Gibson said to the waitress, and immediately she had gone he added to his companion, Sergeant Verney, "Well, what do you make of it?"

"She cleared one difficulty out of the way for us; if she had said he was with her all the evening I don't see that we could have got anywhere."

"Are we going to get much further than that now?"

The waitress brought the coffees and the two men busied themselves with the sugar bowl, and with their thoughts.

It was Sergeant Verney who spoke first.

"I wonder why she didn't back him up," he said. "Scared, perhaps?"

"I don't think it was because she was scared."

"There's no doubt they've been living together, or sleeping together anyway."

"I think she's in love with him."

"And won't support his alibi?"

"We're all liable to do odd things, John; and women in love are liable to do odder than most of us."

"I suppose."

"There's nowt so queer as folk—you and I don't have to be reminded of that."

"No, indeed."

The inspector drew out an old pipe from his pocket and began to fill it with the attention, habitual yet reverential, of the man who takes tobacco seriously.

"Let's have a look at how the thing stands," he said. "Do

a bit of what my old chief used to call reexamination from the ground up.

"We've got the body; we think the weapon was a piece of wood and if so it may well have been one of the logs and thrown onto the fire afterwards. The only prints we've got are too blurred to be of any use. We've got that thick-witted chap who was coming out of the bar of The Stag on Tuesday evening when somebody asked him the way to Heath End Cottage. He himself admits that he hasn't the vaguest idea what the man looked like and he cheerfully adds that he is willing to have a go at an identification parade. What a witness!

"If we ever let him near the box the defense would tear him into shreds.

"Then yesterday we got the betting slip that had blown into the next-door garden.

"That takes us to this Mannington-Travers character."

"Whom I don't like one little bit," John Verney put in. "I wouldn't trust him an inch."

"I must admit I wouldn't want to make a pet of him."

"If I had a daughter I'd take damned good care she wasn't a sleeping-partner of his."

"You can be thankful you haven't got one, John. Girls of twenty-one or two are women nowadays; and women go their own way to hell, or heaven."

"Assisted, in the one case, by such types as Mannington-Travers."

"Could be. Could well be. But that hardly gives us a case against him, does it? His story is that of course he was a client of Edward West and of course he sometimes had losing betting slips—what punter doesn't? But if we are trying to make out that he owed West a lot of money we can take a running jump at ourselves and think again. Because he didn't. Actually he had been winning."

"Which is true. And somehow just what one would expect. 'They toil not, neither do they spin,' if I remember

248

Sunday School correctly, but nevertheless a hell of a lot of young men nowadays seem to get by all right, and to do pretty nicely out of it too. Maybe you and I ought to take up betting, Inspector."

Walter Gibson looked amused. He was amused. He had a bet (with Edward West) three days a week on an average. But he didn't think that it would be helpful to good conduct and discipline to advise his junior officer of this fact.

"Most people say it's a mug's game," he said.

"Some of the mugs seem to do pretty well out of it."

"Mannington-Travers was winning certainly. I wonder why Chess had that particular slip with him down there?"

"You didn't get anywhere at Edward West's over that?"

"Not so far. As far as they can see there isn't any reason. They say he might have taken it because there was (or he thought there was) a query about it. But what query? Nobody can suggest anything. Or is it just possible that he had it in his pocket by accident? Though they admit that that doesn't seem likely."

"Murder itself isn't very likely, come to that."

Gibson laughed. "You've got a point there. But not a jury point. Well, let's get on with our reassessment.

"The only clue we've got takes us to John Mannington-Travers who denies that he even knew of the existence of Chess and equally denies that he was anywhere near Heath End Cottage on Tuesday evening."

"Supporting it by an alibi which we have just heard blown sky high."

"Y-yes."

"Well, haven't we?"

"Suppose the girl wasn't telling the truth?"

"That girl's no liar."

"I'm inclined to agree with you. But—love, hate, jealousy, these things play hell with a woman's heart, and she'll do some unpredictable things when she's suffering from them. This girl may want to put Travers in a hole."

"Could be, sir, I suppose. But I don't quite see it. Not in this particular case."

"Neither do I, actually."

"Which brings us back to the point that his alibi is false."

"A point which he will admit at once, if I read him right, the moment he sees which way the cat has jumped."

"And that won't look any too good for him in court, will it?"

Walter Gibson puffed at his pipe a time or two before answering. Then he said, "I don't see us getting this case to court, John. Not on what we have got."

"Still, giving a false alibi wants a bit of explaining all the same."

"Lots of people dream up false alibis. Usually because they are either scared of the real one coming to light, or else they don't think it would be accepted. That will almost certainly be Mannington-Travers' line. His engagement to this other girl, the admiral's daughter, has just been announced; it's understandable enough that he doesn't want to do anything to queer his pitch there."

"I'll take damned good care I don't get tied up with any admiral's daughter. I was in the Navy once."

"You ought to have chosen a less hidebound service."

"Less snob-bound, you mean. No admiral's daughter for me, thank you."

"Travers seems to like them. This particular one, anyway. He'll say—as he has already said—that he never knew Chess and has never been to the cottage; but being terrified that his name might be mentioned in connection with police inquiries into the case he wanted to choke us off right away by giving us a cast-iron alibi which would kill our case stone dead from the start."

"But if he wasn't with this girl Elizabeth Barton, where was he? Why not produce his real alibi?"

"Possibly because it isn't a provable one. And if you can't

prove an alibi it doesn't exist, you haven't got one. He'll say, 'Actually I was simply in my flat all the evening listening to long-playing records. I had a nightcap about ten-thirty and turned in early. But I know I can't prove that to you so I thought I would try to fix an alibi that was provable, or would look like it anyway. I'm rather glad it came unstuck because it was a lie and fundamentally there's no reason why I should lie. The truth is that I was here, in my flat, alone, all the evening. But I can't prove it.' That's what he'll say."

"Will you believe him?"

The inspector spread his hands. "That's hardly the point," he said. "Whether I believe him or not. The point is that it *is* believable. Certainly it doesn't let him out in the way that a cast-iron, unbreakable alibi would, but we've got to start proving that it wasn't so; that he's lying. Which isn't easy."

"What about the woman who runs that house in Lovell Street?"

"Mrs. Huntley? Well, we had a go at her, didn't we? She's in the basement and Travers is on the top floor. According to her he's in or out. It isn't her business and she just doesn't know. She *thought* she heard him come in about the usual time on Tuesday, but after that she just couldn't say. She's no use to his alibi and equally no use to us in breaking it."

"So on balance you don't think we've got a case?"

"We've got a suspect; but we haven't got a case."

"And the Heath End Cottage killing will go into the unsolved file?"

"It won't be the first."

"The chief won't like it, sir."

"The world contains lots of things that chief constables don't like."

Sergeant Verney laughed. True enough, he thought.

True enough it certainly was, but in this particular instance things didn't happen to work out that way. Fate throws the dice sometimes so that they turn up for the Law.

When Walter Gibson and John Verney got back to the police station they were greeted by a desk sergeant grinning all over his face.

"Bit of luck for you, sir," he greeted the inspector.

"Have I been made chief constable of the county or something?"

"Not quite that, sir, but there's something new on this Chess case."

Both his listeners pricked up their ears.

"What's new about Chess?"

"That chap at The Stag who was asked the way to Heath End Cottage."

"Don't tell me he has suddenly been visited by a startlingly clear mental picture of the man who asked him?"

"He still hasn't the vaguest idea what the man looked like, sir."

"Well then?"

"But he does remember something. On his way out to the back he all but bumped into a stationary car. A Sunbeam Rapier."

"A Sunbeam Rapier?"

"That's right, sir. This character works at the local petrol filling station and he says he just notices cars, it's sort of second nature with him; and their numbers, too, especially if they've got odd-looking ones. CAT 333 was this one. He's sure of it."

Inspector Walter Gibson grinned slowly and hugely. "I'll be believing in Providence next," he said. "Mr. Too-clever-by-half Mannington-Travers is going to have quite a job talking himself out of this little lot now."